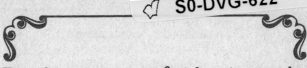

He only meant to comfort her, to ease her heartache a bit, but she looked up at the same time, and his lips naturally found her mouth. Like coming home, he thought, and deepened the kiss. He forgot the words he meant to say, forgot the proprieties, forgot everything except the sweet taste of her lips.

She quit struggling and leaned against him, wanting the moment never to end.

Nick released her arms and slid his hands around her shoulders and back. He felt the curve of her waist beneath the silk wrapper and the swell of her hips as she pressed against him.

A thunderclap shattered the stillness, and lightning rippled over their heads, but neither noticed. . . .

Also by Jeanne Carmichael
Published by Fawcett Books:

LORD OF THE MANOR

LADY SCOUNDREL

Jeanne Carmichael

FAWCETT CREST • NEW YORK

A Fawcett Crest Book
Published by Ballantine Books
Copyright © 1995 by Carol Quinto

Library of Congress Catalog Card Number: 94-94652

ISBN 0-449-22316-7

Manufactured in the United States of America

First Edition: February 1995

10 9 8 7 6 5 4 3 2 1

*For all the charming ladies everywhere
but especially for my
lovely daughter, Dawn Quinto Perry,
and my beautiful granddaughter, Jessica Lee*

Chapter 1

Verity Parnel darted into a narrow alley, nearly tripping over the folds of her black cape. Flattening herself against the wall of the town house, she held her breath until the carriage rumbled past. The clank of wheels on the cobblestone street sounded ominously loud in the darkness. In the distance, she heard the shrill cry of a watchman. Half past one o'clock and all's well. A lot he knew, she thought, risking a step forward. Silence blanketed Harley Street. She pushed up the brim of her hat and looped the cape over her arm. Both were too big. The black beaver hat tended to slide down over her eyes, and the hem of her cape brushed the ground.

A creature slithered in the darkness, distressingly near her slippered foot. A mouse, she told herself sternly, 'tis nothing more. She refused to think of rats with their sharp, gnawing teeth. She stamped her feet, then edged along the wall until she could peer around the corner of the building.

A small light glowed in the distance, but no one was about. The good people of Harley Street were abed for the night, and it would be another hour or two before their servants awoke. Verity thought wistfully of her own bed, where safety and warmth awaited her. Soon, she promised herself, and crept into the street. Lynton's house stood on the corner, shrouded in darkness. Keeping well to the shadows, Verity approached it, heart pounding. She'd studied the house several times and knew every detail of the design—even where the enormous oak tree rose at the rear of the house, its branches stretching upward to the windows. Windows which, according to her observations, were invariably left raised at night.

She'd been surprised, for she'd not envisioned Mr. Lynton as the sort of gentleman who embraced fresh air. She'd met him once while out walking with her papa in the Mall. She still recalled Lynton's pasty complexion, white as flour save for the bulbous red nose, and his immense girth. She doubted he ever exercised, and suspected the gentleman spent all of his hours within doors. Strange he'd sleep with his window open, she thought, but she knew elderly men were often given to odd humors, and it was, after all, to her advantage.

Fancying she heard a noise, Verity glanced nervously over her shoulder. A scrap of paper skittered against the cobblestones, picked up and capriciously carried aloft by the breeze. She shivered as the cold, damp air crept beneath her cape. She prayed it wouldn't rain until she finished this business. Get on with it, she told herself, or the sun would be rising before she finished. Hitching up her sagging pantaloons, Verity climbed awkwardly over the wrought iron fence surrounding Lynton House. Her cape caught on the ornamental gate just as she jumped. Pitched forward, she landed on her side with a thud, the ground hard and cold beneath her.

Verity lay still. She wondered if she'd broken her arm. After a moment, she sat up and gingerly flexed her fingers. She'd be bruised and sore tomorrow, but her bones seemed to be in one piece. She couldn't say as much for her papa's tattered cloak, a large portion of which hung on the fence. Scrambling to her feet, she wrapped the remains of the cape about her and, using the wall of the house as a guide, carefully felt her way toward the back of the yard.

The tree loomed larger than she remembered. Verity surveyed it with dismay, her stomach turning queasily. The lowest limb stretched just above her reach. She tried jumping for it and nearly achieved a handhold, but her hat fell off.

"Bloody hell," she muttered, repeating the strongest curse she'd ever heard from her papa's lips. She felt surprisingly better for the oath, and dropped to her knees to search for the hat. Her fingers brushed against the soft beaver. For a fearful second she believed she'd disturbed some animal. Common sense prevailed, however, and she snatched the hat up.

She wiped the brim with the edge of her cape. Wrinkling her nose in distaste but realizing it was the only way to carry the blasted thing, she clamped her teeth around the brim. Holding it securely in her mouth, she jumped again for the branch above her. Three attempts later, her hand caught the limb securely. She braced her feet against the trunk and swung her other arm up. Now what, she wondered. A pity she'd never learned the art of tree-climbing. Her arms ached, and the beaver hat tasted bitter in her mouth.

Verity swung one leg over the branch, and nearly cried aloud when the limb scraped her foot. Gritting her teeth, she managed to hook her knee over the branch and then, more carefully, to lift her other leg. She now hung upside down directly beneath the limb. Stretching her arms farther along the branch, she brought her torso closer until she clutched the tree to her bosom. Resting for a moment, Verity closed her eyes. Mr. Lynton would pay dearly for her difficulties.

She twisted her foot and, using her knee as leverage, heaved her body upward. After a moment she found herself sitting up in the tree. She yanked the beaver hat firmly down over her curls and then glanced up. At least the branches grew close together. She had only to reach the one above her head and then crawl along it to the open window.

Verity stood cautiously, keeping a firm hold on the tree trunk and her eyes on the partially raised window to her right. The limb she needed rubbed against her waist. Murmuring a prayer, she pulled herself up and straddled it. Still too far from the window, she leaned over and used her hands to inch slowly forward. When she finally drew close enough, she reached down and tugged at the window sash. It slid upward easily.

Verity rested her cheek against the limb, listening for any noise from within the house. She was quite prepared to drop to the ground and flee into the night had she disturbed the occupants. Silence reigned, however, and she reluctantly sat up. Bringing one leg up over the limb, she sat with both legs dangling in front of the window. She scooted over a bit so the tips of her slippers touched the sill. Keeping a tight grip on the branch, she swung her legs down. Her buttocks hit the sill and she barely avoided banging her head against the sash.

"Dear Lord, help me get through this," she whispered, hoping He listened to the prayers of burglars. She ducked inside, her slippers landing on a soft carpet. Holding her hands out in front of her, she cautiously felt her way. She wished she could see better . . . her hand encountered a large wooden object and she felt along the edges. A wardrobe, perhaps?

The curtains fluttered in a sudden gust of wind, and the crescent moon peeped out from behind the clouds. Verity's eyes widened and she murmured a few words of gratitude for the dim light. She stood by the window of a small bedchamber. A nightgown lay folded neatly on the bed, and an elaborate dressing case stood open on the dresser. Judging from the adornments and the enticing smell of perfume on the air, the room belonged to a lady—who fortunately had not yet retired for the evening.

Moving with more assurance, Verity quickly crossed to the door and eased it open. She looked down a long corridor, dimly lit by a gilded sconce hung near the stairs. Hoping the candle had been left burning for the unknown lady and not for Mr. Lynton, she tiptoed into the hall. Verity stood still, straining her ears. When she'd robbed Lord Dinsmore, it had been easy to find his room. He'd snored so loudly, the rumble could be heard through the entire house.

There were no such sounds to guide her here. Verity crept silently to the first door on her right and gently opened it. The room stood empty, the bed stripped and the furniture shrouded in Holland covers. Leaving the door ajar, she tried the next. This one opened on a large, spacious room. Verity held her breath. The heavy, dark furniture and the masculine scent wafting on the air told her she'd found Mr. Lynton's room. She heard the sound of gentle breathing coming from the massive four-poster a few feet ahead of her.

Her heart hammered against her ribs as she stole silently into the chamber. A tall, slant-front bureau desk fitted neatly in a small alcove below the windows. If Mr. Lynton left his purse lying about, as did so many gentlemen, it would no doubt be on his desk. Keeping a wary eye on the bed, she padded quietly across the room and then stumbled. Sprawling across the carpet, she felt the corner of a treacherous footstool poking her rib. She silently cursed the stupidity of persons who kept such furniture where one was most likely to trip over it. She dared not move. The carpet had softened her fall, but the noise might have been sufficient to wake Mr. Lynton.

She breathed in dust and dirt. Really, the maids were lax in their duties. Bessie would never permit such slovenly housekeeping, Verity thought, trying desperately to avoid sneezing. Had Lynton stirred? Did she hear the whisper of sheets moving? She waited several moments, half expecting a blaze of light and the sound of accusing voices. When nothing happened, she cautiously sat up. She could hear Lynton's rhythmic breathing and felt somewhat reassured. Chancing no further mishaps, she crawled to the desk. She found it difficult to keep the cape from tangling in her legs and beneath her hands. Holding carefully to the edge of the desk, Verity slowly stood. The moon had retreated again behind a bank of clouds, and she'd only the shaded light from the hall to guide her. She glanced behind her into the dark shadows of the room. She could not see the bed, but Lynton's regular breathing assured her he still slept. She turned her attention to the task before her. She'd written a note to leave in exchange for his money, and quickly withdrew the folded paper from the deep pocket of her cape. His purse lay in plain sight. She was surprised by the weight of it as she gingerly lifted it. A deep voice spoke behind her, and the purse clattered to the desk.

"Do not move, sir, if you value your life."

Verity could not have moved even had she dared. A candle flared in the room behind her.

"Let's have a look at you. Slowly," he warned.

She didn't need the warning. Hardly eager to face him, she turned reluctantly. Her eyes widened beneath the wide-brimmed hat. The gentleman confronting her was certainly not Mr. Lynton. He'd been old when she'd met him years before and now must be quite elderly. The man leveling a gun at her head could be no more than five-and-twenty. Even in the candlelight Verity could see the rich, dark shade of his hair.

Had she blundered into the wrong house in the darkness? Or stumbled upon some relation? She stared at him. "Who ... who are you?"

His mouth quirked and one eyebrow rose slightly.

6

"I rather think I should be the one asking that question."

"I . . . I fear that I have made a dreadful mistake—"

"Indeed you have. Unfortunately for you, I am a light sleeper. I heard you the instant you opened my door. Now, my good man, remove your hat, if you please."

Not in her worst nightmares had Verity ever imagined such a scene. The blood drained from her face and she hung her head.

"The hat," the gentleman prodded.

Verity took a nervous step backward but immediately halted when the gentleman cocked his pistol, repeating his orders to stand still and remove the hat.

She froze, but made no move to take off the concealing beaver. Far better, she thought, if he just shoots me. She pictured her poor mama, prostrate with shock, when she learned her only daughter had been hauled off to prison. Verity lifted her head and studied the man before her. Would he really shoot? Perhaps he was only bluffing. She would have to risk it. Her eyes measured the distance to the hallway.

She raised her hand and firmly gripped the beaver hat. With a deft motion she yanked it off. Hurling it at his head, she ran for the door. A deafening roar filled the room. The bullet hit her shoulder with stunning force, spinning her about. She glanced down and saw the rip in her cape, and the blood spurting against it. Lifting a hand, she felt the warm, sticky wetness.

He caught her just before she fell. Verity looked up into his face. The room tilted crazily and for a moment she thought *two* men hovered above her. Two men with the same icy blue eyes. She blinked, then gave up the effort. "Not bluffing," she murmured just before her head fell back against his arms.

7

Cursing softly, Nicholas Lynton picked her up and easily carried her to his bed. She weighed next to nothing, he thought, gently laying her against the pillows. Why the devil had she run? He'd not meant to shoot, but his pistols were custom-made and the slightest touch was sufficient to set them off. The hat had caught him off guard.

"Begging your pardon, sir, but I thought I heard—"

He whirled about. Crimstock, his uncle's aged valet, stood hesitantly in the door. Nicholas had no time for explanations. "Get me hot water and bandages at once," he ordered.

The elderly valet's eyes flitted from his young master to the oddly dressed woman on the bed. If he noticed the bloodstained pillows or the pistol carelessly left lying on the floor, he made no mention of it, but merely nodded. "Yes, sir."

"And shut that door," Nick added. He sat down next to the girl and gently removed the dark scarf she'd tied about her throat. Reaching inside the collar of her shirt, his fingers found and measured the pulse in her neck. He rose, somewhat reassured by the slow but steady beat, and considered the situation. Blood saturated her left sleeve. He left her for a moment and searched frantically on the desk until he found a pair of scissors. He cut her sleeve free of the shirt and had nearly stemmed the flow of blood, when Crimstock returned. He directed the man to set the basin of water near the bed and move the candelabrum closer.

"Has my sister returned yet?" he asked, using a fresh length of bandage to blot the blood. It appeared the bullet had only grazed her arm.

"No, sir, nor Mr. Gyffard."

"I suppose the rest of the household is awake?"

"Indeed, sir. However, I took the liberty of informing the staff that you'd accidentally discharged your pistol and suggested they return to bed. I hope that is as you wished?"

8

Nicholas glanced over his shoulder at the old man. He presented a ludicrous sight in his night rail, cap, and slippers. His demeanor might be that of a perfect servant, but Nick thought he detected a conspiratorial gleam in the man's eye. "It is just as I wished. You are a good man, Crimstock. I don't suppose you know anything about bullet wounds?"

"As it happens, sir, I served as batman to your great-uncle. I saw a number of wounds in service. If you would allow me?"

Nicholas stood aside. He held the branch of candles, watching critically as Crimstock gently removed the makeshift bandage. The bleeding had slowed, and the valet carefully cleansed the wound before reapplying pressure.

"There is basilicum powder in the pantry. If you will permit me, sir, I'll fetch it. It should be applied to the wound before it is bandaged to prevent any infection, though this is merely a minor scrape, sir, and nothing, I believe, to alarm us."

"You relieve me greatly, Crimstock."

When the valet had gone, Nicholas gazed at the girl on his bed. He hoped Crimstock proved right, but to his eyes she appeared desperately ill. He flung himself down into the armchair and idly drummed his fingers on the desk. A moment later he rose restlessly and crossed the room. His pistol and the girl's tattered cloak lay in a heap near the door. After stowing the gun safely away, Nick picked up the cape and shook out the folds. A scrap of paper floated to the floor.

He unfolded the note, hastily scanning the lines. *I beg pardon for the intrusion, sir, but seek only that which was unfairly stolen from its rightful owner.*

He muttered beneath his breath, running a hand through his dark hair. The writing appeared neat, the words correctly spelled. No common thief penned those words. But what did she mean by it? He'd certainly never stolen anything.

9

A scratch on the door signaled Crimstock's return. Nick hastily opened the door and took the heavy tray from the valet's trembling hands.

"Thank you, sir," Crimstock panted. He drew a few deep breaths, then pointed to the tray. "I thought tea would be best, when the young lady revives, and perhaps a spot of brandy in her cup would not be amiss."

"*If* she revives," Nicholas answered glumly. "She's not stirred since you left. Perhaps we should send for a doctor?"

"Certainly, sir, if that is what you desire. No doubt you are prepared to answer any awkward questions such a visit would entail. I myself am confident you have a most reasonable explanation for shooting a young female in your bedchamber."

Nicholas hesitated. The circumstances would give rise to the worst sort of rumors, but he was more concerned at the moment with her life than with a possible scandal.

The bracket clock on the mantel chimed the quarter hour.

"Very well. I shall give her until half past two. If she has not recovered by then, you must send for my uncle's doctor."

"A wise decision, sir," Crimstock murmured, moving to the bedside.

While the valet attended the girl, Nicholas helped himself to a generous glass of brandy, ignoring the tea.

Verity's eyes opened slowly. Her gaze took in the ornate ceiling, the blue curtains at the high windows, and the young gentleman slouched in a chair by the desk. Her memory returned in a rush. He'd shot her after all, but apparently not fatally. She glanced down at her bare arm, now neatly bandaged. It ached horribly and a small groan escaped her lips.

Nicholas crossed to her side in an instant. "So, you are awake at last."

10

Verity nodded and made an effort to sit up.

"Lie still," he cautioned. "You have lost a great deal of blood, although Crimstock assures me it is but a minor wound."

"Crimstock?" she asked, her large eyes mirroring her confusion.

"My uncle's valet. He bandaged your arm after I—" He broke off, embarrassed, and took another sip of brandy. Setting the glass down, he faced her. "I am dreadfully sorry, but I shot you. Accidentally, of course, but if I had known you were a woman, I would never have, that is to say . . . well, to be perfectly frank, I have never shot anyone before and I find it a rather unsettling experience." He paused, aware he sounded like a babbling idiot. The brandy had addled his senses. Remembering Crimstock's advice, he suddenly asked, "Would you care for a cup of tea?"

"Yes, thank you," Verity said, and nearly smiled. One would think they were in a formal drawing room.

"Cream? Sugar?" Nick asked politely while doctoring the tea with the remainder of the brandy.

"Neither," she murmured, and struggled to sit up. The gentleman rushed to assist her, supporting her shoulders and rearranging the pillows. When she seemed more comfortable, he handed her the cup.

Verity tasted it, and immediately coughed. "Forgive me," she begged, spilling half the tea on the bed. "It is rather stronger than that to which I am accustomed."

"A new China blend. Orange pekoe and some sort of spices," Nicholas explained smoothly. "Drink it up, it will do you good. When you are sufficiently recovered, we will talk."

Verity glanced up at him, then hastily lowered her eyes. He wore only a dressing gown, thrown carelessly over some sort of nightshirt that opened at the neck, revealing a vast expanse of muscular

11

chest. She dared not look lower, for she'd caught a glimpse of bare legs. She had never seen a gentleman in such a state of dress. A blush suffused her face.

Nicholas mistook her embarrassment for reluctance. "You are in a rather awkward situation, my girl. I suggest you confide in me. You may start by telling me why you broke into my house."

"I thought it was Mr. Lynton's house," she murmured.

"It is."

"You . . . you are not Mr. Lynton," she protested, still keeping her eyes averted.

"Indeed I am, or so my mother has always informed me. Of course, I suppose it possible she mistook the matter, or perhaps you think me an imposter?"

Verity's flush deepened. "There is no need to ridicule me, sir. Mr. Lynton is a . . . a large man, and quite elderly. You do not resemble him in the least."

"Thank you for that, but I believe you must be referring to my late uncle, Rupert Lynton."

"Late?" Verity repeated, stunned. Her gaze flew to his eyes. "I am sorry, sir . . . I did not know . . ."

"Apparently not, though most of his friends attended the funeral. I gather you were not actually acquainted?"

Verity shook her head. The tea was making her feel strangely drowsy. "My . . . my father knew him."

"I see. You broke into this house, thinking it my uncle's, and intended to steal his purse. Might I be permitted to know why?"

"Does it matter, sir? Why do you not call the watch and be done with me?"

Nicholas gazed down at her. The girl had no notion of how utterly enticing she looked. Her face, starkly white, contrasted sharply with her black shirt, still open at the collar. Her silvery blond hair, shimmering in the candlelight, cascaded about her shoulders as though she'd just risen from bed . . . and her brown eyes seemed enormous.

Beautiful eyes, he thought, and felt a moment's compunction for filling them with fear. Abruptly, he remembered he'd caught her lifting his purse. His lips hardened in a firm line. "I assure you, the only reason I hesitate is this strange note I found, which I presume you wrote and intended to leave in place of my purse." He unfolded the scrap of paper and read it aloud.

Verity cringed. She'd penned those lines late one evening, and at the time thought they carried a high tone, amply conveying the injustice done her papa. Mr. Lynton made the words sound silly and childish. Mortified, she wished he'd taken better aim.

Nicholas lounged against the desk, closely observing her. "I admit I was not on intimate terms with my uncle, but I believe him to have been an honorable gentleman, and inasmuch as he left me a small fortune, I cannot think he would steal from anyone."

"Perhaps you think it honorable to deliberately ply a gentleman with whiskey and then take advantage of his weakness by sitting down with him at cards, but I do not," Verity replied a trifle testily. Her arm ached unbearably, and she wished he would just go away and leave her alone.

"Is this gentleman with the lamentable weakness someone close to you? A brother, or perhaps your father?"

A blush betrayed her, but Verity remained stubbornly silent.

"Ah, a close relative. Let us say, then, for the sake of argument, that the gentleman in question is your father. Regrettable, of course, that he should drink and lose, but really, my dear girl, you cannot blame my uncle. It happens every day, and any gentleman worth his name would of course

13

make good his gambling debts, and be wiser for the lesson."

"My father paid what he owed, but your uncle and his friends would not leave him be. They kept inviting him to Whites, and urging him to drink and play cards. Again and again, until they took everything he owned," Verity said angrily, and to her dismay felt tears starting to fill her eyes. She turned her head away so Mr. Lynton would not see. She despised females who wept at the slightest provocation.

Nicholas had seen, of course. He crossed the room and refilled her cup with warm tea, regretting the empty brandy decanter. He handed the cup to her, giving her a moment or two to compose herself. He thought he was beginning to make some sense of this tangled state of affairs, and remarked gently, "I sympathize with you, my dear, but when a man drinks and loses at cards, he has no one to blame but himself."

Verity sniffed. "You do not understand, sir. You do not know how wonderful, and kind and good—" She halted, choking back sudden sobs. Swallowing hard, she regained a measure of control and continued. "Papa wanted only to be liked, but he was very shy in company, and he would . . . he would drink to put himself at ease. Your uncle flattered him, asking him to his club, and when he and his friends urged Papa to drink—" She broke off again with a shake of her head, and took a deep breath. "He could not help himself. Each time he swore he'd never drink again . . . but he always did."

Nicholas sighed. "Nevertheless, you cannot hope to rectify matters in this manner." He tried the effect of a smile. "I hardly think your father would approve of—"

"My father will never know, sir," she interrupted. "He died a month past, on the way home from Whites. He lost everything, and I think the shame killed him."

"Oh, Lord," Nicholas muttered, looking at her helplessly. He could not possibly turn her over to the watch now. But neither could he allow her to continue her career of burglary. The next gentleman she encountered might not be so understanding. Devil take it, it was a wonder she'd not come to harm before this.

He would have to see what could be done to help her. Coming to a sudden decision, he flung open the desk. "Since my uncle was in some part responsible for your plight, I will give you a draft on my bank. How much did your father lose to him?"

"I don't want your charity," Verity said, anger flaring in her eyes as she struggled to rise.

"Lie still," he ordered, glaring at her. Suddenly, the absurdity of the situation struck him, and he laughed. "You are willing to steal into my house and lift my purse, but it goes against the grain with you to accept my draft!"

"It is not your debt," she murmured.

"Egad, a burglar with principles. Well, then, there is only one thing to be done. If you will give me your word—" He broke off, hearing a commotion in the hall, and swore. He locked the door, then faced her. "Apparently, my sister and cousin have returned. If I don't have a word with Kate, she'll be in here to tell me all about her evening. Wait quietly while I fob her off, and then I shall drive you home."

Verity stared at the closed door, unable to believe he meant to let her go—had even offered to drive her home. Of course, she could not allow it. He must never know her identity. She suspected she'd already told him too much. Struggling to rise, Verity climbed off the bed. Her head spun alarmingly, and her arm throbbed, but she remained on her feet. She picked up her cape, crossed slowly to the door, and eased it open. She heard the low hum of voices from a room at the end of the hall.

Moving as quietly as possible, Verity tiptoed to-

ward the stairs. She grabbed the mahogany hand-
rail and, using it for support, crept down the car-
peted steps. Each second she expected to hear a
shout, and was surprised to reach the lower hall
without discovery. Two massive double doors faced
her just beyond the arch leading to the entrance
hall, but no servants were in sight. She rushed
across the marble floor, forgetting caution, and slid
back the heavy bolt. It gave way with a resounding
thud. She flung open the door, racing for the street
as fast as she was able.

Above her a window rose and Nicholas Lynton
leaned out. He saw her small, dark figure fleeing
into the shadows. He lifted his voice in an irate
curse that carried clearly in the night.

Chapter 2

Katherine Lynton Delacourt stared after her elder brother in considerable astonishment and no little amusement. In all of her twenty-three years, she could not ever recall seeing Nicholas so discomposed. He might prefer life in the country to cutting a figure in Town, but he'd *always* conducted himself with the grace and impeccable manners of a polished gentleman. Until now.

It was incredible. Nick has been listening amiably to her account of Lady Granville's ball when they'd heard the front door slam shut. Without so much as a by-your-leave, he'd suddenly raced down the hall to his own room. Kate exchanged a glance with their cousin, Bryce, but he seemed neither concerned nor curious, and recommended with a knowing grin that she allow her brother to attend to his own affairs.

Kate ignored him and followed Nick to his bedchamber. She paused in the door, alarmed to see her brother with his head poked out the window at half past two in the morning, cursing loudly enough to rouse the neighbors.

"Nick! Have you run mad? What in heaven's name do you mean by shouting out the window at this hour?"

"Damn!" He withdrew his head and lowered the window. "The bloody little fool. I should never have left her alone."

"Left who alone?" Kate asked, advancing into the

room, but Nick had vanished behind his dressing screen.

Bryce appeared at the door and lounged against the frame. "I tried to warn you, my dear. Apparently, Nick took advantage of our absence to entertain, and our untimely return has caused his little ladybird to fly the coop."

Kate shot him a scathing look. Having been widowed at nineteen, she knew well enough the desires of men, and she did not doubt her handsome brother had his share of conquests. But *not* in his own home and definitely *not* when she was present.

Nick stepped out from behind the screen, buttoning his shirt. "Toss me my coat, Kate," he directed as he sat down to pull on his boots.

"You are not going out? Nicholas, I demand you tell me what this is about."

"Not now, Kate. There isn't time."

"It seems obvious to me," Bryce commented, watching his cousin dress with unusual haste. "She must be something special to throw you in such a taking."

Nicholas stepped around his sister and retrieved his coat from the chair on which he'd tossed it earlier. He shrugged it on as he crossed the room. "You have a foul mind, Bryce, and I'll thank you to keep a proper tongue in your head before my sister."

"Nick!" Kate cried, but he disappeared out the door, leaving her questions unanswered. A second later they heard the front door slam again.

"Bit testy, I'd say."

"You would be wise not to provoke him, Bryce," Kate warned, sitting down on the settee near the fireplace. "I may find you an amusing rogue, but Nick does not half approve of you. Give him cause and you shall soon find yourself on the doorstep without a shilling."

Bryce shrugged as he sauntered into the room. "I rather doubt it. Our sainted Nick has too ingrained a sense of fairness. He knows I should have inherited Uncle Rupert's fortune."

"A pity our uncle did not think so," she said, watching him move restlessly about the room.

"The old curmudgeon! Imagine cutting me off because of a few gambling debts, when he played cards every night of his life—well, well. What have we here? Tea for two and an empty brandy decanter. How cozy."

"I'm sure there is a perfectly reasonable explanation—"

"Of course, my dear, and I gave it to you."

Kate paid no attention, but suddenly rose and crossed to his side. Bryce stood just beyond the four-poster, his back to the bed, intent on examining the tea tray. "Bryce," she whispered, grabbing hold of his arm. "Do my eyes deceive me, or are there bloodstains on the pillows?"

"Extraordinary!" her cousin confirmed a moment later. "Now, what can our Nick have been about?"

"You . . . you do not think he was hurt somehow?" she questioned, growing pale at the thought.

"Come now, Kate. You saw the way Nick raced out of here. He's in superb condition. I'd stake my life on it."

"Yes, of course. I cannot imagine what possessed me to think otherwise."

"But something is deuced odd. Much as I should like to, I really cannot imagine my cousin resorting to violence to seduce a bit of muslin, not when there's a score of them more than willing—"

"Do try not to be so ridiculous," Kate interrupted stiffly. Lifting her skirts, she stepped away from him. "We must wait for Nick to return and explain what has occurred." She resumed her seat near the fire and added tartly, "And I hardly think he will appreciate you rummaging through his papers."

"Just curious," he murmured, but he moved swiftly away from the desk when they heard the front door. He was seated in a wing chair near the fireplace by the time Nicholas entered the room.

One glance at her brother's face was sufficient to persuade Kate to withhold her questions. Bryce, however, knew him less well and drawled, "Lose her, did you?"

Nick strode past him without comment, his eyes glinting furiously. He crossed to the table and picked up the empty decanter, and then slammed it down again.

"Don't look at me," Bryce protested, holding up his hands. "I swear I haven't had a drop, have I, Kate? It was empty when we came in. I rather assumed you and your ... friend ... finished it off earlier. Shall I ring for Crimstock?"

"Do not disturb him," Nick ordered curtly. "Kate, would you leave us, please? I wish a few words alone with our cousin."

"No, I will not." She glared at her brother, her eyes just as blue and just as determined as his. "I am not in the nursery any longer, Nicholas, and I have just as much right to hear what you have to say as does Bryce. Indeed, more, and I am *not* leaving this room until I have an explanation from you."

Bryce stared from one to the other, mentally wagering five pounds on Kate. His cousins were an amiable pair, but he'd already learned Kate's pretty, dark curls and sweet-as-cream smile hid a stubborn streak a foot wide.

Nick sighed, half tempted to climb into bed and leave his sister and cousin to do as they pleased.

"There are ... there are bloodstained pillows on your bed, Nick," Kate said, her voice wavering slightly.

He saw the fear in her eyes and, instantly contrite, moved to sit beside her. "It is nothing to be concerned about, Kate," he assured her, taking her hand in his.

Bryce laughed. "Never tell me you were compelled to use force, old man, for I shall not believe it!"

"How gratifying," Nick replied with a cool smile. "However, one more such remark, and I shall personally see your bags are packed and thrown out the door."

"Egad, but I have truly offended you. Nicholas, I am sorry and most humbly beg your pardon. I meant only to ease the tension with a bit of humor, but I can see you are out of sorts and in no mood for levity. What can I say? Just tell me what I can do to make amends. Stay right here and I will fetch some brandy. Then we can discuss this more reasonably." Not waiting for a reply, Bryce rose quickly and disappeared out the door.

Nick met Kate's eyes and smiled ruefully. "Are you certain he is our cousin?"

She nodded. "Can you doubt it? He is the image of Uncle James."

"Perhaps, but I never met a more unprincipled rapscallion, and I cannot like you standing on such intimate terms with him."

Kate withdrew her hand. "Will you never realize I am no longer a green girl? Bryce at least treats me as though I have some sense, and he is the perfect escort when you are too busy to bear me company, which of late has been all too frequently."

"Then, for your sake, I shall try to bear with him."

"For your own, too, brother dear. Were it not for Bryce, it would have been you accompanying me to Lady Granville's ball tonight."

"There is that," Nick murmured.

"Indeed, and when I think you told me you intended to spend a quiet evening reading—Nick, what did happen tonight?"

He glanced up to meet her searching eyes. Kate had known a great deal of sorrow. She'd lost her parents at a young age, and her husband after only a year of marriage. But Nick had always been there to comfort her, and money, or the lack of it, had never been a consideration. He thought again of the haunted look in another young woman's eyes. He suspected she had no one to comfort her or ease her sorrow.

"Drinks for all," Bryce announced, returning with his arms full. "Brandy for Nick and me, champagne for you, Kate." He poured them each a generous measure, then lifted his glass in a salute. "To the best of cousins."

Nick smiled. It was difficult to remain angry with Bryce when he set out to please. The brandy helped, too, though he'd already consumed more than usual.

Kate took a sip, watching her brother over the brim of the glass. The fury had left his eyes and she felt safe in prodding him. "You were about to tell me what happened."

Nick cradled the brandy glass in his hands. Avoiding their eyes, he murmured, "A burglar broke into the house and tried to lift my purse."

Kate nearly dropped her glass. Her gaze flew again to the bloodstained pillows on the bed, then searched her brother's face. "Nick, swear to me you are not hurt."

"Not in the least, save for my pride. She escaped while I was talking to you."

"She!"

"I knew there was a woman involved," Bryce said. "But the bloodstains, old man? Never tell me you shot her."

"I did, though not intentionally. She was dressed like a man, and in the darkness I didn't realize—I had my pistol leveled at her, and when I ordered her to remove her hat, she threw it at me. The gun went off and grazed her arm."

"Zounds! She sounds a resourceful lass—"

"Bryce, this is no laughing matter," Kate interrupted furiously. "Why, Nick might have been killed." She turned to her brother. "Did you call the watch?"

"No, Kate. The girl meant me no harm. Actually, it was Uncle Rupert she intended to rob. She apologized rather prettily when she realized her mistake."

"Egad, but this is better than a play," Bryce said as he refilled his glass.

Nick removed the folded note from his pocket and tossed it in Kate's lap. "I found that on the floor."

Kate scanned the neatly written lines and then passed the paper to Bryce. "I do not understand any of this."

"I do," her cousin said after he read the note. "She had this prepared and a story to fob off anyone who chanced to catch her. Clever girl, but I own myself surprised that you fell for such flummery, Nick. My advice is to call the watch and have them search for her at once."

"To what point, Bryce? She took nothing. My purse, you will observe, is still on the desk."

"No doubt an oversight on her part," he retorted, earning another black look from his cousin. Unrepentant, he grinned. "Pretty, was she?"

"I suppose one might say so."

"Just as I suspected. She's counting on her looks to protect her."

"No, I do not think so. She truly believes our uncle and three of his cronies conspired to cheat her father at cards. They left him penniless, and she is exacting her revenge. There was an item in the *Gazette* last week that ties in with this. Both Lord Dinsmore and Mr. Ravenscar, friends of Uncle Rupert's, had their houses broken into, and yet the only thing stolen was their purses."

"Well, you'd best warn Lord Ashford, then. He was the other one Uncle Rupert played cards with regularly, and is no doubt on her list. Lord, Nick, 'tis plain as the nose on your face that this girl is nothing but a thief."

Nick stood. "I will bid you good-night, Bryce. I am too fatigued to argue with you any further. Kate, my dear, can your questions wait until morning?"

She rose and kissed his cheek. "Of course, Nick."

When they'd left him alone, Nick strode to the window and stared down at the empty street. He hoped the girl was safe. He undressed slowly, and after tossing the stained pillows off the bed, tried to sleep, but he could not get the girl out of his mind. She must have been desperate to have conceived such a plan, and brave to have carried it through. He smiled in the darkness, remembering the way she'd faced his pistol. Fearless and foolish, he thought, a dangerous combination.

He turned on his side, but sleep eluded him. Bryce's words rang in his ears. Lord Ashford would be next. Good Lord, he hoped not. He knew the gentleman well, and found him cold, unfeeling, and arrogant. Ashford also possessed a sadistic sense of humor that frequently led him to find his amusement at the cruel expense of others. If he found the girl in his room, he'd shoot her without blinking an eye. Or, worse, Nick suddenly thought, easily picturing Ashford forcing the girl to his bed.

At the other end of Harley Street, Verity crept cautiously out of the alley where she'd hidden for over an hour. She'd seen Lynton searching for her, striding determinedly up and down the street. She'd been close enough to hear him flag a hackney carriage and question the driver, but the man had not been in sight when she scurried into hiding and knew nothing. The moon befriended her again, slipping behind the clouds and cloaking the night in darkness. Nicholas Lynton, standing not ten feet distant from her, had sighed loudly. Verity heard his boots scrape against the cobblestones and cowered, but his footsteps slowly receded until the sound was swallowed by the night.

Tired, cold, and discouraged, Verity turned in the direction of Welbeck Street. She'd not far to walk, but even that short way seemed nearly impossible. Head down, her arm aching unbearably, she doggedly placed one slippered foot in front of the other.

The night seemed as though it would never end. She finally reached the small, respectable town house that was her home for yet another month. Verity climbed in the window she'd left raised, careful not to disturb the two Siamese cats, fast asleep on the hearth rug. She moved slowly up the stairs and then down the long hall, hesitating a moment outside the door of her mother's bedchamber. For once Verity ached for someone to comfort her, to hold her warmly and tell her not to worry. She longed for someone who could make everything right with her world, but there was no one save herself. She sighed and stole quietly past the door.

In the safety of her room, Verity awkwardly undressed. She could barely lift her left arm, but it had been neatly bandaged and she saw no signs of fresh bleeding. Her dressing gown lay on the bed where Bessie had left it, and Verity drew it on, thankful the long sleeves would conceal her wound. Then, gathering up her tattered black garments, she stuffed them into an empty hatbox and stored them at the back of her wardrobe. She'd burn them at the first opportunity. Never, ever again would she try to recoup her father's losses, not even if it meant the poorhouse. Lord Ashford could keep his ill-gotten gains.

Verity pulled the covers up to her neck, wishing she could hide beneath them forever. I must have been mad, she thought, fighting back tears. It would have served her right had Mr. Lynton called the watch. But even though she'd tried to steal from him, he'd treated her with kindness, if one discounted the gunshot which, she admitted fairly, was not entirely his fault. He had gently tended her arm and then repaid her villainy with generosity. Verity burned with embarrassment, recalling his offer to give her a draft on his bank. He no doubt thought her contemptible. Or pitiful.

She sniffed and determinedly closed her eyes. She should get some sleep and think no more of Mr. Nicholas Lynton . . . think no more of the one man in London whom she could admire but must never see again.

If only Mama had not become ill, Verity thought, her eyes growing heavy with sleep.

"Miss Verity! Lord, child, you sleep like the dead!"

Verity felt a hand on her shoulder and tried to shrug it off, but Bessie's strident voice roused her from her lethargy. She slowly opened her eyes.

"A body would think you were up half the night instead of retiring early to bed like you did," the stocky housekeeper said, going to the windows and pulling open the curtains.

Verity closed her eyes against the bright sunlight flooding the room. "Just give me a moment, Bessie. I shall be down directly."

"Best hurry, your mama's been asking for you this last hour." Her voice softened and she added, "She seems worse this morning. Maybe we'd best send for that doctor again."

"I shall look in on her. Thank you, Bessie."

When the door shut, Verity glared at the morning sun. It was a beautiful day. It should have been dark and rainy, she thought, struggling out of bed.

She rubbed her eyes, regretting the absence of a breakfast tray, a luxury she'd dispensed with since her father had died. The maids had been let go weeks before, and Verity had tried to dismiss Bessie, too. But the housekeeper had refused to leave, even when Verity told her there was no money for wages.

26

"I been with Miss Lavinia since she had curls down her back and took her meals in the nursery, and I ain't about to leave her now. You just do what you got to, Miss Verity, and don't worry none about me."

Verity had not argued further, thankful to have the older woman's assistance. She promised herself to make it up to the housekeeper one day, and in the meantime did what she could to help, which was not much. Bessie would not allow her to cook, wash the dishes, or mop the floors. She begrudgingly agreed Verity might polish the furniture if she had time, and if Miss Lavinia did not need her.

The clock on the mantel chimed and Verity gasped, shocked to realize the time. She tried to hurry, but dressing was suddenly a chore beyond her capabilities. She'd chosen a high-necked, long-sleeved black day dress, and after struggling with the tiny buttons lining the back, gave up the effort. Her hair was equally impossible to dress. Verity realized she'd have to invent a reason for being unable to use her left arm, and sighed. Her morals were rapidly eroding. Since Papa had died, she'd become a thief and an accomplished liar. What next? Unable to face her reflection in the looking-glass, she picked up her comb and hurried to her mother's room.

Lavinia Parnel was sitting up in bed, and, as usual, her pretty blond curls were covered by a becoming lace cap. Her color was far from normal, however, and her eyes were red and watery. She coughed into a linen handkerchief, her slender body racked with the exertion. When she regained her breath, she held out her hand to her daughter. "Come in, my dear, come in."

"How are you feeling, Mama?" Verity asked, crossing to sit on the side of the bed.

"Utterly wretched, darling. This dreadful cough makes it nearly impossible to breathe. But do not let us speak of that. Tell me what you have been doing?"

"Something foolish, I fear," Verity replied, brushing a damp curl away from her mother's brow. "I bumped my arm on the wardrobe yesterday, and this morning it is horribly sore. I cannot even lift it to put my hair up, or button my gown. Could you help me, Mama?"

"Of course, darling, turn around." Lavinia quickly did up the buttons and then instructed her daughter to bring her hairpins and a comb. She worked gently to untangle Verity's long tresses and deftly pinned them into place. "This reminds me of when you were a little girl, Verity. I loved brushing your hair. Your papa used to say the color was moonlight and sunlight all mixed together . . ."

"I remember, Mama," Verity said softly, hearing the unshed tears in her mother's voice. She leaned over and dropped a light kiss on her brow. Was it only her imagination, or did her mother feel unnaturally warm?

Lavinia, blinking back tears, eyed her daughter critically. "You look very pretty. Hattie could not have done better, if I do say so myself. Now, where are you going today? I hope someplace nice."

Verity smiled. "Hardly. Mr. Swithin is calling this morning."

A shadow crossed Lavinia's eyes at the mention of her late husband's man of business. She'd always felt Swithin disapproved of her. Whenever she and George had argued about money, he'd begun by saying, "Mr. Swithin said we must economize." The man disliked her, she was certain of it. He'd even had the audacity to tell her she must not order mourning clothes, as though she could be so disrespectful to George's memory. She'd ignored his advice, of course, and had directed the modiste to make up several dresses. She knew a thing or two about business, and the best way to keep a tradesman from dunning one was to increase one's business. Lady Beckworth had taught her that piece of sage advice.

Verity, unfortunately, had sided with Swithin and refused to order any gowns for herself.

Lavinia eyed her daughter warily. "I will not see him. You may tell him for me—" She broke off as a spasm of coughing shook her body.

Verity poured a glass of water and held it tenderly to her mother's lips. "Just rest, Mama. I shall deal with Mr. Swithin. Do you wish me to send for the doctor?"

Lavinia shook her head. "He would only say we must leave London at once, and I have already told him we cannot."

Verity glanced at her in surprise. Perhaps Mama was finally beginning to understand that they had no money.

"Remove from London, indeed," Lavinia muttered. "You could not possibly meet an acceptable gentleman in Brighton or Southampton, not when everyone who matters is in London for the Season. I do not know what Dr. Talbot could be thinking. Which reminds me of something I meant to speak to you about, Verity. Bessie told me that nice Mr. Guilford called yesterday and you refused to see him. Do you think it wise, child? I am certain that with a little effort, you could easily bring him up to scratch."

"Mr. Guilford is twice my age, Mama, and he reminds me of a fish. His . . . his eyes bulge and his lips are always wet," Verity replied with a shudder.

"You are a great deal too nice in your tastes, child. Lord Bideford you considered a bore, and Mr. Wallace too fat. John Selby, who I am sure was perfectly amiable, you characterized as an arrogant know-nothing. You find something amiss with every gentleman you meet."

Not *every* gentleman, Verity thought. She had no fault to find with Nicholas Lynton.

"I sometimes fear you will never marry," Lavinia fretted. Sniffing audibly, she wiped her eyes. "I don't know what is to become of you."

"Hush, Mama, and try not to worry. I asked Swithin to try to find us a home in Brighton and we—"

"Brighton! Verity, tell me you do not mean it. We cannot possibly leave London now. Why, 'tis the height of the Season."

"Indeed we can, and I think we must. Dr. Talbot said it is imperative if you are to recover."

"What does he know?" Lavinia demanded. "I shall tell you what will restore me to health, and that is the knowledge that my only daughter has finally met a gentleman she likes well enough to marry!" Her agitation set off another round of coughing.

Verity watched her mother helplessly. The spasms were growing worse, and of longer duration. She would have to send for Dr. Talbot again, though she knew what he would advise. She prayed Swithin had been able to find them some sort of lodgings.

"I . . . I am sorry, dearest."

"Try to rest, Mama." Verity dampened a handkerchief with lavender water and bathed her mother's brow. She could not bear the fearful look in her eyes, and in an effort to soothe her, murmured, "I have met one gentleman I liked very well indeed. His name is Nicholas Lynton."

"Lynton? Do I know the family?" Lavinia asked, her feverish eyes suddenly brighter.

"I believe so, Mama. His uncle, Rupert Lynton, was a friend of Papa's. Now, do try to rest while I speak to Swithin."

"I shall try, darling, but you must promise to bring Mr. Lynton to see me. I must meet this paragon."

"As soon as you are better, Mama," Verity promised rashly while cursing her wayward tongue.

Whatever had possessed her to mention Nicholas Lynton? He was the one person she must avoid at all cost.

Chapter 3

Nathaniel Swithin was a small, earnest man as careless with his appearance as he was meticulous with his work. He invariably had an assortment of stains on his coat, his stock was never tied neatly, and his trousers were snagged and ill-fitting. Verity suspected he was so immersed in his papers that he neither knew nor cared what went on about him. She watched as he set down his cup and saucer with a jolt, the tea sloshing over the brim.

When he dipped his head to refer to his notes, Verity could see the pink scalp showing beneath his sparse brown hair. She stared at it while mentally counting up her small hoard of money.

"It is an excellent location, Miss Parnel, and I am assured the staff is most competent," Mr. Swithin said. When Verity hesitated, he added, "It belongs to the Earl of Lewes. His aunt, Lady Belton, lived there until her death last year."

"The house sounds wonderful, Mr. Swithin, and just what Mama needs, but this stipulation that the staff be employed . . . I am sorry, but I do not see how I could possibly afford it. I do not have to hide my teeth with you, sir. You know our situation—"

"But that is the best of it," he said, gesturing broadly with his hand. The papers on his lap went flying, disturbing the Siamese cats sleeping near Verity's feet. The female of the pair yowled her displeasure and glared disdainfully at the man clutching the fluttering sheets. Verity soothed the cat, gently caressing the animal's dark ears, then retrieved two of the papers and returned them to Swithin.

He took little notice. "You see, Miss Parnel, Lord Lewes cannot pension off the staff. He confided in me that they have lived all their lives at Brighton and would not know how to go on elsewhere. It makes leasing the house rather difficult because so many persons prefer to bring their own servants and those who do not, well, suffice it to say that many are not quite the sort he would wish to have living in his aunt's house." He reddened slightly and took a sip of the tea, droplets from the wet cup dribbling down onto his stock. "I took the liberty of explaining your situation, and Lord Lewes thinks it an ideal solution. The servants come with the house, at no added expense to you."

Verity breathed a sigh of relief. "Then there is no more to be said, save to express my gratitude and inquire how soon we may remove to Brighton?"

"As soon as you wish."

Verity rose, and extended her hand. "Thank you, Mr. Swithin. I shall begin preparations at once and you may inform the staff to look for us by Tuesday next."

"Tuesday?" He rose and glanced about the cluttered room. He knew she had only the elderly housekeeper to assist her and a great deal of work to be done before the house could be closed. "Are you quite certain, Miss Parnel?"

"Indeed, sir. Mama's health is such that I feel it necessary. Bessie and I shall begin packing at once."

"I admire you, Miss Parnel, and if there is anything I can do to assist you, please do not hesitate to ask." He bowed awkwardly over her hand, and in the process dropped his papers again.

Verity helped him to collect them and then walked with him to the door. "There is one thing you could do for me. Mama, Bessie, and I shall

33

travel by public coach, but we will need a carter to convey some of the furniture and our trunks. If you could find someone—"

"Consider it done, Miss Parnel," he interrupted. "I shall notify you when the arrangements are complete." He stumbled as he left, tripping over one of the Siamese cats.

"Cleo!" Verity scolded, scooping up the animal in her arms. "I apologize, Mr. Swithin, she always seems to be underfoot."

"However do you tell them apart?" he asked, glancing back at the other cream-colored cat peering around the door. To him the pair looked identical.

"Easily," Verity said with a smile. "Cleopatra is slightly smaller than Antony, and she follows every gentleman who enters the house."

"I see," he said, but did not quite dare to reach out and caress the silky fur. Cleo's blue eyes stared at him without blinking. "Well, then, I had best be going. I shall send you word in a day or two. Please convey my regards to your mother."

"I shall, and thank you again." Verity closed the door and stood leaning against it. There was so very much to be done. But before she could even begin to make lists, she heard the sound of a bell. She sat Cleo down, admonishing the cat to behave, then hurried up the stairs to her mother's room.

"Is he gone?" Lavinia asked weakly, looking pale and drawn as she leaned against the pillows.

"He is, and we are much indebted to him, Mama. He has found us a wonderful house in Brighton."

"I do not *wish* to go to Brighton," Lavinia protested.

"But, Mama, the house includes staff," Verity coaxed. "Just think, we shall have a butler, cook, and two maids to assist us. Will that not be lovely?"

"Indeed, but to leave London now—Verity, I cannot help but believe it to be a mistake, and I have made plans."

"What plans, Mama?" she asked with a laugh, knowing her mother had not been outside the house in weeks.

"I wrote and invited someone to dinner next week, just an informal evening, you know," Lavinia replied, and would not look at her daughter. Her hands nervously pleated the cover.

"Whom did you ask, Mama? You are not well enough to receive visitors—"

Lavinia suffered a spasm of coughing, her face growing red with the effort to regain her breath. Verity held her, smoothing the hair back from her mother's brow. When the fit passed, she eased her back against the pillows. After pouring a glass of cool water, she held it while her mother took a small sip.

"I am sorry, dear," Lavinia said after a moment. "Sometimes it is such an effort to speak. Perhaps, we should talk later. . . ."

"I'll leave you to rest, Mama, just as soon as you tell me who you invited to call. We must cancel the invitation, as we will not be here next week."

"Not be here? Surely, you cannot intend to remove so soon?"

"I do. The house is available at once, and the faster we leave the dust of London, the faster you will recover. Now, tell me, Mama, whom did you invite?"

"Only . . . only Mr. Lynton."

Verity felt faint. She stared at her mother, praying she'd not heard right.

"He was a good friend to your father, Verity, and I felt it only right to take our leave of him. What is amiss, child? Why, you look as though you've seen a ghost."

"Mr. Lynton passed away soon after Papa," Verity told her, and absently sipped from her mother's glass.

"But . . . but you did not tell me! You said you'd

met his nephew, but you never said anything about Mr. Lynton passing on."

"I know, Mama." She sank down on the bed beside her mother. "I did not wish to distress you, or I would have told you Mr. Lynton suffered a stroke. Mr. Nicholas Lynton, his nephew, inherited the estate."

"Oh. Well, I'm certain he'll understand my confusion. Perhaps he will even call in his uncle's stead."

Verity fervently prayed he would not. Her voice trembling, she asked, "When did you suggest he come?"

"On Monday," Lavinia murmured, closely observing her daughter. "Perhaps it will still be possible. Surely we need not leave till Wednesday or Thursday?"

Verity rose. "You must excuse me, Mama, there is much to be done, and I must speak to Bessie at once. Do try to rest."

"But, Verity—"

"I am sorry, Mama. We shall talk later." She escaped out the door, then leaned against it, her heart racing. It was entirely possible that Mr. Lynton would disregard the invitation, but she could not risk the chance. Even if it meant working day and night, she intended to see they were packed and ready to leave on Saturday.

Nicholas Lynton strode into the drawing room late Thursday afternoon and immediately crossed to the sideboard. Pouring himself a generous glass of whiskey, he glanced over his shoulder at his sister. "Lord, Kate, how on earth do you bear with those women? I have seldom seen a more vicious, nasty set of cats."

Katherine, trailing into the room after him, laughed. "But, Nick, you said you wanted gossip, and you must own you received an earful this afternoon. Maria and her friends know simply everything about everyone in London."

"Except my mysterious intruder," he replied, shrugging out of his close-fitting coat.

"Well, you might have learned more if you had merely listened instead of subjecting every person you met to an inquisition. Really, Nick, I have seldom seen you behave with such a lack of finesse."

"Was I rude?" he asked contritely. He poured her a glass of sherry and brought it to her side.

"Other than cutting Lady Pauline off in the middle of a sentence, and snubbing Sir Frederick, do you mean?"

Nicholas chuckled and Katherine reached out a hand to him. "You might possibly have enjoyed yourself were you not so obsessed with this girl. Why is it so important you find her?"

He squeezed her hand, sobering abruptly. "I cannot explain it, Kate, but if you'd have seen her, you'd understand. She was terribly frightened. I cannot forget the haunted look in her eyes." He shook his head as though to erase the memory. "I swear I meant to help her. If only she had not run before I had the chance."

"I should imagine one would find it rather difficult to believe a gentleman means well when he has just shot one," Katherine said, though not unkindly.

Nick groaned.

Taking pity on him, she added, "I think you're going about this the wrong way. The odds of finding this girl at a ton party, or hearing word of her there, must be enormous. Why, you do not know if she is even received in polite society."

"She is," he answered with certainty. "Her father played cards at Whites with Uncle Rupert and the others. They must be a respectable family."

"Except that she is inclined to burglary."

Nicholas rose and paced the room. "You don't understand, Kate. I'm convinced she was driven to it, and our uncle was partially responsible. I *must* find her."

Katherine watched him for a moment, then remarked softly, "Bryce believes she tipped you a leveler."

"Is he teaching you boxing cant now? How wonderful."

She ignored that. "He said the way you described her hair, and her eyes and her . . . her figure, you sounded quite besotted."

"He would think so."

"Well, you must own, Nick, your present behavior lends credence to his opinion. This girl is all you think of."

He stared at her for a moment. "Of all people, I should expect you to have some sympathy for this child's plight. Would you have me abandon her?" Not waiting for a reply, he flung himself into the chair facing his desk and picked up the mail.

Katherine wisely kept her opinion to herself. When her brother seemed more calm, she asked, "Have you spoken to those friends of Uncle Rupert's? Surely, they could give you the names of the gentlemen they regularly played cards with."

"I thought of that," Nick replied, rifling through a stack of correspondence on his desk. The invitation from Mrs. Parnel was cast aside with others addressed to his uncle. He rose restlessly and crossed to the window, staring moodily out at the street. "Ravenscar and Lord Dinsmore left Town together, and are not expected back for several days."

"What of the other one you mentioned? Lord Ashford?"

"Impossible. He would think it most strange were I suddenly to initiate a conversation with him when we've not spoken in three years. I know Ashford. He would try to find some way to use this girl to his advantage. I would rather wait for Ravenscar or Dinsmore to return."

"Good. Then you will be free to accompany me tomorrow. I thought I would call in at Wedgwood and Byerley's to look at new china."

"Take Bryce, he's a better judge of such things," her brother advised.

"And much better company."

He turned and glanced at her, amusement turning up the corners of his mouth. "*Touché*, Kate. I am a poor excuse for a brother."

"You did promise to show me the sights of London, but since we've come to Town, you have either been shut up in Uncle Rupert's library or chasing after that girl. However, I do not mean to complain."

Nick grinned at her. "I planned to make some calls in the morning, but if you will wait for me to return, I promise to take you not only to Wedgwood's, but to Gunter's Tea Room for an ice afterward."

"Wonderful, but I could go with you, Nick, and then you would not have to come back here to collect me."

"Afraid I would forget, Kate?"

She laughed. "You have been rather absentminded lately."

"You are welcome to come with me if you wish, though you will no doubt be bored. I mean only to call on some physicians in the area. Do you not think it likely she sought treatment for her wound?"

"It is possible," Kate agreed, but without any real conviction. She sought only to soothe her brother. "Come sit down, Nick, and try not to think of her for a bit."

He obliged her, but even while he listened with every pretense of interest to Kate's chatter about balls, routs, and alfresco picnics, his thoughts were on his blond intruder. She had invaded not only his house, but his mind. He couldn't forget the terror in her large, dark eyes, or the fragile feel of her slender body when he'd carried her to his bed.

Bryce was waiting for his cousins when they returned late the following afternoon. He greeted them lazily, and after one look at Nick's dark face, added, "Poor hunting, I gather."

"We had no luck finding the girl, if that's what you mean," Kate replied. She carried a large, heavily wrapped parcel across to the sideboard and carefully set it down. "But I found the loveliest dessert service, and just come see this vase."

The male cousins shared a commiserating look, and Nick stretched out on the sofa next to Bryce. "It's your turn," he murmured. "I have admired tea services and dessert services ad nauseam."

Kate heard him and whirled about, hands on her hips. "Did I complain when we traipsed through some of the worst parts of Town I have ever seen, and climbed dozens of dingy stairs to speak to dozens of idiotic doctors who thought we had run mad?"

Nick laughed. "Not a word, though the way you glared at Dr. Mayhew had him cowering in his boots."

"Insolent fool," she muttered. "But you are hardly any better, Nicholas Lynton. A gentleman who cannot appreciate the finer things in life cannot be counted a gentleman at all."

"Oh-ho!" Bryce said, rising and crossing to her side. "Has Nick turned our gentle Kate into Kate the Shrew?"

She looked up at her cousin. "Do I sound shrewish?"

"Of course not, my dear, a trifle discomposed, perhaps . . . but show me your treasure."

"I warn you, Bryce, if you admire that hideous thing, I shall likely disown you," Nick threatened as he rose to pull the bell rope. "Kate, will you have a cup of tea, even if it is served in Uncle's old china cups?"

"Ignore him, Bryce, as I intend to do. He has the

taste of a plebeian," Katherine advised, turning her back on her brother. While Nick ordered tea brought in, she carefully unwrapped a tall basalt vase. She turned it around so Bryce could admire the delicate hand-painted classical figures on the front, and the palmette border. "Is it not exquisite," she breathed.

"Careful, Bryce, or she will be apt to present it to you as a wedding present."

"Nicholas, hush! Heavens, I shall be glad when you find that dratted girl. Perhaps then you will be more amiable."

"It is, uh, rather unique," Bryce said, picking up the vase and holding it aloft by the looped handles. "But what will you do with it?"

"The vase will go perfectly in the entry hall at our house in Newbury," Katherine replied, admiring it anew. She watched her cousin carefully replace it and then crossed to the wing chair. "And if my brother continues in his present mood, I shall return there next week."

"No, say you do not mean it," Bryce begged. "Why, the Season has just begun. You would miss the masquerade, not to mention Lady Lovell's ball."

Kate shrugged her pretty shoulders and glanced at Nick from beneath her lashes.

He regarded her with barely concealed amusement. "Relax, Bryce, Kate is not that eager to return home. But what of you? Have you any plans for the future?"

It was Bryce's turn to shrug. "Difficult to say, old man. I had rather counted on inheriting from Uncle Rupert, you know. Not that I begrudge you his fortune, but it leaves me at loose ends."

"What would you have done?" Kate asked curiously.

"Done? Why, nothing, my dear, save enjoy life like a gentleman."

"Do be serious, Bryce. You must have had some plans had you inherited the estate."

"None, my dear."

She stared at him, but the moment was saved from awkwardness by the arrival of the maid with tea. Kate covered her confusion by fussing with the cups. She knew several gentlemen in Town who seemed solely preoccupied with their dress or with their horses, but neither she nor Nick were of that persuasion. At home she worked tirelessly on behalf of the local school and orphanage, and frequently tended to the needs of the tenants.

Her brother had a wide range of interests, too. In addition to managing the estate and overseeing his other properties, he played an active role in educating two local boys. Kate knew he personally paid for the boys' schooling, and supervised their progress. She took it for granted that her brother would involve himself in the affairs of their small village. Every Lynton did so. Duty before pleasure was a precept drilled into them from the time they were toddlers.

"My dear, do not look so shocked," Bryce scolded, easily reading her thoughts. "I really am not fit for anything else."

"I find that hard to believe," Nick said, accepting a cup of tea from Kate. "Have you given any thought to the army? If you wished, I'd be willing to purchase you a commission."

"Perish the thought! Not that it ain't generous of you, cuz, but can you really imagine me in the army? I understand the regiments rise at near dawn, and while I should not be averse to traveling abroad, I shudder to think of being involved in an actual battle. War is so barbaric, do you not think?"

Kate laughed. "I must agree with you on that point, but perhaps there is something else you wish to do. Nick, what of that farm in Yorkshire? Did you not say you were having trouble finding a decent land agent? Perhaps Bryce could—"

"Katherine, my dear, if ever you had a kind

thought for me, do not suggest such a thing. I would as lief join the army."

"But . . . but what will you do?"

"Must I do something? I rather thought I'd visit with you for a spell, and when you return home, if you do not wish my company, I might remain here and keep an eye on the house."

"I mean, how will you manage to support yourself? I do not wish to pry, Bryce, but you told me yourself that your income is barely adequate to clothe you."

"It falls lamentably short of that," he replied with a laugh. "If Uncle Rupert had come across with the ready, there would be no problem. As it is, I suppose I must rely on my luck at the faro table and the kind generosity of my cousins. One day, if I am very, very fortunate, I shall meet an heiress who does not too closely resemble a horse, and who would condescend to wed me. In the meantime, you must not fret, my pretty Kate. At the moment I am quite flush."

Kate shook her head, her dark hair falling across her cheek and her eyes full of amusement. "Well, if I were an heiress, I do not believe I would consider a gentleman with so little ambition."

"Nor would I allow it," Nick added.

"Ah, but you have not considered the advantages of such a match. A gentleman without ambition would be free to devote himself entirely to the fine art of pleasing his chosen mate."

"I doubt I could be pleased for long with a gentleman short of funds," Kate teased. "I have very expensive tastes."

"Witness the basalt vase," Nick said, his blue eyes full of laughter as he gazed at his sister over the brim of his cup.

"You are a mercenary wench, Kate," Bryce declared. "And speaking of mercenary, Nick, I believe I might have a lead for you to your little burglar. That is, if you're still interested in finding her?"

"What?" Nick demanded, rising abruptly to his feet. "Why did you not say so at once?"

"Sit down, cousin. There is nothing to be done tonight, and, in truth, it may not come to anything. However, it occurred to me that, provided the girl was not lying, old Addlethorp might set you on the right trail. He knew everything there was to know about Uncle's affairs. If this girl's father was in the habit of losing heavily, he undoubtedly signed a number of vowels. Addlethorp would know his name."

"Of course! I should have thought of that at once." Nick headed for the door, and would have rushed off had not his cousin stopped him.

"He's out of Town," Bryce said. "I took the liberty of strolling around to his quarters this afternoon. His clerk told me he'll return in the morning."

"Blast! Why is everyone I wish to see suddenly leaving Town? One would think there was an epidemic afoot."

"Perhaps it is an omen that you are not meant to find this girl," Kate suggested, but subsided when Nick glared at her.

"Addlethorp hasn't gone far, just over to Tilbury to read a will. His clerk assured me he'll be in his chambers in the morning." Bryce searched the pocket of his vest and pulled out a small scrap of paper. "Wrote out his direction for you," he explained.

"Kind of you to take the trouble," Nick said gratefully.

"See? I do have my uses. Now, cuz, if you will persuade Uncle's housekeeper to hand over the key to the wine cellar, I shall gladly go down and select a decent bottle of wine for dinner. That stuff they've been serving lately smacks distinctly of vinegar, and I know Uncle Rupert had some devilish good stuff laid up."

"If I find this girl tomorrow, you may help yourself to every bottle in the place," Nick promised. He glanced at the clock on the mantel, wondering how early he might reasonably call on the solicitor.

The evening passed slowly. Nick refused to attend the theater with Kate and Bryce, planning instead an early night. But he was still awake when they returned, and lay in bed listening to their idle chatter as they passed down the hall. He thought once the house quieted for the night, he'd be able to sleep. His mind, however, refused to rest, and he composed endless imaginary conversations with his blond burglar. Consequently, it was close to dawn before he fell into a restless slumber, and he did not rise until the clock chimed nine, and the clatter of street vendors woke him.

He dressed hurriedly, not bothering to ring for Crimstock. He was nearly ready when the elderly valet scratched on the door, and entered a moment later with a cup of chocolate.

"I have not time this morning," Nicholas told him while hastily making a last adjustment to the immaculate white linen stock at his throat.

"You will not leave the house without some nourishment?" Crimstock asked. "I brought it up special, sir, as soon as I heard you stirring."

"I appreciate it, but I am in a bit of a hurry."

The valet blocked the door. "Haste makes waste, sir, if I may be so bold as to say so. Start the day without proper nourishment, and you'll find one thing after another going awry."

Nicholas opened his mouth to argue, but realized it would be quicker to drink the blasted chocolate. "Thank you, Crimstock," he murmured, accepting the proffered cup.

The valet watched him approvingly, and when Nick had drained the cup, he stepped aside. "Feeling a bit better, sir?"

Nicholas nodded and escaped before the man could suggest breakfast. The way the servants fussed over him was gratifying, but if he remained in London much longer, he would soon be as portly as his late uncle. The curricle waited at the door, and Nick took his reins from the stable lad.

He set his grays to a brisk pace, enjoying the feeling of the cool morning air against his face. He had a premonition that today he would finally learn the name of his blond intruder.

Chapter 4

Until Nicholas faced his uncle's aged retainer, he had not quite considered how he would pose his questions. There was no reason for this man not to reveal the information he required, but Nick wished to be certain his questions aroused no suspicions about his blond intruder. Mr. Thaddius Addlethorp might be getting on in years, but his mind was razor-sharp and his shrewd eyes missed little.

"I would have been pleased to wait on you, sir, had you sent me word you desired to see me," Addlethorp said politely.

"I was merely passing by," Nick said. "It is of no great importance, but I thought perhaps you might be able to help me with a trifling detail."

"Certainly, sir, if it is within my power."

"I understand my uncle played cards on a somewhat regular basis at Whites," Nick began.

"Indeed, yes. While I cannot condone excessive wagering, your uncle was extremely clever, and, fortunately for you, Mr. Lynton, he nearly always won."

"So I've heard. However, I'm somewhat concerned about a gentleman who lost heavily to Uncle Rupert."

"You need not be, Mr. Lynton. A man who is in the habit of losing, yet continues to play, deserves no sympathy. Remember what the ancients say, for as you sow, so are you like to reap."

"Perhaps. However, the gentleman in question

died soon after my uncle, leaving his family in dire circumstances. I'd like to do something to assist them."

"Commendable, but you needn't feel obliged, Mr. Lynton. If they've come to you for assistance, I advise you to send them on their way at once. Charity only weakens one's moral stamina."

Nicholas picked up his gloves and stood. "I shall keep your advice in mind, but the family did not come to me. I heard of them only by chance, and I desire to see them myself. All I require of you, Mr. Addlethorp, is the name and direction of a gentleman who lost heavily to my uncle."

Though Lynton smiled, something in his manner flustered the older man. He looked up, startled. "I say, for a moment there you quite put me in mind of your uncle."

"The name, sir?"

"Oh, yes. Well, let me see," he replied, pressing the tips of his fingers together. "I think, if the rumors you've heard are true, you must be seeking George Parnel. He played frequently with your uncle, my lords Dinsmore and Ashford, and Mr. Ravenscar."

"Do you know anything of him?"

Addlethorp chuckled. "I know he lost a small fortune—"

"Do you have his direction," Nick interrupted, his patience rapidly eroding.

"Well, of course, sir. He leased a house on Welbeck Street, number forty-six, I believe. But I really would not advise visiting the family. Mr. Parnel left two vowels as yet unpaid, and though I've written twice, I've had no response."

"Tear up the vowels," Nick ordered, striding toward the door.

The solicitor's face turned red, then drained of all color. "You cannot be serious, sir! Why, the debt is well over a thousand pounds. It's part of your inheritance."

Nicholas slammed the door in answer, and took the narrow steps two at a time. Welbeck Street, he thought, amazed. He'd searched half of London for Miss Parnel, and all the time she'd lived a stone's throw from his own house on Harley Street. He might have met her out walking at any time. Tossing a coin to the lad holding his horses, he took control of the reins.

Nick drove as fast as he dared, but the streets were teeming with traffic. Vendors hawked their wares, draymen cursed loudly, and huge, lumbering wagons blocked the road. He had to rein in his horses every dozen feet or so. He turned with relief onto Oxford Street, but it was little better. Cursing quietly beneath his breath, he narrowly avoided running down a street urchin. But he finally reached Welbeck Street.

Nick found number forty-six without difficulty, but he stared at the house in dismay. The windows were shuttered and the knocker off the door. He'd felt so certain he'd find her today that he couldn't believe she was gone. Summoning a young boy to hold his horses, he approached the house. Not a sign of life anywhere, but he still banged his fist against the door.

"The house is empty, sir," a young man emerging from the adjoining town house informed him. He would have walked on had not Nicholas blocked his way.

"I am trying to find the Parnels—"

"Sorry, sir, but I'm afraid I don't know the name."

"The family lived here," Nick insisted, indicating the house behind him. "It's extremely important I find them. There was a daughter, blond, slender—" He broke off, aware the man was regarding him strangely. "I apologize, sir. I must sound like a madman, but I assure you I'm not a creditor. I want only to offer my help to the family. My name is Nicholas Lynton." He held out his hand in a gesture of friendliness.

49

"Thomas Young," the gentleman responded, shaking hands. "I think I know who you mean. I spoke to the young lady when we chanced to meet in the street, but we weren't really acquainted. All I can tell you is that she left this morning. I wouldn't have known, except I forgot an important paper and when I came back to fetch it, I saw the post chaise and wagon. The young lady saw me and came across to say farewell. I'm afraid you just missed them."

"Did she say where they were going?"

"She did mention something about taking her mother to the seaside for her health." He thought for a moment, then shrugged. "I'm sorry, but I don't recall any particular town."

Verity found Brighton lonely with little to occupy her except worrying over her mother's health and their steadily decreasing finances. The move had been more expensive than Verity anticipated, for Lavinia refused to arrive in Brighton by public coach. An extravagant gesture since no one had seen their arrival other than a flock of screaming sea gulls, and some fishermen too busy spreading their nets to pay any heed.

The house, at least, had met with Lavinia's approval. Tall and elegantly styled, it was trimmed in the prince regent's colors of buff and blue—though the paint was fading now and the rich red of the brick had mellowed. The elderly staff had turned out to meet their new mistress and treated Lavinia with a deference that did much to restore her good humor.

Wythecombe, the white-haired butler, pointed out the house was ideally situated just off the Steine, within easy walking distance of the shops, vapor baths, and Donaldson's library. To Lavinia's disappointment, and Verity's relief, he'd explained apologetically that most of the shops were closed at present. They would reopen in the summer, when the prince regent visited.

Lavinia sighed and asked to be shown to her bed-chamber. Olive, who'd served Lady Belton, stepped forward and begged the privilege of leading the way. A tiny woman, her dark skin contrasted sharply with her gray hair. She smiled, exuding such warmth and desire to please that Lavinia accepted her assistance and motioned Bessie to follow them.

Verity, assured her mother would be properly looked after, allowed the talkative Emma to show her to her room. The maid, as round as Olive was thin, kept up a lively flow of chatter, and her double chin quivered as she laughed. She promised Verity she'd enjoy her stay in Brighton, nodding her head for emphasis so that her fat sausage curls shook and looked to be in danger of coming undone.

Her words proved true, however. Within a few weeks, both Verity and her mother felt quite at home. Were it not for the circumstances, Verity thought as she tended the garden, she could be almost content. Emma watched over her like a mother hen with a new chick.

Indeed, all the staff were pleasant and eager to please. Verity could seldom sit in the library for more than a few moments before Emma or Dorcas looked in with offers of tea or a bit of cake. Their chef, Tobias, was married to Emma and just as broad of girth as his wife. He clearly appreciated his own cooking, which Verity admitted was excellent, but she worried over the cost. Tobias had assured her that Lady Belton had been the same, and he knew how to hold the line. He explained the fish, caught fresh by his nephew, cost them little. The fruits and vegetables were from the Earl of Lewes's greenhouse, supplied every fortnight without charge. The earl looked after his own, Tobias told her.

Verity sniffed the air, catching the tantalizing

aroma drifting from the kitchen window. Two pies cooled on the sill, the smell making her mouth water. If she didn't watch herself, she'd soon be as large as Tobias.

Emma's face appeared in the window above the pies and Verity waved. A moment later the maid waddled out to the garden, carrying a large-brimmed bonnet.

"Good heavens, miss, you don't want to be out here with nothing on your head. I brought you Lady Belton's old hat," she said, extending a straw monstrosity. "She always wore it when gardening. Not that she had a skin like yours, miss. My lady was as dried up as a prune when I came into service here, and that was twenty years past."

Verity, having learned it was useless to argue, accepted the hat. It was too large and slid down over her brow, but if she protested, Emma would only go search out another. Her new maid was as bothersome as Bessie when it came to what she considered proper for Verity.

"The garden's looking lovely, miss," Emma said. "His lordship will be pleased when he sees what you've done. It was him that had that brick wall built to protect his aunt's roses from the salt blowing in off the sea."

"What is he like, Emma?" Verity asked, sitting on her heels and rubbing her aching back.

"Just as kind and sweet a gentleman as you'd ever want to meet," the maid declared. "No one took better care of Lady Belton. There's some who'd hide their old relatives away and never give another thought to them, but not his lordship. He was here every week, sitting and talking with his aunt, and whatever she wanted, he saw to it that she had."

"He sounds very nice," Verity agreed, smiling.

"You'll see for yourself, miss. Like as not, he'll be here today. He comes himself, once a month, to see that everything's as it should be."

"Today?" Verity asked with a twinge of alarm.

"Indeed yes, miss. Did I forget to mention it?" She shook her head. "It's a terrible thing to get old and lose your memory. I declare, sometimes I don't know what day of the week it is."

Verity barely heard her. She glanced down at the ragged blue muslin dress she wore. Patched and stained, it was good for little but gardening. And with her hair hanging down her back beneath the ill-fitting straw hat, she must look a sight. Hardly the lady of quality the Earl of Lewes had specified as a tenant for his aunt's house.

She rose hurriedly to her feet. "I should change at once—"

"Forgive me for coming through, but Wythecombe said I would find you out here," a deep voice said from behind her.

Verity, her face flushed, turned slowly. The tall, lean gentleman before her was elegantly clad, though in the style of years past. His blue velvet cutaway coat had long sleeves that reached to his knuckles and contrasted sharply with the snowy white stock tied neatly about his throat. Her gaze traveled over the tight-fitting knee breeches, fastened at the knee with the sort of gold buckles she remembered her grandfather wearing.

"I am Lord Lewes," he explained, his gray eyes twinkling as he handed her his card.

Anthony Edward Claude Eden, the eighth Earl of Lewes, Verity read silently from the impressive card. She glanced up to meet his eyes and found him regarding her kindly.

"When I first stepped out, I nearly mistook you for my aunt Penelope," he said. "I used to come here as a boy, and always found her in the garden, wearing one of her old gowns and, if I am not mistaken, that very hat. She had long blond hair, too, though it turned pure white when she grew older." He smiled suddenly. "You evoke some delightful memories, Miss Parnel."

53

"It does take one back, does it not, my lord?" Emma said, then sighed. "I suppose I'd best go in. I'll make sure Tobias has the kettle boiling, miss." She dropped a curtsy to the earl, then ambled off, not in the least disconcerted by his presence.

Verity, too, relaxed under his benevolent gaze. Smiling up at him, she extended an invitation. "Do come into the house, sir. If you will allow me a few moments to change—"

"Verity, child, what are you thinking of to keep our guest standing out there?" Lavinia scolded from the doorway. "His lordship will think you have no manners."

"On the contrary, I find her most charming," Lord Lewes responded gallantly, then offered Verity his arm. He escorted her to the door, and when she'd performed the introductions, bowed over Lavinia's hand. "It is easy to see how Miss Parnel comes by her beauty."

Astonished, Verity watched her mother flutter her lashes as she gazed admiringly up at the earl. Lavinia invited him into the drawing room, assuring him the staff had tea ready. Glancing over her shoulder at her daughter, she added, "Run along, darling, and change your gown. I shall try to entertain his lordship until you return."

Bemused, Verity obeyed her. She'd not seen her mother looking so pleased in more than two years. Or so well. She was far from recovered, and still tired easily, but she'd improved greatly since coming to Brighton. Lavinia attributed it to the vapor baths she now visited twice weekly, but Verity suspected it had much to do with the way the staff pampered her mother.

She watched after her for a moment, then hurried to her room. Bessie was waiting to help her change her muslin for a dark gray linen day dress. A lighter gray sash trimmed the high waist and accented the long sleeves. Bessie brushed Verity's curls and secured them in a knot before threading a dark gray ribbon through them.

"There, child. No one would think to look at you that you're wearing one of your mama's made-over gowns."

"It is perfect," Verity told her. "I do not know how we would ever manage without you, Bessie."

"Go on with you, child," the maid said, shooing her charge toward the door, but her face was flushed with pleasure.

Verity hurried down the steps, worried now about her mother. Lavinia had clearly anticipated the earl's visit. Verity just hoped she'd not over-taxed her strength in preparing for it. Even mild excursions left her mother weak and dreadfully tired. Pausing in the doorway of the drawing room, Verity listened to the sound of light, infectious laughter. Delighted to hear her mother enjoying herself, she forgot her concern and entered the room with a warm smile for the earl.

He rose as soon as he saw her, and remained standing until Verity was seated next to her mother on the upholstered settee.

"I was just telling his lordship how pleased we are that he called," Lavinia said as she filled a delicate china cup with tea and handed it to her daughter. "He promises me that, though we may be quite bored with the lack of company at present, once the prince regent arrives, we will yearn for these quiet days."

"I assure you, Miss Parnel, Brighton is gay beyond belief in the summer."

"For myself, sir, I am content, and consider us most fortunate in securing a lease on this house. Your aunt had some beautiful things," Verity replied, waving a hand to encompass the room. The curtains and wall coverings had faded with time, but the mahogany furniture gleamed with polish and loving care. The sun, pouring through the south windows, cast a mellow, warm glow and picked up the gold of the daffodils gracing the top of an inlaid Pembroke table. "This is a perfect room."

"Thank you, though not everyone shares your taste. One lady who came down from London told me I should throw everything out and redecorate, following our regent's lead in using the Orient as an inspiration."

"Good heavens," Lavinia said with a laugh. "I cannot imagine this room with red dragons and black japanned furniture."

"Nor I, dear lady." His long, narrow face took on a melancholy look. "I suppose 'tis foolish of me to preserve it, but I spent much of my boyhood here. My parents traveled frequently, and I considered it a high treat to stay with my aunt Penelope."

"She must have been an exceptional lady," Verity said softly. "The servants speak very highly of her."

"As well they should. She didn't believe in standing on ceremony, and encouraged her staff to speak their minds." He hesitated, then glanced at Lavinia. "If they should overstep the line now and then, I do hope you will make allowances."

Her silvery laugh rang out. "I am far more likely to steal them away from you. They watch over me as though I were a tender girl in the first blush of youth."

He smiled, his eyes as full of mischief as a young boy's. "Perhaps it is because you look so young."

Lavinia tried to speak, but a spasm of coughing shook her slender body. Verity rose at once and poured a glass of water, but it was several moments before Lavinia was able to take a sip. Lord Lewes watched in concerned silence.

Eyes watering, Lavinia begged his pardon. "This dreadful cough is the reason we were forced to remove to Brighton. Though I am much better, it still catches me unawares."

"Do not apologize, Mrs. Parnel. I once suffered

the same affliction, but I'm sure Brighton will restore the roses to your cheeks."

Lavinia smiled weakly. "You are most kind, Lord Lewes, but I must beg to be excused."

Both Bessie and Olive had come to the door when they'd heard their mistress coughing. At a nod from Lavinia, they hurried to assist her.

Verity rose as well, but her mother waved her back. "Remain here with his lordship, child. See that he finishes his tea and cake. I shall be better directly."

When Lavinia had left the room, Lord Lewes inquired gently, "Has she been ill long?"

Verity nodded. "This past year. She grew worse when Papa died, but she's been so much better of late that I'd hoped she was recovering."

"Give her time, my dear," he advised, his voice warm with sympathy. He hesitated, then spoke frankly. "Mr. Swithin told me something of your circumstances. We have been acquainted a number of years, and he thought I could perhaps help. I should like to do so, and if you agree, I'll send my own doctor to see your mother. He is an excellent man."

Warm tears sprang to Verity's eyes. She was able to endure hardships stoically, but sympathy invariably broke down her defenses. She murmured her thanks, blinking rapidly.

Nicholas, settled comfortably in his bed at the Old Ship Hotel in Brighton, tried to concentrate on his book. But after reading one page numerous times, he laid it aside, wondering if his sister had been right after all. Kate had been incredulous when she'd learned he meant to search the southern coast for Miss Parnel. He closed his eyes, recalling the scene in their London sitting room three weeks earlier.

Kate had come in laughing, her hair tousled from the wind and becoming color in her cheeks. Bryce had followed on her heels, his low voice conveying some choice bit of gossip. They'd both paused in the doorway, surprised to see Nicholas sprawled in a chair, a glass of brandy in his hand. But that was nothing to the astonishment they'd felt when he made his announcement.

Kate had crossed the room in her brisk stride. "You are mad, Nick, quite, quite mad. I believe this girl has bewitched you. You do realize that what you're proposing is preposterous? Why, she could be anywhere in England."

"Her neighbor said Mrs. Parnel was ill, and they were removing to somewhere near the sea," he answered wearily.

"Oh, I do beg your pardon. You have only the entire coastline to search."

"I believe I will find her somewhere in Sussex," Nick said, a trace of stubbornness creeping into his voice. "She is without funds and cannot travel far."

"You are wasting your breath, Kate," Bryce drawled from his seat near the fire. "Obviously Nick has made up his mind and nothing we say will sway him. I, however, have not the slightest desire to go traipsing down England's coast." He shuddered, adding, "Not at this time of year."

Nick, carefully avoiding his sister's eyes, merely nodded. "You may both remain here or accompany me as you wish, but I leave tomorrow morning."

"Tomorrow," Kate breathed. "It's impossible. Nick, you have not considered. We have engagements—"

"I have none. Stay here with Bryce, Kate, and keep your engagements. I'll return as quickly as possible."

"I shall," she retorted, stung that he so little wished her company. "I have no taste for fool's errands."

"Now, Kate, be reasonable," Bryce coaxed. He glanced slyly at Nick. "Your dear brother is of an age when gentlemen frequently behave a bit foolishly over a ladybird. He's obviously taken with his little blond thief." He winked lewdly at his cousin. "I shouldn't wonder if more occurred that evening than Nick is telling."

"You have the mind of a mucker, Bryce," Nick replied, his voice ominously low. "I suppose it is beyond your comprehension that I feel responsible for the girl. Let me remind you that our uncle was partially to blame for her plight, and I compounded her problems by shooting her. Any *gentleman* would feel it to be his duty to find the girl."

"Of course, old man, of course. No offense intended—only I can't help wondering how hard you'd search if she were old and haggard."

"Just as diligently," Nick swore, but his voice lacked conviction. He saw Bryce's knowing grin.

After condemning his cousin as a care-for-nobody, Nick had retired to his bedchamber and pulled out a sturdy valise. His cousin's remarks rankled, but there was no sense in losing his temper with Bryce. His cousin would never feel deeply about anyone or anything. And in fairness, Bryce had never seen Miss Parnel. Never seen the innocence shining in her large, dark eyes, or the vulnerable way she'd cowered against the pillows when he'd approached her.

Nick could still picture her, the way her long blond hair had rippled over the pillows, like spun gold shimmering in the candlelight. He recalled the soft feel of her skin, and the contrast of her black shirt against her slender white neck. Nick sighed, annoyed with himself for the turn his thoughts had taken. He haphazardly tossed several shirts and linen stocks on the bed. He was searching his wardrobe, when Crimstock scratched on the door and entered.

"Might I be of assistance, sir?"

Within moments the elderly valet had his clothing neatly sorted and folded. He coughed and when Nick glanced at him, he gestured to the valise.

"There is an art to packing, sir. If not done properly, you'll find your shirts sadly wrinkled and your stocks beyond wearing."

"Thank you, Crimstock. I'll keep it in mind, but I fear I'm all thumbs when it comes to this sort of thing."

"Then, if I may be so bold as to suggest it, perhaps you would be wise to take a valet with you."

"Have you someone in mind?" Nick asked absently as he fingered a dark blue dress coat.

"I should be pleased to go, sir."

"But I'd be traveling fast," Nick began. He saw the twinkle in the old man's eye and smiled. "I apologize, Crimstock. You've proved your worth and I'd be grateful for your assistance—but can you be ready to leave in the morning?"

"Within the hour, if necessary," the valet declared.

"The morning will do," Nick said, laughing silently at the old man's enthusiasm. Although he had doubts about the wisdom of taking an elderly valet on a fast-paced journey, Crimstock's presence had proved a blessing.

At their first stop in Rye, the valet preceded him into the Mermaid Inn. Crimstock announced his master with all the pomp and ceremony generally accorded a visiting duke. The effect had not been lost on the inn's proprietor, and Nick had enjoyed the finest of accommodations. It had been the same everywhere they stayed.

But not even the resourceful, indomitable Crimstock had been able to unearth a sign of Miss Parnel. Not in Rye, or Hastings, or Eastbourne, or in Newhaven. His thoughts drawn back to the present, Nick picked up his book once more.

A scratch at the door made him glance up as Crimstock entered. "Will you be needing anything else, sir?"

"Nothing, thank you. Just make sure I'm awake early." He hesitated, then added, "This is our last stop, Crimstock. If we don't find Miss Parnel in Brighton, we go back to London."

"As you wish, sir." After adjusting the curtains, the valet tottered toward the door. He paused with his hand on the knob. "May I say, sir, that I have enjoyed our jaunt tremendously?"

Nick smiled. "I am pleased to think it has not been a complete waste."

"Do not lose heart, sir. It looks to be a fine day tomorrow, and I should not be at all surprised were you to find your young lady here."

"But I should be," Nick muttered when the door had shut. He discounted his valet's encouragement. Crimstock had said the same thing in every town they'd visited. It meant nothing, and Nick was beginning to think Kate had been right. He was on a fool's errand.

Chapter 5

Nicholas awoke the following morning with a strong desire to burrow beneath the covers and stay there. Several sleepless nights, combined with the frustration of the last few weeks, had left him tired and irritable. Although Crimstock provided him with a steaming cup of coffee, it did little to improve his mood and nothing at all to ease the throbbing behind his eyes. He listened wearily while Crimstock told him the places in Brighton where they'd most likely hear news of Miss Parnel.

"I should think the vapor baths or the library most promising," the valet said as he drew open the curtains.

"If she's here," Nicholas replied moodily. He groaned aloud as he glimpsed a gray, cloudy sky. "Not another rainy day. It's an omen, Crimstock. We might as well pack and leave at once."

"I'm told the clouds will blow over and the sun shine before noon. 'Tis often that way on the coast, sir."

"Then wake me at noon."

"It will be nearly that by the time you are shaved and dressed," Crimstock said, consulting his large pocket watch. "I thought you were feeling out of sorts, sir, and took the liberty of allowing you to sleep late. However, as it is after ten—"

"Ten! Good heavens, man, why didn't you say so?" Nick climbed out of bed and stretched. He allowed his valet to drape a brocade dressing gown about his shoulders, then strolled to the windows.

"I think you are overly optimistic, Crimstock. More than likely, we'll be caught in a thunderous downpour."

He was wrong, of course. By eleven, when he was attired to fit Crimstock's notions of propriety, the sun peeped through a patchwork quilt of gray and white clouds. By half past the hour, when he reached Donaldson's Circulating Library on the east side of the grassy enclosure known as the Steine, the sun appeared in full force.

Nick's spirits lifted along with the temperature, and he doffed his hat to two elderly ladies. He crossed the veranda in front of Donaldson's, where subscribers were encouraged to sit and gossip, and stepped into the library. He greeted the clerk with a friendly smile and renewed hope.

"Good morning. I wonder if you might help me," he said, leaning against the counter. "I am trying to find some friends. Can you tell me if you have a Mrs. Parnel listed among your subscribers?"

The clerk's helpful smile disappeared as his sparse brows drew together and his thin lips compressed in a frown of stern disapproval. "I am not at liberty to dispense such information."

"But I only wished to know if the lady is in Brighton—"

"There are rules, sir."

Nicholas, wishing he'd not left Crimstock at the hotel, straightened and withdrew several pound notes, which he edged across the counter. "Of course, I quite understand. Only Mrs. Parnel is quite an old friend, and I should hate not to see her if she's here."

"Parnel, you say?" the clerk asked while greedily reaching for the notes. "I suppose there can be no harm in mentioning that a Mrs. Parnel and her daughter recently leased Lady Belton's house."

Nicholas reminded himself that Parnel was a common name, but he couldn't quite suppress the sudden surge of hope that lightened his eyes and curved his lips in a smile. "Is the house in town?"

"Just a few blocks east of the Steine," the clerk said. "However, it appears your luck is in, sir. I believe that is Miss Parnel just coming in the door."

Nicholas swung around and met Verity's astonished gaze. She dropped the parcel of books she carried, but her eyes, as large and frightened as he remembered, remained fixed on his face.

An older, buxom lady moved between them as Nick stepped forward. "Miss Parnel, I have been searching everywhere—"

"No," Verity cried, backing away. "Oh, no!"

Before Nick could reach her, she disappeared out the door, her books left scattered on the floor. He tried to follow, but the heavyset woman blocked his path. Colliding with her, he was nearly knocked off his feet, and half the lady's packages tumbled from her arms.

Nicholas apologized as he edged around the woman, but she entangled him in a mesh of fleshy arms and bulky bundles.

"Just a moment, young man," she ordered, firmly holding onto his arm. "The least you can do is retrieve my packages. It's disgraceful the way you young people tear about with no thought or consideration for anyone."

He bent quickly, scooped up her bundles, and piled them in her arms. "I beg your pardon, ma'am," he muttered as he strained to keep an eye on Miss Parnel's rapidly departing figure.

"Let me tell you, sir, in my day gentlemen had manners—now, just look what you've done—a whole pound of coffee, wasted. You shall pay for this, sir!"

Nick's appalled gaze followed the trail of ground coffee pouring from a tear in one of the packages, down over the woman's dress, into a growing mound on the floor. Mouthing profuse apologies, he hastily withdrew a stack of notes and thrust them into the woman's hand.

Dodging the clerk, who knelt near the door picking up Miss Parnel's books, Nick raced into the street. Only a few ladies were abroad, none of whom resembled Miss Parnel's slender form.

"Damn," Nicholas swore softly.

The heavyset woman, who had followed him to the door, sniffed in loud disapproval. "Foul language, too. Shocking, simply shocking behavior." Turning to the clerk, she prodded him with her umbrella. "Really, Mr. Thistle, if you are going to permit persons of such low character into the library, I shall have to cancel my subscription."

"I'm sure the gentleman meant no harm, Mrs. Ponsonby."

"Gentleman? Why, one can look at him and see he's a hardened rake, a rogue of the worst sort—"

Nicholas judged it time to leave. He wanted to ask the clerk for directions to Lady Belton's house, but didn't quite dare in the face of Mrs. Ponsonby's wrath. He strolled in the direction of his hotel, the lady's discourse on his birth, breeding, and morals ringing in his ears. Her words had little effect, however. All Nick could think of was Miss Parnel. She was there, in Brighton. It was a small town—she could not possibly elude him for long. Unless she disappeared again. He quickened his steps.

In the temporary safety of her room, Verity paced restlessly. The sound of every passing carriage brought her rushing to the window to peer out anxiously. She felt certain Mr. Lynton's arrival in Brighton was not a coincidence, and it would be only a matter of hours before he knocked on the door. And then . . . her mind whirled as she contemplated the possibilities. Would he denounce her as a thief? Have her arrested and hauled before the authorities? Verity closed her eyes, thinking of what the shock would do to her mother.

She'd not expected ever to see Nicholas Lynton again. She had been so certain that once he discovered her gone, he would quickly forget her. But he'd obviously taken the trouble to learn her name, and had somehow followed her to Brighton. She'd told no one in London where they were going, so it could not have been easy to find her. That Lynton had done so, and within a month, worried Verity. What did he want with her?

The sound of a carriage approaching filled her with dread. She peered out the window until it passed, then sank into a chair, trembling with relief. But she knew it was only a temporary reprieve. Sooner or later he'd find her. She should have stayed at the library and talked to him, begged him for mercy.

The chatter of voices drew her to the window again. She saw her mother coming up the walk with Bessie, and watched her for a moment. Dear Mama. She was so much improved since coming to Brighton. If only there were some way to protect her from learning the truth about her daughter—but that seemed impossible with Mr. Lynton in town. Perhaps I should tell her myself, Verity thought. The shock might be less.

A light tap on the door heralded her mother's arrival. Lavinia, in a swirl of black silk, stepped into the room.

"Darling, are you not well? Emma said you had a dreadful headache, so I came up at once. I cannot ever recall you being ill, Verity."

"It is nothing, Mama—"

"Oh, I am so glad, dearest, because I have the most delightful surprise for you. We are entertaining tonight, and I have invited someone special to meet you." She reached out a hand and squeezed her daughter's. "I know it must be terribly dull for you here, Verity, but I think the gentleman I asked to join us this evening will amuse you. He's just returned from London, and knows all the latest gossip."

"Playing matchmaker again, Mama?" Verity asked, making an effort to smile. "I wish you would not."

"Nonsense. I've invited a pleasant young man to dinner, that's all. If you do not like each other, there is nothing more to be said. Of course, if you do . . . darling, you must know it is my fondest wish to see you wed."

"I know," Verity replied, staring miserably down at her hands. "But, Mama, the truth is, I'm not fit to be married. No respectable gentleman would offer if he . . . if he knew some of the things I've done."

The color drained from Lavinia's face. "What on earth do you mean? You are not—not soiled?"

Verity glanced up. It took her a moment to comprehend her mother's meaning, and then she nearly laughed. "No, Mama! I've never even been kissed, but there are other things—"

"Nothing else matters, Verity! Heavens, child, you gave me a fright." Lavinia pressed a hand to her breast. "I can feel my heart beating fit to burst. Help me to my room, darling."

Verity, beside her in an instant, placed a supporting arm about her mother's waist and walked with her to the large bedroom at the end of the hall. Bessie met them at the door. After one anxious look at Lavinia's face, she hurried to turn down the cover on the four-poster. Olive ran for the smelling salts.

Feeling as though she were in the way, Verity watched the two maids fuss over her mother. After a moment she slipped silently from the room.

Much to Verity's relief, the day passed without any word from Nicholas Lynton. By the time the dinner hour drew near, she'd half convinced herself that she'd only imagined his appearance in Donaldson's Library. There was a sameness about many stylish young gentlemen, and it would not be the first time she'd mistaken one for another. After all, she reasoned, she'd seen Nicholas Lynton only once in her life, and then in a dimly lit room when she was near to fainting.

Only once . . . but she'd dreamed of him often. No doubt she had embellished his image, confused the real Nicholas Lynton with her dreams. Dozens of men might have dark, wavy hair that glistened a deep blue in candlelight, but surely no man could actually have eyes the vivid blue she recalled, eyes so heavily lashed, they appeared at odds with his thick, dark brows and imperious Roman nose.

She recalled the wide, firm mouth she'd dreamed of, his strong chin softened only by a dimple when he smiled . . . it had to be her imagination. She had probably bestowed her dream image on some poor gentleman she'd met once in London at a cotillion or ball. And he, poor fellow, recalling her name, had scared her witless today. The real Nicholas Lynton was probably a hundred miles away.

A knock at the door set her heart pounding furiously, but it was only Emma.

After one glance at Verity, Emma chuckled aloud. "Your mama sent me with a message, miss. She said I was to tell you she does not wish to see you in that old gray muslin dress again. You are to wear your dark blue silk with the black ribbons."

"But we are in mourning," Verity protested, looking down at her gray dress. It was true it was not precisely becoming, but it was one of the few somber colors she owned.

"She said the black ribbons would be enough, as it's been three months since your papa passed on."

"Three months." Verity sighed as she allowed Emma to unbutton her dress. "In some ways it seems much longer, and in others as though it were only a week or so. . . . Emma, how is Mama? Is she well enough to entertain a guest tonight?"

"Oh, yes, miss. She slept for hours this afternoon, and Olive said she's as excited at having company as a young girl waiting for her first beau."

Verity didn't doubt it. Her mother had always shown a great deal of interest in any gentleman who called. The young man coming tonight was only the latest in a long list of eligible bachelors Lavinia had invited to the house in the hope that one of them would appeal to her daughter. Unfortunately, none of them did. Verity had learned to tolerate such occasions with good grace, if not enthusiasm. It was little enough to do if it made her mother happy.

Emma helped her change into the blue dress, then stood back to admire the effect. "You're pretty as an angel, miss."

Verity crossed to the looking-glass. The dress had been made up before her father died. The skirt was fuller than her other gowns, and Bessie had added a lacy frill at the hem, edged with black ribbons. The skirt swung outward as she walked, revealing her black satin pumps.

Verity liked the feel of the skirt, but not the revealing bodice. Cut in a low square, it barely covered the top of her breasts, and her bust was further emphasized by a black ribbon running beneath it. She asked Emma to fetch her cashmere shawl, then draped it over her shoulders, hiding much of the bodice.

"You need a nice string of pearls to set if off, miss," Emma advised.

Verity agreed, but all their jewelry had been sold. She shrugged, pretending indifference. "It is only a quiet dinner with Mama and a young man she's invited. I should not like him to think I dressed exceptionally fine to please him."

"Well, even without jewels, you look lovely, Miss Verity."

"Thank you, Emma. I believe I hear the clock

chiming and had best go down before Mama comes looking for me."

She found her mother in the drawing room and stood still for Lavinia's scrutiny.

"I hardly think you need a shawl, darling. The night is so warm, I had them open the windows to catch the breeze."

Verity dropped a kiss on her mother's brow, ignoring the hint. "I am glad to see you recovered, Mama. 'Tis a pity Lord Lewes is not here to see how beautiful you look."

A delicate blush colored Lavinia's cheeks and, as her daughter intended, she forgot her train of thought. She raised a hand to her blond hair, tucking a stray curl into place. "I am sure I do not know what you mean."

Verity smiled, but her mother did look exceptionally lovely. Black became her, the dark crepe setting off her ethereally pale complexion and silvery blond hair. Verity sat down opposite her and made an effort to put her worries aside. "Tell me about our guest, Mama. Who is he, and how did you chance to meet?"

"A most distinguished young man with excellent manners and the most exquisite taste. Mrs. Leamington introduced us, for it happens they used to be neighbors in Kent."

Another dandy, Verity thought with a groan. Her mother seemed to have a propensity for fashionable young men whose every thought and effort were expended on their wardrobes. She schooled her features to give the appearance of attention while her mother enumerated this particular gentleman's many virtues, but she was preoccupied with her own problems. She could not get Mr. Lynton out of her mind.

The knocker sounded and Lavinia leaned over and whispered, "Leave your shawl off, Verity."

Wythecombe tapped on the door, then entered. "Mr. Charles Haversham, ma'am."

Lavinia rose at once and Verity stood just behind her, a welcoming smile on her lips.

Wythecombe coughed, then added, "And Mr. Nicholas Lynton."

Lavinia looked in some confusion at Mr. Haversham, a tall, heavyset young man whose face still held the pudgy roundness of youth.

"I must beg your forgiveness, Mrs. Parnel, for bringing an unexpected guest," he apologized, his face bright red. "But when Mr. Lynton learned I was dining here, he pleaded for the privilege of accompanying me. It seems he knew your daughter in London, and is most eager to renew their acquaintance."

"Oh, we are always delighted to receive another guest," Lavinia said with a laugh. "Brighton is rather dull just now, do you not find? Do come in, gentlemen."

She stepped aside and Verity stared into Nicholas Lynton's eyes, eyes as vivid blue as she'd remembered.

He crossed to her side at once, and bowed over her hand. In a low whisper he told her, "I have searched half of England for you." For the benefit of the others, he added in a louder voice, "Miss Parnel, will you forgive me for not waiting to pay a proper call? When Charles told me he was dining here, well, I could not resist the opportunity to see you again."

"That's putting it mildly," Haversham said, sounding aggrieved as he took the chair next to Lavinia. "He wouldn't give me a moment's peace until I agreed to bring him along."

"Really?" Lavinia asked, her eyes brightening as she glanced at Lynton. She'd thought Haversham an attractive young man, but he paled to nothingness beside his friend. She could see why the man appealed to Verity, but what was wrong with her daughter? She'd barely uttered a word since their guests had arrived.

"Verity, my dear, would you ask Wythecombe to see that another place is laid for dinner?"

Verity started to rise, but Nick stayed her with a hand laid gently on her arm. "I would not dream of upsetting your table at this late hour. I only thought to visit for a few moments."

Lavinia laughed. "What nonsense is this, sir? You must not think you are intruding. As it happens, I sent you an invitation to dinner—admittedly, it was last month in London, but you were nevertheless invited. When my daughter told me you were Rupert Lynton's nephew, I sent an invitation at once. You must know your uncle and my late husband were great friends."

"Your daughter mentioned it," Nick murmured.

Her face flaming, Verity rose. "I shall just speak to Wythecombe," she said, and hurried from the room before Lynton could detain her. Outside in the hall, she leaned weakly against the door. Several deep breaths helped to steady her racing pulse, but she knew she could not linger long. Heaven only knew what Mr. Lynton might say to her mother—or she to him.

However, when she returned to the drawing room, she found the three in animated conversation, discussing the regent's proposed renovations to the Pavillion in Brighton. The gentlemen rose at once. Self-consciously, Verity took her seat, regretting that she had not thought to ask Wythecombe to set dinner ahead.

"I was just telling your mother of an evening I spent at the Pavillion last summer, Miss Parnel," Charles Haversham explained. "You would not credit how excessively warm the rooms are kept. Why, half the guests were near to fainting from the heat."

Feeling unusually warm herself, Verity allowed her shawl to slip off her shoulders. She heard her mother ask if the rumors they'd heard were true, of dinners lasting for four hours with more than thirty removes.

Under cover of Haversham's reply, Nicholas leaned forward and spoke softly. "I am pleased to see your shoulder has healed, Miss Parnel."

Verity, her eyes wide and questioning, glanced at him.

"I should hate to be the one responsible for marring such perfection," he continued in a low murmur. His gaze fastened on her bodice, memories of another night stirring his blood. "Dare I hope you have forgiven me?"

She shivered at the intensity of his eyes and hastily rearranged her shawl. "I know it is I who should be seeking your forgiveness, sir, but I pray you will not speak of . . . of our meeting before my mother."

He glanced at Lavinia, who seemed intent on keeping Charles occupied, then back at Verity. "She does not know, then?"

Her hands clenched tightly in her lap, Verity shook her head. "Mama has been ill. I fear the shock would be too much for her heart. Please, Mr. Lynton, I beg you, do not expose me, if only for her sake."

Nicholas studied her. She looked far too grave for a girl of her age, sitting there as slim and dignified as a princess, except for her eyes. They gave her away. Those enormous dark eyes filled with fear. What kind of life had she led to make her look so wary? He had promised her his help, yet her fear was palpable. He felt the same instinctive urge to protect her that she'd aroused in him the night they'd met.

"Gracious, but you two look serious. What on earth were you discussing?" Lavinia asked, feeling a trifle uneasy at the sudden silence in the room.

"I was trying to persuade your daughter to drive out with me tomorrow," Nick improvised, turning to Lavinia with a warm smile. "But I suspect she is

73

afraid to leave you. She has been telling me of your unfortunate illness."

"Oh, that, 'tis nothing," Lavinia replied, dismissing her poor health with a wave of her hand. "Verity worries too much. She treats me as though I were made of porcelain. I assure you, Mr. Lynton, I am perfectly well and, if you wish to take my daughter driving tomorrow, you may do so with my blessing."

"Now, just a moment," Haversham protested. "I was going to ask Miss Parnel to go for a drive."

"Sorry, Charles, but I believe I have a prior claim." Nick turned to Verity, who refused to meet his gaze. "Are we agreed, then? I'll call for you at two o'clock."

She nodded. "If you wish, sir."

Wythecombe, on the stroke of six, opened the door of the drawing room and announced dinner was served.

Nicholas rose, offering Verity his arm, which left Haversham to escort Mrs. Parnel. As they walked from the room, he bent his dark head close to hers and whispered, "I do wish it, my dear. It appears we have much to discuss."

Chapter 6

Verity waited in the drawing room for Mr. Lynton's arrival, praying silently that he would arrive before her mother returned from the baths. Every other day Lavinia walked down to the beach to the small single-story building with its round-headed windows, and the elegant inscription outside, HYGEA-DEVOTA. Beneath that, in smaller letters, was the more practical designation HOT AND COLD BATHS. One could bathe in cool seawater pumped into the building by means of a steam engine, or, for those who so desired, heated to a warm temperature. Lavinia and the other ladies partaking of Dr. Awsiter's cure need not shiver in the cold sea. Nor were they subjected to the inquisitive gaze of gentlemen loitering on the beach with their telescopes trained on the bathing machines.

Afterward, Lavinia promenaded on the Steine with her faithful Olive in attendance. She generally called in at some of the small stores, where one could purchase lace, tea, or other smuggled goods at bargain prices. If she was not too tired, she visited the library to hear the latest gossip. When she returned home, she partook of a light luncheon, followed by Dr. Awsiter's tonic. Verity had watched Tobias prepare the concoction, and wondered how her mother endured it. He boiled four ounces of seawater together with four ounces of milk, then added sufficient cream of tartar to produce a whey. After it had been strained and cooled, her mother drank the entire portion.

Lavinia declared the tonic not at all unpleasant, but she'd made a horrid face when first sampling it, and Verity refused to taste it at all. She would admit, however, that the tonic seemed to do Mama a world of good, and she knew Dr. Awsiter was highly regarded in London.

After checking the clock for the fourth time, Verity wondered if she, too, should visit the good doctor. Perhaps he had a tonic that might soothe her nerves. She had seldom felt so restless and out of sorts. She rose, shook out the folds of her gray walking dress, and adjusted the fall of the silk pelisse she wore over it. The clock on the mantel chimed two just as she heard a carriage arriving. Fighting a rising tide of nervousness, her palms sweating beneath her kid gloves, she hurriedly seated herself once more on the sofa, pretending an interest in the *Brighton-Hove Herald.*

Wythecombe opened the door of the drawing room, announcing Mr. Lynton's arrival with sufficient pomp and dignity to do justice to a visit from the prince regent himself.

Verity rose. Stealing herself to meet Mr. Lynton's gaze, she unconsciously lifted her chin. But there was nothing threatening in his countenance. Indeed, she thought his eyes, beneath those ridiculously heavy brows, held a hint of amusement. She heard him greet her, and knew she answered, but had little notion of what she'd said. She was far too aware of her hand resting on his hard, muscled arm as he escorted her out to his carriage.

A yellow curricle glinting in the sun, drawn by two superbly matched roan horses, waited for them. Nicholas saw her seated comfortably before he climbed up beside her. After stating it was a beautiful day for a drive, he inquired if there was any particular place she would like to visit.

"If you drive up East Street and follow that to the road to Lewes, we will pass the Downs, which is said to be exceptionally pleasant," Verity replied, her eyes straight ahead.

Nicholas nodded, and after turning his horses, glanced at her again. He'd thought her beautiful by candlelight, but she was equally lovely in the unforgiving light of the sun. Her long blond curls, just visible beneath the black feathers of her hat, seemed an entrancing mixture of gold and silver. Her complexion was flawless, a soft ivory with just the merest trace of pink on her high cheekbones. He couldn't see her eyes, but her mouth was lush and full, even though she kept her lips compressed in a tight, firm line.

He was determined to find out the truth about her today, but he thought his inquisition could wait a bit. Miss Parnel looked braced for the worst. He longed to see her delicate lips curved in a smile, and glimpse her large eyes when they were not filled with the fear he seemed to arouse in her.

He waited until they passed the Castle Inn on East Street. Intending to be pleasant, he remarked, "How is your mother today? I do hope her illness has not driven her to bed."

Verity flushed and replied stiffly, "Mama is at Dr. Awsiter's Baths this morning. He believes the seawater to be beneficial in treating her and has prescribed a hot bath every other day."

"It must be working. She looks remarkably well," Nick said agreeably, his attention on the road.

Verity clenched her gloved hands, anger overriding her caution. "I am aware, Mr. Lynton, that you have every reason to doubt my word, but my mother *is* extremely ill. She may not wish to discuss her health in polite company, and she may appear to be well, but she tires most easily, and when a spasm of coughing takes her, she must fight to get her breath. There are still many days when she cannot leave her bed."

Nick checked his horses slightly and gazed at her, his brows arching in genuine surprise. "My dear Miss Parnel, I did not mean to imply otherwise."

She could not doubt the sincerity of his eyes, and glanced away, embarrassed. "I must apologize, then."

Silence reigned between them for several moments until she felt compelled to explain. "Last night, when Mama passed off her illness so lightly, I feared you suspected I had exaggerated her poor health. Then, when you called today, and she was not at home, I . . . I thought you must believe she could not truly be ill."

When he did not reply, Verity stole a look at him.

Nick turned to meet her gaze. It was the first time she'd looked at him without fear. He thought it fortunate he had his hands full with his horses. Otherwise, he'd be tempted to take her in his arms, urge her to cry on his shoulder, and then promise to make all right with the world, as he sometimes did with his sister. But this was not Kate, and Miss Parnel did not look like she wanted to cry. To the contrary, her wide brown eyes gazed up at him with valiant dignity and something very like courage.

He tried the effect of a smile. "Do you think you could bring yourself to trust me a bit if I swear I intend you no harm?"

She ducked her head, staring down at her hands. Nick silently cursed himself for thinking he could discuss anything with her while handling a pair of fresh horses. He reined in his team, guiding the curricle to the side of the road.

"What . . . what are you doing, sir?"

"Just halting here for a few moments while we talk." He looped the reins over his hand and turned to face her. "You did not answer me, Miss Parnel."

Verity shrugged. "I should like to believe you, sir, but why did you follow me to Brighton, if not to have me arrested?"

Nick laughed, the sound seeming unnaturally

loud in the quiet of the country. There was no traffic in sight, and save for a few startled blackbirds, which flew up at the sound, no other sign of life. He was aware of Verity staring up at him and struggled for some semblance of control. "I have searched for you for weeks, my dear, but only because I feared you might be in dire straits and in need of assistance."

"Why should you care?" she asked softly.

Had no one ever been kind to this girl? Kate would have accepted his concern as her natural due, and any of his tenants would take an offer of help in stride. His gaze traveled down her slender throat to her shoulder, covered now by her green pelisse. He knew if he peeled back her coat and gown, he would see a small scar where his bullet had grazed her delicate skin.

Verity felt the intensity of his eyes and noted the direction of his gaze. She had heard about gentlemen who could undress a lady with a glance, but she'd not thought Lynton of that sort. She shifted uncomfortably and pulled her pelisse closed at the throat. "You are sadly mistaken, sir, if you think I would trade my favors for your silence."

Her meaning was abundantly clear, and Nick flushed. He was not here to offer her a carte blanche, but just thinking of the wound he had inflicted on her delicate shoulder had aroused some decidedly immoral thoughts. He recalled all too clearly the way her breasts had swelled beneath the black silk shirt, and the softness of her slender throat when he had felt for her pulse. The image of her in his bed, her blond hair spread in tangles over his pillow, would not leave him.

He sighed, and forcing his attention elsewhere, asked, "Do you mind if I smoke?" When she did not reply, he withdrew a cigar and lit it. He blew out a cloud of smoke, regaining some small measure of control, then risked a glance at the girl beside him.

She sat stiffly, her back ramrod straight, her hands neatly folded in her lap.

He could hardly blame her for her reaction, but obviously helping her was going to be more difficult than he had envisioned. "Let us try this again," he suggested after a moment. "I know you are . . . respectable. I believe that only desperation could have driven you to attempt to rob my uncle Rupert. But if he was in any way responsible for your situation, then I, too, am at fault, and seek only to make amends."

She looked at him then, her liquid-brown eyes easily reflecting her emotions. Surprise registered, along with a flicker of hope.

"I do not understand, sir. Why should you go to so much trouble?"

"I offered you a bank draft, but you left without it," he said, a wry smile on his lips. "And I had wounded you. I was concerned. I had horrible visions, imagining you dreadfully ill and without the funds to seek medical help."

"If I had died, it would've been due entirely to my own folly," she replied. "You, sir, cannot be thought to be in any way responsible."

"That is a matter of opinion, Miss Parnel," he said, leaning back against the seat of the carriage. "And there is another matter that concerns me greatly. Lord Ashford."

She looked alarmed again, and he hastened to reassure her. "I am aware that you successfully robbed Lord Dinsmore and Mr. Ravenscar, but you must give me your solemn promise not to ever attempt such a thing with Lord Ashford."

"How did you know about the others?" she asked, her voice low and her head bowed.

"Easy enough to piece together from your note and reports in the London *Gazette*. But Ashford is—he is a vindictive man, Miss Parnel, cruel and not precisely given to chivalrous impulses. I should hate to think of you in his hands."

"You need not worry on that account, Mr. Lynton. I assure you I would never, ever again attempt to rob anyone. It was only that Mama was so ill, and there were no funds left. . . . Papa lost everything at Whites, even our house in Shrewsbury. I know that is hardly justification, but—"

"You need say no more, my dear," he interrupted. With one hand he reached out and lifted her chin so that she faced him. "Let us put the past behind us and speak of it no more. Shall we cry friends?"

Receiving a tremulous smile as his answer, he released her.

Verity returned home late that afternoon, far later than she had intended, and found Lavinia waiting. She'd not meant to worry her mother, but Mr. Lynton had proved such charming company, such a delightful conversationalist, hours had passed before she realized the time.

Lavinia had tea ready in the drawing room and was much disappointed when her daughter entered the room alone. She scolded Verity for not inviting her young man in for tea.

Verity accepted a cup from her mother's hand and sat down opposite her. "He is not my *young man*, Mama."

"Well, he might be if you would but make an effort to attach his affections. I saw how he looked at you, my dear. You must trust your mother's instincts in these matters."

Verity flushed. "You are imagining things, Mama. We are merely friends."

"When you are a little older, you will learn that there is no such thing as mere friendship between a gentleman and a lady," Lavinia said, her face becoming a little pink at such plain speaking. "One must always be aware of the differences in their . . . their natures. Friendship is merely a prelude to an attachment of a stronger sort."

"What sort, Mama?" Verity asked absently, leaning down to feed Cleo a piece of cake.

"Why, marriage, of course. The natural order of the world is such that men and women are attracted to each other, and it is a woman's responsibility to nourish that attraction. She thus encourages the gentleman to enter into the blessed state of matrimony, and children may then be produced."

It was the same lecture Lavinia's own mother had once given her, but it seemed to have little effect on Verity. Lavinia stared at her daughter in confusion. Unnatural girl.

Antony crawled out from beneath the sofa where he'd been sleeping and rubbed against Verity's legs, seeking his share of food. She caressed his silky ears and then broke off a piece of cake for him. When he had licked her fingers clean, she became aware of her mother's gaze and looked up. "I am sorry, do go on, Mama."

"What is the point, when you do not attend to a word I say?"

"I was listening," Verity replied, wiping her fingers with a handkerchief. "You were discussing the attraction between ladies and gentlemen."

"Then you will make an effort to encourage Mr. Lynton? He is such a delightful young man—" She broke off as Verity resolutely shook her head. "Good heavens, why ever not?"

"There can be no question of marriage between us. The differences in our stations must preclude—"

"Nonsense. You come from a fine, distinguished family, Verity, and do not forget it. Why, Lynton should consider himself fortunate if you condescend to wed him. He may be very well-looking, but he is not titled."

"No, but he did inherit his uncle's estate, in addition to his father's. From what he has said, it is apparent that he is extremely wealthy. And we, Mama, are nearly destitute."

"If he comes to care for you, such distinctions will not matter," Lavinia replied with a shrug of her pretty shoulders. "I remember Mama telling me about the Gunning sisters. They both married dukes, you know, and not a penny to their names. I dare say, neither was as pretty as you."

"I believe you must be prejudiced, Mama, but thank you. Is there any more tea?"

"If you will only apply yourself, Verity, I am certain you could easily bring Mr. Lynton up to scratch," her mother coaxed while refilling Verity's cup. "I could call on that seamstress Mrs. Leamington told me about, and have her run up a few new gowns for you."

"You must not, Mama. I have told you we have no funds for such frippery. Indeed, I must soon find a position, or I do not know how we shall contrive next year."

"But, Verity, we would not have to pay her anything, not for ages. And if Lynton makes you an offer—"

"You must forget Mr. Lynton, Mama. He will look higher than a penniless girl for his bride." Or a thief, she added silently. The thought saddened her, but she knew it to be the truth, and was determined not to be depressed over her situation. She smiled brightly for her mother's benefit. "Did I tell you that I have spoken to Lord Lewes. He is very kind, is he not? He is going to inquire among his acquaintances to see if anyone is in need of a governess."

"Oh, no, child, no! Good heavens, I could not bear to see my only daughter hiring herself out as a drudge. Oh, my dear, you must not think of such a thing. . . ." Her words trailed off as ready tears sprang to her eyes.

"Mama, please don't cry," Verity begged, reaching out a consoling hand. "You will make yourself sick again. It is not so terrible, I promise you. And if I find a good position, you will be able to remain here in Brighton, with all the staff to care for you."

"If only your dear father were still alive. He would know what to say to you."

Verity, too, wished for her father's presence, but wishing would not bring him back. She rose wearily. "Come upstairs and rest awhile, Mama. We can discuss my plans when you are feeling better."

"I shall never feel better if you persist in talking such foolishness," Lavinia said, but allowed her daughter to help her up. She glanced with hope at Verity. "You did not mention to Mr. Lynton this notion of becoming a governess, did you?"

"No, Mama." Not precisely, Verity amended silently. She had said only that she hoped to find some sort of position that would enable her to support herself and her mother.

"Thank the dear Lord for small blessings," Lavinia murmured. She might yet have time to bring her daughter to her senses.

While Verity struggled to convince her mother that employment as a governess did not herald the end of the world, Nicholas Lynton dined at the Old Ship Inn. He'd invited Charles Haversham to be his guest, feeling he owed the fellow some extraordinary civility for encroaching on his evening with the Parnels. The supper room was not at all crowded, and the food well prepared and deftly served. It should have been a pleasant evening. His guest ate heartily, making up for Nick's more spartan appetite, and seemed disposed to linger over brandy and cigars. Haversham's capacity for spirits seemed bottomless.

Having nothing better to do, Nick motioned the serving girl to refill his guest's glass for the fourth time. During the lull in their conversation, he caught the soft sounds of an orchestra playing somewhere in the distance, and glanced up in surprise. Brighton was rather thin of company, and he had not expected much in the way of entertainment. He glanced across the table at Haversham. "Is it my imagination, or do I hear music?"

Charles waved his glass toward the back of the hotel, nearly spilling the brandy. "It's coming from the ballroom," he explained. "It's Thursday, you know."

"Thursday?"

Charles nodded. "Thursday, ball at the Old Ship. Monday, ball at the Castle Inn. Been that way for years. This is Thursday."

"I see," Nick replied, wondering at once if Miss Parnel might be in attendance. He took a small sip of brandy and asked casually, "Do many people attend?"

"Not this time of year," Charles said, watching the cloud of smoke above his head slowly disperse. "Once the regent comes, then it's a squeeze. Not now, though."

The man's conversation was tedious enough to make Nick wish for his cousin Bryce's acerbic presence. He tried again. "What of Miss Parnel?"

Haversham brightened. "Deuced pretty girl, Miss Parnel. Taking her driving tomorrow."

"Yes, I know." Charles had told him at least six times that he was driving out with Miss Parnel. It was not something Nick cared to dwell upon. "I meant," he explained patiently, "does she attend the assemblies?"

Haversham looked confused, but gave the matter his consideration. "Shouldn't think so," he opined at last. "Still in mourning, you know. Poor girl lost her papa. Needs someone to take care of her."

"She seems remarkably resourceful to me," Nick muttered.

Charles shook his head. "Not good. Not good for a girl to be alone in the world. Should have a man to look after her. Did I mention I'm taking her driving?" he asked, his words beginning to slur.

"I believe so." Nick rose abruptly, feeling an urgent need for fresh air. "Would you care to stroll on the Steine?"

"Rather have some more brandy."

"I dare say you would, but I believe some fresh air would be more beneficial. You will want to be clear-headed tomorrow."

"Why?"

Nicholas rounded the table. "You are taking Miss Parnel driving," he reminded the young man as he helped him to his feet.

"Right you are," Charles declared, weaving slightly. "Deuced pretty girl, Miss Parnel."

"Indeed, she is."

Haversham glanced slyly up at his companion and nudged him in the ribs. "I say, Lynton, you casting eyes her way?" He chuckled loudly and added, "Shouldn't like to cut you out."

"You may do your best," Nick replied as they stepped out into the cool night air.

It had occurred to him that Charles Haversham, other than his lamentable incapacity for brandy, would make an excellent match for Miss Parnel. She had confided her need to find a position, and, while he admired her determination, he hated to think of her employed as a servant in some dreadful household. If her situation became dire, she might even be driven to attempt robbery again. Marriage to Haversham was a much better alternative, if the younger man could be brought to the sticking point.

Brandy clouding his own usual good sense, and intending to inspire Haversham with a bit of jealousy, Nick confided, "I heard Miss Parnel was rather sought after in London. We must think ourselves fortunate so few gentlemen are in Brighton."

"Why?"

"Oh, for heaven's sake," Nick fumed, losing all patience.

"Beg pardon." Charles moaned suddenly and turned away from him. He was wretchedly sick all over the new grass of the Steine.

It was several moments before Haversham could face the world again. Nicholas helped to mop his face with his handkerchief while listening to profuse apologies.

"It must have been the fish," Charles declared, his face a pasty hue. "Dreadfully sorry, Lynton."

"Do not give it another thought," Nick said, but the distinct aroma rising from Haversham's clothes was making him nauseated. With exquisite tact he suggested, "Perhaps the best thing would be for you to retire early. Do you need assistance back to the inn?"

"Not at all. I must thank you for a . . . a pleasant evening," Charles said, managing to execute an awkward bow. He turned then and tottered off in the wrong direction.

Nick went after him. By the time he'd settled Haversham at the Castle Inn and returned to the Old Ship, it was nearly eleven o'clock. The assembly over, a number of elderly people were just leaving the inn. Nick waited on the veranda until they passed, then hurried inside. His timing was regrettable.

Amelia Ponsonby, who had paused to speak to the inn's proprietor, Mr. Hicks, was just emerging. Engaged in conversation, she neglected to look where she was going and walked straight into Nicholas Lynton.

She stepped back, her aristocratic nose instantly detecting brandy fumes. "You again!"

"Sorry, ma'am," Nick apologized, and cravenly hurried past.

"Upon my word, Mr. Hicks, I should think you would be more careful about admitting ruffians to the Old Ship."

The proprietor was noticeably surprised. He had judged Mr. Lynton to be a respectable young man, well-heeled, and nothing pinch-fisted about his ways. But he refrained from comment. Mr. Lynton would be gone before long, while Mrs. Ponsonby resided in Brighton year-round.

Nicholas heard her. Indeed, he suspected everyone remaining in the Old Ship heard her loud, carrying voice. Were he to remain in Brighton much longer, his reputation would be in shreds.

He entered his room and found Crimstock still awake, and waiting for him. Nick received the old man's ministrations with welcome relief. Here, at least, was one person who approved of him without reserve. When Nick was at last ready for bed, and his offensive garments had been removed, he thanked the elderly valet warmly.

"My pleasure, sir," Crimstock returned with a ghost of a smile. "But if you would not think it impertinent, I should like to inquire about your plans. If we are to remain in Brighton, I must make proper arrangements for the care of your clothing."

"I had not thought on it," Nick said softly. Of course he must return to Town soon. He had business affairs that required his attention, and he disliked leaving Kate in Bryce's company for long. And, after all, there was no reason for him to remain in Brighton now. He had found Miss Parnel, assured himself that she was well and not in need, and extracted a promise from her that she would refrain from robbery in the future.

"I shall let you know on the morrow," he said at last. Crimstock nodded and withdrew, but Nicholas continued to think about his plans. Long after the candle by his bed had gutted, he lay awake, the thought of leaving Brighton strangely unsettling.

Turning on his side, Nick considered the matter. He had thought Haversham an ideal solution to Miss Parnel's problems, but now entertained serious doubts. Perhaps it would be wise to remain in Brighton a few more days and observe Haversham's progress with the girl. And it would only be civil, Nick thought, to pay Miss Parnel a call.

He could write Kate, ask her to come down for a

few days. She might enjoy Miss Parnel's company. His eyes suddenly flew open as an ingenuous idea struck him. Of course, he should have thought of it sooner! Climbing out of bed, he lit a candle and searched the desk for a quill and paper.

Chapter 7

Nicholas drew on his dressing gown and crossed quickly to the writing desk built to fit snugly beneath the window. He lit two tall candles, then searched through the desk until he found a stack of stationery in one drawer and a few quills in another. Ink for his pen was in a small pot atop the desk. Using his own knife, he sharpened a quill, dipped it in the ink, then began to write furiously.

After a few lines he paused, read what he had written, and crumpled the paper. "My dear Kate," he wrote on a clean sheet. "I have found Miss Parnel (the young lady I was searching for) here in Brighton, and was pleasantly surprised to find she is a lady of genteel birth and breeding. She is possessed of an intelligent mind, a keen sense of humor, and beautiful dark eyes." He scratched out that last bit and then abruptly tore the paper in pieces.

"My dear Kate," he wrote again on a third page. "I have missed you greatly and loathe leaving you alone in London with only Bryce and the servants to watch over you. It occurs to me that perhaps we should employ a companion for you for those times when I must be away, someone to bear you company and amuse you. I know you find Bryce tolerable, but I was thinking more of a young lady. I have found the ideal person here in Brighton. Her name is Miss Verity Parnel, and she resides with her mother." He paused to read the words aloud, shook his head, and wadded the sheet into a ball.

Kate would know at once the young lady must be his blond intruder, and his sister would not appreciate his roundabout approach. Better to be straightforward with her. Simply tell her he'd found the girl and she needed their help. Kate had a kind heart and she'd understand if he could only find the words to describe Miss Verity Parnel. He idly wrote her name, liking the look of it against the parchment. Verity meant truth, he mused, and chuckled aloud. The perfect name for a thief . . . but she was not really one, he would stake his life on that.

Verity was true . . . true and courageous. She had refused the money he'd offered her. A more mercenary girl would have taken it and thanked him prettily. But not Miss Parnel. Nor, he strongly suspected, would she marry merely for the sake of money. Charles Haversham was not wealthy, but he could offer her a comfortable life. Nick had seen the way Charles looked at her over dinner, the admiration in his eyes apparent. She could have had him dancing attendance on her if she wished. But although Miss Parnel treated Charles kindly, she offered him little encouragement.

Nick sighed, looking at the crumpled pages before him. At this rate he could ride to London and back before he completed the blasted letter. He briefly considered the merits of such a plan, but discarded the idea almost at once. He disliked the idea of leaving Miss Parnel alone, well, practically alone. She had her mother, of course, and the servants seemed devoted to her, but they would be of little help if she ran into any sort of trouble. He did not reflect on what sort of trouble would require his assistance. It was sufficient that he felt she needed him nearby.

Running a hand through his hair, Nick drew out a fresh sheet and started anew. After greeting Kate, he leaned back in his chair. How did those writer fellows get a person down on paper? He had read *Mansfield Park* and felt the author succeeded admirably, almost wickedly, in describing the characters. One practically knew them. He wished he could do that with Miss Parnel, to manage somehow to set down the goodness of heart he saw so clearly reflected in her eyes. She was beautiful, one noticed that at a glance. But what drew him to her went beyond mere beauty. She had a warmth about her, a sweetness ... and despite her attempt at robbery, she possessed a deeply ingrained sense of morality. He wanted Kate to understand that and not judge the girl harshly. He wanted to draw a picture with words that would show Miss Parnel's true nature, her ready sense of humor, and sharp wit that bespoke a mind above the ordinary.

His pen scratched quickly, but this effort was no better than the last. His words were stilted and he sounded as though he were compiling a list of admirable virtues rather than describing a real person. Nick sighed and started over. Ink stained his fingers and a smudge decorated his brow where he rubbed his hand across it while thinking.

As the hours advanced, the pile of crumpled pages grew steadily, littering his desk and overflowing onto the floor. The candle burned to a mere stub before he finally completed a letter. He signed it with a flourish and quickly folded it before he could read it again and change his mind. He had never had such difficulty composing a letter. But Kate would understand.

He rose wearily, crossed to the bed, and dropped his dressing gown where he stood. Tired as he was, he smiled with satisfaction as he settled in bed. He could imagine Miss Parnel's pleased delight when he told her of his plan. He knew she and Kate would like each other.

The following week passed quickly for Verity. Lord Lewes called and invited both her and her mother to dinner as his guests at the Castle Inn.

He was a kindly man, and her mother seemed to blossom in his presence, responding like a flower opening to the sun to his rather gallant courtesy. Verity enjoyed his visit, too, but she was disappointed to learn he had no news of a position for her. Her small supply of funds was rapidly dwindling, and she knew she must seek employment in earnest. She'd written to Mrs. Beauchamps, who ran a small, very select school for young ladies, and inquired if there might be a position. Verity had been a superior student and hoped that if her old mentor could not employ her, she might at least provide a recommendation.

Verity watched the post daily and tried to hide her despair when no letter arrived. Unwilling to rely solely on either Mrs. Beauchamps or Lord Lewes, she studied the Brighton paper, scanning the pages for employment. Only a few positions were listed, and those required experience and references. Verity marked the advertisements, thinking she might ask Mr. Lynton his advice when next he called.

He'd become a frequent visitor at their home, along with Mr. Haversham. Lavinia encouraged both gentlemen and welcomed them warmly, always inviting them to stay for tea or dinner, an invitation they seldom refused. Mr. Lynton insisted on repaying their hospitality, inviting them to dine at his inn as his guest. Not to be outdone, Mr. Haversham took them to the Castle Inn for dinner. Verity enjoyed both evenings, and tried not to think too much of the dreary future in store for her. At least she would have this spring to remember.

Monday dawned bright and sunny. A gentle breeze drifted, carrying the salty smell of the ocean to Verity's window. A perfect day to work in the garden, she decided, breathing in the warm air. She hurriedly changed into a faded gown of her mother's, deftly avoided Emma, who would insist on providing her with a hat, and slipped outside.

The sun felt pleasantly warm against her face as she surveyed the garden, but she frowned at the sight before her. The weeds had made inroads, and wilted blossoms hung their heads from the bushes, as though shaming Verity for her neglect. She set to work at once with her scissors, snipping the dying flowers, and then settled down on the grass to remove the pesky, persistent weeds. She worked diligently, but all too often her mind drifted to thoughts of Nicholas Lynton. She turned her spade in the earth, breaking the soil with her gloved fingers.

It was flattering to have two personable young men calling on her, even if it meant nothing. Mama, of course, was cast in high transports, envisioning a wedding before year's end. Verity hated to disillusion her, but she knew Mr. Lynton was only being kind. It was his nature, she thought, remembering how he'd told her of caring for his sister. As for Charles Haversham . . . she sighed. One could not discourage a gentleman who had yet to proclaim his suit. Verity was almost certain he meant to offer for her, but thus far Mr. Haversham had observed every propriety, treating her with the same gentle courtesy and consideration he showed her mother.

He was an earnest young man, and Verity wished she could feel more strongly attracted to him. Marriage to someone like Mr. Haversham would solve all her problems. But try as she might, she could feel no more than a friendly regard for him. A pity, she thought, for he was a nice person, and really quite handsome unless one compared him to a certain dark-haired gentleman. Mr. Haversham did not show to advantage when Mr. Lynton was near. *He* had only to walk into a room and the conversation suddenly sparkled, the wine tasted sweeter, and the world seemed a brighter place.

"This will never do," Verity muttered, attacking a

94

stubborn weed. "He will disappear one day. Continue hoeing this row, my girl, and you will harvest only empty dreams." Nicholas Lynton was not for her, and she knew she must put him out of her mind. But he was like the weeds in the garden, taking hold and refusing to be ousted. She heard the sound of the door and glanced around. Her good intentions floated away on the breeze.

A smile curved her lips and warmth lighted her eyes. "Mr. Lynton! I did not expect to see you today."

"I hope I am not intruding?"

"Not at all, sir," she replied. Rising, she stripped off her gloves and gave him her hand. "We are always delighted to see you, and I was just about to stop for a cup of tea. Would you join me?"

She suited the garden, Nick thought, likening her to some mythical nymph. The sunlight caught and danced in her hair as the breeze stirred tiny tendrils of curls about her brow. Her gown might be patched and streaked with dirt and grass stains, but she wore it with the innate dignity and bearing of royalty.

He accepted the hand she offered, holding it a fraction longer than etiquette dictated, and looked around the small garden. "I hate to go inside when it's such a pleasant day. Might we have tea in the garden?"

Dimples appeared in her chin. "I think Emma anticipated your wishes," she said as the door opened again, and her maid emerged, carrying a large tray.

They settled it between them on the wide wrought-iron bench, sheltered by the seawall. Nicholas, eyeing the assortment of cakes and freshly baked lemon cookies, remarked, "I think I must envy you your cook."

Verity nodded as she poured a cup of tea for him. Her fingers brushed against his when she handed him the cup. The slight touch set her blood tingling. She blushed furiously, and sought desperately for some diversion. "Our chef is a master. Indeed, all the staff here are wonderful. I fear I shall miss their pampering."

"You are not leaving?" he asked, a tinge of alarm creeping into his voice. Had she accepted an offer from Haversham?

"No, we are settled here at least until the end of the year. Then—" She broke off, shrugging. "Who knows? If I am successful in finding a position, I shall be able to renew the lease for Mama."

Nicholas longed to wipe the frown from her forehead, to erase the worry from her dark eyes, but he could say nothing until he heard from Kate—and his sister was taking a damnably long time to answer his letter. He swallowed a sip of tea and stared at the daffodils. "Did I ever tell you I am blessed with the sight?"

Verity smiled. "Are you now? Tell me what you see among the flowers. Or must I cross your palm with silver first?"

"Laugh if you must, but I'm willing to wager you will shortly be offered a wonderful position with a kind and generous lady."

"I wish you would tell Mama so," Verity said, laughing at his nonsense. "She imagines the most horrendous fate for me. Mama believes the only proper life for a girl is marriage." She regretted the words instantly.

"Marriage is not always the ideal solution," Nick replied, suddenly serious. "My mother was the same and encouraged my sister to wed during her first Season."

"Oh, I thought—from things you said—that your sister lived with you."

"She does now. Kate did not choose wisely. She married a handsome, personable young man. Unfortunately, he was given to excessive drink and addicted to sport. He was a bruising rider, and one afternoon, after he'd downed more wine than he should, he took a spill over a stone wall. Broke his neck instantly."

"I am so sorry," she murmured.

"Don't be. The man was a fool and Kate is better off without him."

"Still, it must have been difficult for her."

He nodded. "It took her a long time to recover, but she seems content enough now—though I sometimes wonder if she will ever be tempted to wed again."

"She is fortunate to have you looking after her," Verity replied, her hands twisting around her cup. "Many young ladies have no choice other than marriage."

"True," Nick agreed, watching her. He disliked the shadowy sadness in her eyes and sought to set her laughing again. With a teasing smile he said, "I doubt Kate would have been bold enough to think of burglary. She is not as enterprising as some ladies of my acquaintance."

Verity flushed. "It is not something I would ever attempt again."

"I am relieved, my dear, but confess to curiosity. Were you not frightened?"

Verity shook her head. "Not at first. I was so angry at the way those men had cheated Papa—" She broke off, abruptly aware that one of those men was Rupert Lynton. "I'm sorry. I did not mean—"

"Go on," Nick told her, much amused. "What put the idea in your mind?"

"I read a notice in the *Gazette* that Lady Lichfield had been robbed. Someone climbed in an open window and took forty-two pounds, which had been carelessly left lying about. I thought at first that it was a pity it had not been Lord Dinsmore. The same paper reported he'd just won four thousand pounds at Whites in one evening."

She looked down at her hands, remembering the awful desperation she'd felt. Tradesmen were dunning them and her mother was dreadfully ill, but there was no money to send for the doctor. Verity had even asked Swithin to pawn her jewelry. He had reluctantly told her the few pieces she owned were paste. The real jewels were replaced over the years by her father, to pay his gambling debts. She didn't want to speak of those dark days, but her eyes came up to meet Lynton's. "Had I been a man, I would have called Lord Dinsmore out."

"I think he got off lightly," he said, smiling at the martial light in her eyes.

"Perhaps. But it would have been more honorable. As it was, I crept into his house in the dead of the night."

Hearing the distress beneath her words, he spoke lightly. "I am still astonished you managed it. It was wrong, of course, but I can't help admiring your cleverness. May I ask how you contrived to get inside?"

Verity suddenly smiled. "He sleeps with his windows open, and let that be a lesson to you, Mr. Lynton. Especially if an old tree grows near those windows."

"You climbed that tree?" A sudden vision of Verity tumbling from the high branches upset him. "Good God, you could have broken your neck."

"Or been shot," she retorted, her dimples showing as she teased him. "But the worst to befall me at Lord Dinsmore's was losing my boots. I'd borrowed Papa's and they were rather large. They slipped off my feet when I was halfway up the tree."

Nick laughed. "One must give you credit for ingenuity."

"I didn't feel very ingenuous. I was frightened and nearly screamed aloud when Lord Dinsmore started snoring. I will tell you in confidence, sir, that he makes enough noise to wake the dead."

"I trust I do not snore so loudly?"

"Not . . . not at all," she replied, her voice a bare

whisper as she recalled seeing Mr. Lynton in his bedchamber.

"And Ravenscar?"

"Oh, he was much easier. His footman obligingly left the door open while he slipped out to meet a lady friend."

"Considerate of him," Nick commented dryly, but beneath his amusement was grave concern. He didn't wish to worry her, and phrased his next question carefully. "Did you leave both those gentlemen the same sort of note you left me?"

She nodded. "I wanted them to know the theft was to repay a debt they owed. I know that seems odd to you, but I didn't regard my actions as robbery. I was reclaiming Papa's money."

"I understand," he replied, managing to keep his voice sympathetic. The problem, though Miss Parnel did not realize it, was that either of those gentlemen could discover her identity from the note—if they cared enough to pursue the matter. He'd have to do something about that when he returned to Town.

A tan paw reached up from beneath the bench, swiping at a lemon cookie just as Nick reached for it. He drew back his hand as he heard Verity's musical laugh.

"I must apologize, sir. It appears one of the maids allowed Cleo to escape the house."

"Cleo?" He leaned over to peer beneath the bench. A cream-and-dark-brown Siamese with large blue eyes returned his regard. Apparently deciding he was worthy of her attention, the cat arched her back, then rubbed against his boots.

"She's a shameless beggar," Verity warned.

"Is she now?" Nicholas broke off a bit of cookie and offered it to the cat. She swiped at his hand, deftly knocking the tidbit free.

"You've done it now," Verity said. "And earned a friend for life."

"Have I?" he asked softly, his gaze fixed on her.

She blushed, uncomfortably aware that Mr. Lynton was not referring to the cat. She was saved from answering as the kitchen door swung open.

"There you are!" Charles Haversham stepped out into the sunlight. "Your mama told me I should find you out here, Miss Parnel. Oh, tea in the garden. Now, that is what I call a splendid notion."

Katherine Lynton Delacourt glared at her cousin across the breakfast table. "Must you always be so critical?"

Bryce shrugged. "The world is hardly perfect, my dear, nor the people in it."

"Yourself included," she retorted.

"I would be the first to admit my faults," he replied easily, effectively taking the starch from her sails. "I am utterly without ambition, completely intolerant of others, and not entirely trustworthy. You're likely to hear any number of less than flattering remarks about my character, to which I would not take exception. But I am equally certain you will never hear it said that I rig myself out like a dashed popinjay. However did you keep from laughing at your Mr. Donahue?"

"He is not *my* Mr. Donahue, and you were extremely rude." But she couldn't help smiling a little. "I will own the spotted waistcoat was dreadful, but your manners were worse. Really, Bryce, if you continue to insult our hosts, we shall cease to be invited anywhere."

He motioned to the waiting footman to refill his coffee cup. "I think you need not be concerned, dearest Kate. A young lady with an inheritance will always be courted by the ton."

"Well, thank you! And I thought it was my beauty and charm that endeared me to my friends. How naive of me."

"Quite."

When she lifted a buttered roll as though to toss it at his head, he quickly raised his hands and begged pardon. "You do rise to the bait beautifully, my sweet, which makes teasing you nearly irresistible. Shall I tell you that Miss Cartland sat in the corner with her mama all evening? And she, dear cousin, has a portion twice the size of yours. Now then, tell me what has put you in such a bestial mood this morning."

Kate sighed and pushed away her breakfast plate. "I am growing tired of London, I suppose. Sometimes it all seems so pointless. One meets the same people over and over. One ball is much the same as another."

"Rather a dull lot in Town this year," Bryce agreed.

"That is not what I meant."

"But true all the same. Many more Seasons like this one and you'll find yourself as cynical as I. Should you care to run off to America with me?"

"America? What on earth put that notion in your head? Of course, I know you're not serious."

Bryce smiled. "No? Well, it was only a thought. When you shunned me for Donahue's company, I retired to the billiard room and spent an entertaining hour listening to tales of the colonies from his cousin. Calvert, I believe his name is—and the man seems surprisingly civilized."

"Giles Calvert! I have heard Caroline Greene speak of him, but I didn't realize he was present last night. Why did he not come up to the ballroom? Does he not dance?"

"I did not ask, my dear. It appears he mightily disapproves of our frivolity. Apparently they take a more solemn view of life in the colonies."

"Then life there would certainly not suit you, cousin."

"Touché ... I'm much inclined to agree with you, except he talked of vast opportunities, of vast lands free for the taking." He looked down at his cup and spoke almost as if to himself. "An enterprising gentleman could acquire extraordinary wealth, I think."

"Bryce!"

He glanced up, amused by her outburst. "An enterprising gentleman, I said, which we both agree I am not. 'Tis only mere speculation."

"For a moment you sounded most serious."

"Heaven forbid. Tell me instead, my sweet, what pleasures await us. I see Roberts has brought in the mail. A towering stack, too. Your beauty and charm are much sought after."

She made a face but began sorting the dozens of invitations, now and then laying one aside. "Lady Fitzhugh invites us to a rout party. I think we should attend—her parties are always so amusing."

"Indeed. A droll creature. Would she have me, I would wed her."

"She is twice your age, Bryce."

"And twice my size, too, but she controls half the wealth in England."

Kate shook her head at his nonsense as she sorted the cards and letters. Halfway through the pile, she scooped up an envelope with a glad cry. "Bryce, this is from Nick!"

"My day is complete," he murmured, and gestured to the footman. "George, see that my cup runneth over."

The servant obliged him, filling the cup to the brim, while Kate quickly scanned the two pages from her brother. Bryce saw the color drain from her face. "Kate, my dear, what is it? Nick is not hurt, is he?"

"No, but he shall be when I get my hands about his neck!" Anger brought the color flooding back to her cheeks, and her eyes darkened ominously. "George, leave us, please." She waited until the footman closed the door of the dining room, then turned to her cousin. "You will not credit this. Nick has located that girl who attempted to rob him—

she's in Brighton—and he has been there with her all this past week."

"Now, Kate, darling, do be reasonable. I grant you I'm surprised he wrote to tell you of it, but there's nothing to be alarmed about. A gentleman must have his little flings—"

"I could overlook a *fling*, as you so nicely put it, but not this. Bryce, he wants me to offer the girl a position as my companion. He writes that he will await my answer, and if I'm agreeable, he'll escort her back to London himself."

"Egad! 'Tis worse than I thought. I knew he was besotted, but to foist a common thief off on you goes beyond all bounds." He tapped his long fingers restlessly against the table, even less pleased with the news than Kate.

Bryce had been cruelly disappointed when his uncle left his fortune to Nick, but he'd not despaired. Nicholas, he'd noted, carefully avoided all the lures set out for him by this Season's reigning crop of beauties. While Bryce had little doubt his cousin had his affairs, they were brief, and conducted with discretion with little chance of a lasting attachment. The situation suited Bryce perfectly. As long as Nick remained a bachelor, Bryce knew there was still reason to hope that he might one day inherit his uncle's estate. In the meantime, he could live off his expectations.

"She has bewitched him," Kate fumed, scanning the letter again. "That is the only possible explanation. He writes nothing of the robbery, only that she is of genteel birth and has endured much hardship. He desires I see she is properly clothed and take her about with me."

"I had not thought it possible, but I own I'm shocked at my cousin proposing such a thing. It's an insult to you, Kate."

"It is indeed, and so I shall tell Nick." She rose abruptly. "Will you give me escort to Brighton?"

Bryce considered quickly. If Kate wrote, refusing

to accept the girl, there was no telling what Nick might do. "I think you are wise to go, and certainly I will accompany you. When do you wish to leave?"

"At once," Kate replied. "I fear there is no time to be lost."

"Today, you mean? But, Kate, you cannot have considered. Why, we must pack. Surely, tomorrow—"

"I am leaving this afternoon, Bryce. With or without you." She turned and marched from the room.

Bryce sighed. He was of half a mind to let her go alone, and he knew she would. But he also knew Kate adored her brother. Left alone, Nick might well talk her into acceding to his wishes.

Reluctantly, Bryce followed her up the stairs. For such a charming girl, there were times when Kate could be quite fatiguing. He winced, envisioning the fireworks certain to take place in Brighton.

Chapter 8

Katherine fumed and ranted for two hours after leaving Town. Initially angry with her brother, she soon directed her rage toward Miss Parnel, and by the time they reached Crawley, thirty miles south of London, she would have willingly ordered the young girl beheaded.

Bryce, for his own purposes, had encouraged her wrath. But after endless miles of listening to nothing but Kate's unabated fury, he grew tired. Hungry and irritable, he failed to mind his words and carelessly remarked that Nick had much to answer for.

Kate turned on him immediately. She might castigate her brother endlessly, but she'd never allow anyone else to. She faced her cousin with blazing eyes. "How can you say so? You, to whom he has been all kindness and generosity, dare to criticize him for helping a penniless girl?"

Bryce sighed wearily. "I thought we were agreed her poverty was a sham, a mere ploy to—how did you put it—to ensnare Nick in her toils?"

Kate flushed. "Do not mock me, Bryce. I'm convinced the girl is a fraud, but Nick obviously believes her tale, and seeks only to help her. One cannot fault him for that."

He did not reply, but the cynical gleam in his eye was sufficient for Kate to guess his thoughts. She fumed, "Do not judge all men by your own base instincts, cousin. You know nothing of being a gentleman. Oh, you dress the part well enough, but it is all gilding. Beneath your pretty ruffles and fine linen shirts, you are nothing but a black-hearted rogue! Nick is ... Nick is—"

"A saint," Bryce suggested, much amused.

Kate, knowing her brother would be the first to scoff at such an appellation, bit her lip.

"You are damnably beautiful when you're angry, my sweet, but much as I admire the way your eyes flash with righteous indignation, I pray you'll spare me the sermon."

"Does it please you to make sport of me?"

"Very little, though it does break the monotony of the drive."

"Beast!"

Bryce reached over and lifted her hand to his lips. "You take life much too seriously, my dear. It would be well for you to realize that your sainted brother, while in every instance an estimable gentleman, is still very much a man—with a man's desires and needs."

Kate jerked her hand from his grasp, faint color rising in her cheeks. "I am aware of that! Nick has had ... affairs in the past, but he conducts them discreetly. He would never invite one of his ... *doxies* to reside with us."

"Katherine! You shock me. What would Nick say if he heard you using such language?"

"Very likely that I am too much in your company."

"He would indeed think so, and I, being such a black-hearted rogue, no doubt deserve it. Perhaps that is why he seeks to provide you with a companion."

"A thief to teach me my manners? Thank you, but I much prefer the rogue. A least I need not hide my jewels from you."

"Not at the moment, though were I in need of funds ... I suspect those diamond clips at your ears would fetch a pretty price. Not paste, are they?"

She raised a hand to one ear and caressed the large pear-shaped diamond in its gold filigree setting. "Nick gave these to me for my birthday. Bryce, I do wish you would be serious."

"I was never more so, my dear."

"No, you are miffed only because I called you a rogue. Must I apologize?"

"Not at all. I have been called far worse, but if you wish to make amends, I beg you to instruct the coachman to call a halt. We are just approaching Cuckfield, and a tolerable dinner can be had at the King's Head Inn. It might be well to change horses, too. We shall make better time with a fresh pair." When she hesitated, he cajoled, "I am famished, Kate. My stomach has been growling this last hour."

She laughed but glanced worriedly out the carriage window. The sun was well down, and it would be growing dark soon. She had hoped to reach Brighton while it was still light.

Bryce, easily reading her mind, chuckled. "Nick will still be there, Kate. Even if we were to drive straight through, it is likely you would have to cool your heels at the inn waiting for his return. Saint or not, I somehow doubt he spends his evenings in his room."

"You are right, of course," she acknowledged. "Tell Johns where you wish him to stop."

Bryce leaned out the window and yelled up to the driver. The man nodded and a few moments later drove the carriage into the deserted yard at the King's Head Inn. Business was slow for a posting house, and two ostlers hustled out to attend to their needs.

Bryce bespoke a private parlor, and dinner was, as he had promised, tolerable. Indeed, Kate thought she had seldom tasted better than the Cornish hens with chestnut dressing, or the Marlborough pudding served for dessert. Bryce seemed inclined to linger, having discovered the innkeeper's private hoard of brandy. He told Kate that it was probably smuggled in from France. He also sampled a fine Bordeaux wine, and exasperated her by haggling over the price of a case for above a quarter hour with the innkeeper.

Bryce triumphed and Kate waited impatiently while a postboy was sent to the cellars to fetch a case.

"All this fuss over a few bottles of wine," she muttered, tapping her foot.

"Not merely wine, cousin, but a case of perfectly aged, vintage red Bordeaux. Really, Kate, you must learn to appreciate the finer amenities of life." He directed the boy to stow the crate on the seat of their carriage rather than in the *foregon* with their baggage, and at Kate's incredulous look, explained, "It must not be jostled unduly, my dear."

"It is you who shall be jostled if you do not order Johns to drive on at once," Kate warned as she stepped into the carriage. "If you continue tarrying, it will be dawn before we reach Brighton."

"At least then we might be assured of finding Nicholas in his bed," Bryce murmured, pulling out his pocket watch. "However, I reckon we shall arrive between eight and nine. Not an unreasonable hour."

Kate glanced out the window, refusing to be drawn into further argument. They rode in peaceful silence for several miles, and then she turned to ask Bryce the time. But he appeared to be sleeping, his dark head resting against the cushioned back of their seat. Just as well, she thought. She'd enough of Bryce's dry wit for one day.

At precisely half past eight, their carriage rolled to a stop on North Street in front of the Ship's Inn. Bryce stirred sleepily, checked his watch, grunted in satisfaction, and then opened the door. He climbed down gracefully and helped Kate to alight. When she was safely on the ground, he turned back to the carriage.

"Bryce! Do leave that stupid wine alone. One of the servants can see to it."

"You speak blasphemy, Kate."

She stamped her foot in vexation, then whirled about and headed for the inn. "Stay with your precious wine," she called back. Without thought to her appearance or the time, she pushed open the door and walked into the common room.

Dozens of people seemed to be present, all of whom turned to stare at her until silence enveloped the room. A young woman, especially a young woman as pretty as Kate, arriving alone in the night was a rarity for Brighton.

Kate hesitated, searching vainly for some sight of Nicholas. She heard the low murmur of voices start up again, and guessed she was the topic of conversation. A blush suffused her face, and she backed up a step.

Bryce, entering behind her, placed a reassuring hand on the small of her back. He inclined his head and spoke softly. "I thought you might be missing me, cousin." He guided her across the room to a cushioned seat in an alcove, then directed his attention to a redheaded maid descending the stairs.

A warm smile and lift of his hand brought the girl to his side at once. "Where might one find the innkeeper?" he inquired pleasantly.

The maid, a buxom young girl, dropped a curtsy as she smiled boldly up at him. "He'll be out in a moment, sir, but I'd be more 'an pleased to help you."

Katherine muttered beneath her breath while Bryce grinned. Before he could answer, however, the landlord appeared.

He was a large man, big-boned and ham-fisted, with the air of one who would tolerate no foolishness. One stern look from beneath his dark brows sent the girl scurrying about her business. Then, carefully drying his hands on the apron tied about his broad girth, he nodded to Bryce. "What can I do for you, sir?"

"We shall require several rooms—"

The big man shook his head regretfully. "Wish I could accommodate you, but we're full up. Might try the Castle Inn.

"We got a grand gentleman staying with us, just passing through on his way to London, but with a score of folks. Took the last of our rooms."

"I see. Well, then, can you tell me where we can find my cousin, Mr. Nicholas Lynton? Mrs. Delacourt here is his sister."

The innkeeper shot Katherine an appraising look. "That so? Fine gentleman, Mr. Lynton, but you're short of luck, ma'am. Saw him go out not an hour past."

Katherine thanked him politely and wearily stood. "Let us find rooms, Bryce. I am so tired, I cannot think clearly."

Her cousin nodded and, after receiving directions to the Castle Inn, scrawled a message for Nick on the back of one of his calling cards. He entrusted it to the landlord and then escorted Katherine back to the carriage.

It took only moments to reach the Castle Inn, but Kate chose to remain in the carriage while Bryce bespoke rooms. She glanced idly out the window. The prince regent's pavilion with its odd domes and long spirals could be seen just ahead, and opposite them the grassy Steine where a few people strolled leisurely about. The night was warm, brightly lit by a near-full moon and hundreds of low-hanging stars. How pleasant it looked, she thought, and rather romantic. Catching the sound of light laughter on the ocean breeze, she turned to watch a young lady with her escort.

They halted on the promenade path, and though the gentleman had his back to the carriage, Kate could clearly see the pretty face tilted up to his. The lady's countenance was all admiration, and she seemed to hang upon his every word. Kate smiled, imagining she was witnessing a courtship.

The couple strolled on after a moment, and Kate caught a glimpse of the gentleman. Nick! She flung open the carriage door just as Bryce stepped up to it. It hit him with a sickening thud.

Bryce tumbled backward, landing unceremoniously on the cobblestone street. "What the devil!"

"Oh, Bryce, I am so sorry," Kate cried, climbing down as Johns hurried around the carriage. "I saw Nicholas just now over there on the Steine."

Bryce withdrew a handkerchief and held it to his head as Johns helped him up. The door had caught him on the shoulder and a sharp corner cut his brow just above the eye. Blood quickly soaked his handkerchief.

"Oh, dear heavens, you are hurt," Kate fretted. "I suppose we must get you inside."

"Kind of you to be concerned," he remarked, leaning heavily against Johns. "But I think . . . I think I'd best sit down for a moment."

The driver eased him down to the steps of the carriage, and Bryce sat there, his head tilted back and his eyes closed.

"Let me see," Kate demanded, removing his hand. Blood flowed freely from a jagged cut, and she gasped at the ugliness of it. She quickly replaced the handkerchief and ordered the coachman, "Johns, go inside and tell someone we need a physician immediately."

Several people had gathered and stood back a few feet, watching curiously. Dulcie, seeing the crowd about her mistress's carriage, elbowed her way through. "Miss Kate! Lordy, what did you do to Mr. Gyffard?"

"I didn't do anything," Kate retorted, but honesty compelled her to add, "At least, I did not mean to. The carriage door hit him—Dulcie, do not just stand there! Fetch me a clean handkerchief."

"Perhaps I can be of assistance," a deep, melodious voice offered from behind her.

Kate glanced over her shoulder and up at the sympathetic face of an elderly gentleman. He stepped around Dulcie and close to the carriage, accompanied by an attractive older woman.

"May I?" he inquired politely, removing the makeshift pad from Bryce's head and replacing it with his own clean one. "Perhaps it would be best to get the young man inside."

"I tried to, but he said he needed to rest for a moment."

Bryce opened his eyes. His vision blurred as he squinted at the gentleman applying firm pressure to his head. "I ... I believe I can walk, if ... you would help me."

"Keep this pressed to your head," the man ordered, transferring the bandage to Bryce's hand. "Now, young lady, if you will take his arm on that side, I think we can manage."

Together they half lifted Bryce to his feet and made a stumbling, halting passage across the way to the door of the Castle Inn. Dulcie ran ahead and opened it for them just as Johns emerged.

"They sent a boy for the doctor, Miss Kate," he reported, and immediately took her place next to Bryce. Nodding to the stranger assisting them, Johns gestured toward a door. "There's a private parlor to the right, with a long bench in it. The innkeeper said we could bring him in there."

Bryce, his eyes glazed, suddenly groaned and slumped against Johns. The brawny coachman picked him up as though he were no more than a sack of potatoes and carried him into the parlor.

"Oh, Miss Kate, is he going to die?" Dulcie wailed, ready tears running down her pudgy face.

"No, of course not." The bracing words came automatically, but Kate trembled inside. She twisted her hands together, then, realizing how stained her gloves were, pulled them off. Bryce's blood, she thought, looking down at the dark blotches. She felt a comforting hand on her arm and glanced up.

The blond woman she'd seen in the street stood next to her. For the first time, Kate realized the lady was clad entirely in black. A widow, she wondered, gazing into the woman's warm, compassionate eyes.

"Lord Lewes will not allow anything to happen to the gentleman," the lady promised. "And Dr. Awsiter will be here soon. He is my own doctor, and I can assure you a most excellent physician. Do not fret, my dear. I am certain your young man will be fine."

"My cousin," she corrected the woman whose encouraging words had helped. Kate lifted her chin before following the men into the private parlor. The widow and Dulcie trailed after her, but Kate was unaware of their presence. Her gaze was drawn immediately to Bryce's still form laid out on the padded seat.

She crossed quickly to his side and knelt next to the bench. "Bryce? Bryce, I am so dreadfully sorry—" Tears choked her voice and clouded her vision.

Her cousin stirred, a low moan escaping his lips. A second later he opened his eyes. "Kate?"

His voice was a bare whisper, but she smiled, elated at this small sign of life. Of course Bryce would not die. He was far too contrary. She squeezed his arm. "I am here, Bryce. Is there anything I can do? You have only to ask."

He turned his head, grimacing at the sudden pain, but his mouth twisted into a semblance of a grin. "The wine," he rasped. "Take care of my wine."

"I cannot imagine where Mama and Lord Lewes could be," Verity said, glancing about the empty supper room at the Ship's Inn. "I distinctly told her we would return here."

Nick, uncomfortably aware that they had dallied on the promenade much longer than he had intended, patted the delicate hand resting on his arm. "Perhaps they strolled out to meet us, and we missed—"

"Oh, dear heavens. Nicholas, suppose Mama became ill?"

He shook his head. "Lord Lewes would certainly have left word for us. I suspect they merely grew tired of waiting and walked out to meet us. We shall probably find them on the promenade."

Verity considered the matter. She, her mother, and Lord Lewes had dined at the Ship's Inn as Nick's guests. Dinner had been a lengthy affair, and though the company was delightful, she had tired of sitting for so long. When Nicholas suggested a stroll on the Steine, she had agreed at once. Lavinia, however, protested. Sated with rich food, she felt far too comfortable to move. The earl had chuckled, echoing her sentiments, and urged the young people to go off without them. When Verity hesitated, Lord Lewes assured her he would take good care of her mother.

"Unless you do not trust me," he'd added, giving his best imitation of a wicked leer.

Verity laughed, but she was unaccustomed to relying on anyone else, and her uneasiness showed.

Lavinia settled the matter. "Good heavens, child, go along with Mr. Lynton. I shall be perfectly fine. Better, perhaps, for not having to listen to the nonsense you children speak."

Nick came around the table and assisted Verity to rise. "I think they are wishing to be rid of us," he teased, amusement turning up the corners of his lips, accenting the cleft in his chin. "Surely you do not wish to be disobliging?"

Verity found it difficult to deny Nicholas anything when he smiled at her in such a way, though she knew it was not wise to stroll with him in the moonlight. Nicholas would disappear from her life soon. It was foolish to imagine otherwise. But just this once would not hurt, she thought, giving in to a growing desire to walk with him beneath the stars. And she would have one evening to remember him by.

The warm, balmy night had drawn dozens of couples to the Steine, but Verity had been conscious only of Nick's tall figure walking next to her. He was attentive, his dark head bent close to hers, while asking endless questions about her life in Kent. She found it easy to confide in him, and talked of her childhood and the carefree days before her papa had begun drinking. The minutes sped swiftly away, and it was Nick who finally remarked the hour was growing late. He suggested they return by way of Ship Street, walking around to the rear of the inn and entering through the assembly rooms.

Verity had shamelessly agreed, knowing it would prolong their stroll. It had seemed harmless enough, but now her mother had disappeared, possibly taken ill. She twisted her gloved hands together helplessly, worry shadowing her eyes.

"We shall find them outside, I am certain," Nick said, eager to erase the frown from her pale brow. He escorted her through the door leading to North Street, and they walked rapidly toward the Steine. They were nearly opposite the Castle Inn when Dr. Awsiter's carriage drew up. Verity recognized his rig at once and halted Nick, but had no chance to question the physician. He stepped down from his carriage and rushed inside.

A small crowd had gathered outside the inn, and a buzz of speculation arose with the doctor's arrival. Nick, deciding there was nothing to be learned there, directed Verity toward the young boy holding the carriage horses. "What brings the doctor here?"

The lad shrugged. "They said someone got hurt on the promenade and was carried into the Castle."

Nick thanked him and tossed the boy a coin. He glanced down at Verity's white face. "It is no doubt a mere coincidence, my dear, but if it will make you feel more at ease, we can inquire within."

Verity, unable to speak past the lump in her throat, nodded.

Nicholas guided her past the small cluster of the curious people gathered in front of the inn, and held the door for her. He was certain no harm had come to Mrs. Parnel, but it was with a measure of relief that he saw her speaking to a young woman across the room. There was something decidedly familiar about the shapely back of the lady . . . she reminded him of Kate, he thought. Then his astonished gaze noted Dulcie standing next to her mistress, and his coachman, Johns, leaning against the wall.

Verity espied her mother at the same moment, and with one accord the pair hurried across the room.

"Mama! I have been so worried about you."

"Kate, my dear, what are you doing in Brighton?"

The ladies turned at once. Mrs. Parnel looked fondly at her daughter and spoke to her younger companion. "Ah, here is Verity now—"

She broke off as Kate hurled herself into her brother's arms. "Oh, Nick, Bryce is injured and it is all my fault."

Verity stepped back, freeing his arm. She watched the dark-haired girl, knowing that this must be Katherine, of whom Nick had spoken so fondly. But what was she doing with Lavinia, and who was Bryce?

The door behind them opened and Lord Lewes stepped out, closing it softly behind him. "Mr. Gyffard is recovering—" he began to say, but stopped short at the sight of Mrs. Delacourt in young Lynton's arms.

Kate, hearing his voice, released her hold on Nick and turned anxiously to Lord Lewes. "Is he really recovering, sir? What does the doctor say? Oh, this is my brother."

Lord Lewes nodded at Nick, then spoke to Kate. "The doctor is still examining him, but he believes the young man will be fine after a good night's rest."

"Kate! I wish you would tell me what is happening."

"I shall, Nick! Oh, it is so wonderful to see you," she said, hugging him again. "I was so frightened—promise you will stay with me for a while."

"Are you putting up here?" he asked, uncomfortably aware of the sudden tension about him.

Kate laughed shakily. "I do not even know if Bryce bespoke rooms. He came in to see the landlord and just as he returned, I saw you on the promenade. I was getting out of the carriage and the door hit poor Bryce. Nick, it was such a dreadful cut above his eye, and we could not stop the bleeding. He could not even walk. Johns had to carry him inside."

"But how did you come to meet Mrs. Parnel and Lord Lewes?"

Kate's gaze flew to the kindly widow. They had introduced themselves, but in the confusion, Kate had not caught the lady's name. If she had only known, she would have cut the woman cold. She turned her attention to the older gentleman and reached out a hand. "I shall be forever indebted to you, sir, for your assistance."

Lord Lewes appeared embarrassed. He turned to Nick. "Assure you, it was nothing, Lynton. We walked out in search of you and chanced upon this young lady. I had no idea she was your sister."

"And even now we have not been properly introduced," Kate said, looking up at her brother.

He performed the introductions rapidly. Kate was not much surprised to learn her elderly rescuer was an earl. Even in the confusion and amid her concern for Bryce, she'd noticed the air of courtly

117

dignity about the gentleman. She was astonished, however, to find him in such company as the Parnels. Stealing another glance at Lavinia, she decided the widow could not know about her daughter's nefarious activities. Mrs. Parnel had been extraordinarily kind and compassionate, and Kate thanked her now with a warm smile. Then Nick introduced Miss Parnel, a note of pride in his voice. Kate's smile disappeared. She acknowledged the girl with the briefest of nods before deliberately turning her back. She spoke softly to her brother.

Verity caught the dislike in Kate's glance. There could be no mistaking it. Distressed, she spoke quietly to her mother, "Perhaps we should leave, Mama. Lord Lewes can see us home."

"Oh, but, darling, I could not possibly leave until I am certain that young man is recovered," Lavinia protested. "He's dear Mr. Lynton's cousin, you know."

The door behind them opened again, and Dr. Awsiter emerged with a shaky Bryce leaning on his arm. The small group surrounded them, asking dozens of questions at once, except for Verity. She remained standing near the wall, feeling very much alone.

Bryce grinned at his cousin. "I see Kate found you."

"By chance," Nick said. "But how are you? I hear you took a devilish bad hit."

"Bled like a stuck pig," Bryce agreed before glancing at Kate. "Like as not, I'll have a scar."

"It will give you a rakish look and you'll thank me for it one day," she predicted. Her relief at seeing him on his feet made her feel light-headed.

"If you don't mind," the doctor interrupted, "I think this young man needs his bed."

Bryce nodded weakly. "I fear he's right. But you could do me a favor, Nick."

"You need not ask. I shall look after Kate."

"Kind of you, but what I had in mind was the

118

wine I left in the carriage. A case of the finest Bordeaux you've ever tasted. Ask the innkeeper if he'll store it in the cellars."

Nick grinned. "Consider it done. Now, off to bed with you." He watched as the doctor escorted his cousin from the room. Then, noticing Verity, he quickly crossed to her side.

"I must apologize, my dear. Allow me a few moments to see my sister settled, then I shall see you home."

Verity smiled up at him, though it took every ounce of her willpower. "Thank you, Nicholas, but you need not trouble yourself. Lord Lewes can drive us back."

Katherine joined them, slipping her arm possessively in Nick's. She looked up at him with a proprietary air. "That's a splendid idea. I confess I'm still a little shaken, and should be glad of your company."

Lord Lewes, accompanied by Lavinia, joined them. After one look at Nicholas helplessly sandwiched between his sister and Verity, the earl smiled. "Well, Lynton, looks as though you've your hands full. You must allow me to see our ladies home."

"It is a privilege I envy you, sir," Nick replied, his gaze fixed on Verity, who was avoiding his eyes. She'd worn her dark blue gown with the black trim. Earlier, he'd thought the color flattering to her, but now it seemed to imbue her with a deep aura of sadness. He felt a rare flash of annoyance with Kate and wished her elsewhere.

Lavinia saw nothing wrong. She liked Katherine Delacourt tremendously and felt much inclined to mother the girl. She took one of Kate's hands in her own. "It was a pleasure meeting you, my dear, and I hope we shall see you on the morrow. Now, do not let your brother keep you up late talking. A young girl needs her rest. You don't want shadows beneath those pretty eyes."

Kate murmured politely that she doubted she'd be able to stay awake for long.

Nick took advantage of their conversation to speak softly to Verity. "I shall call tomorrow to see how you do."

"Please don't bother," Verity replied. "I'm sure you will be much occupied with your sister and cousin. You must not give us another thought."

He wanted to protest, but Verity had turned to Lord Lewes. "If you are ready, sir?"

Nick watched her leave, his heart unaccountably heavy.

"She stands much on her pride for a thief, does she not?" Kate asked, abruptly releasing his arm.

Chapter 9

Lavinia gazed across the breakfast table at her daughter. Buttering a biscuit, she remarked casually, "I do hope you intend to change your gown after we eat, my dear. I think it likely we shall have callers before the afternoon is out, and you will want to look your best before Mrs. Delacourt."

Verity stared at her mother. Had she not noticed the frost in the air last evening? Mrs. Delacourt's manner had been sufficiently cold to nip the flowers in bud. Remembering the snub, Verity said, "I doubt the lady will call, but if she does, she must accept me as I am. There is little point in pretending to be what I am not."

"And just what are you, may I ask?" Without waiting for a reply, Lavinia continued. "I shall tell you what you are, and that is a girl of good, if impoverished, family. A girl with the opportunity before her to make a splendid match."

"Mama, you mistake Mr. Lynton's attention to us as something more than mere kindness."

"If he were only being kind, I doubt he'd ask his sister to come to Brighton to meet you. A gentleman does not do such a thing unless his intentions are serious. I think he means to make you an offer, darling, and wants his sister's approval."

"Which she is not likely to give, even if what you surmise is correct." Striving to remain calm, she broke off a piece of bacon and carefully laid it on the edge of the table. A cream-colored paw flashed in the air, and the bacon disappeared. "And Mr.

Lynton," Verity continued, "did not invite his sister here. Her arrival was a complete surprise to him."

"Even so, he must have written to her about you, and I'm certain she's come to see for herself the delightful girl who has won her brother's heart. Now, don't be difficult, darling."

"You live in a dreamworld, Mama," Verity replied, but knew she was wasting her breath. There were not sufficient words in Mr. Johnson's dictionary to persuade her mama otherwise once she took a notion in her head. Verity only hoped her mother would not be too disappointed when Mrs. Delacourt failed to call.

She rose, came around the table, and dropped a fond kiss on her mother's brow. "I'll be in the library if you need me."

"Dearest, *must* you do the accounts this morning? You know it gives you a headache, and you invariably end with ink stains on your fingers, not to mention your brow—though how you contrive to smudge your face has always puzzled me—but I wish you would not today."

"Don't worry, Mama. If we should have callers, you may send Emma or Bessie to fetch me. I promise I'll run up the back stairs and change before presenting myself." Verity spoke the words lightly, wishing that she had her mother's ability to picture the world as she desired it to be.

Lavinia was capable of utterly ignoring anything not to her liking. She refused to see Katherine Delacourt's patent disapproval of her daughter, knowledge that weighed heavily on Verity's heart. Nor could her mother be brought to understand that they were almost entirely without funds. Whenever Verity broached the matter, it was dismissed as unimportant.

Staring down at the ledger sheets before her, Verity could not be so cavalier. The list of expenses seemed to grow at an alarming rate, while their small hoard of savings rapidly diminished. And there was nothing left to sell.

She sighed, her fingers idly tracing the design on the mahogany and rosewood table beneath her journal. It was a beautiful piece of furniture with its giltwood front and carved cabriole legs, and lovingly polished as were the book cabinets lining three walls. Every piece of furniture in the library gleamed with a rich, warm patina that bespoke prosperity. Hardly the room in which to labor over accounts, Verity thought.

Mama might believe Nicholas Lynton intended to offer marriage, but Verity knew better. Poor Mama. She thought her daughter's only bar to making an excellent match was her penniless state. Lavinia was astute enough to realize such a consideration would not weigh with a man like Nicholas—but she didn't know her daughter was a thief.

Verity closed her eyes, regretting for the hundredth time her rash behavior. Nicholas understood her reasons and had forgiven her. She knew he would always stand her friend, and do whatever lay within his power to help her. He'd even laughed when she'd told him about Lord Dinsmore snoring. But he wouldn't be amused by such conduct in his wife. She idly traced his name in the corner of her ledger. She was certain Nicholas Lynton had never done a dishonorable thing in his life, and he would search for a lady of equally high moral standards when he married.

One could not blame him, she thought, but she wished she'd met Nicholas before Papa had died. If only . . .

A soft tap on the door brought Verity's attention back to the present. She glanced up as Emma stepped in.

"Begging your pardon, miss, but company's arrived and your mama wants you to change."

"Who is it, Emma?" she asked, hope soaring as

she searched the maid's face. Had Nicholas come after all?

"A young gentleman wishful of seeing you," Emma replied with a broad grin. "That nice Mr. Haversham."

"Oh, how . . . how pleasant. Tell Mama I shall be in directly."

It took Verity only a few moments to change her gown. She wore a gray and black walking dress Bessie had cleverly sewn from the remnants of two of Lavinia's cast-off gowns. After using spirits of salt to quickly remove the ink stains from her hands, she rubbed in a cream smelling faintly of roses.

"Best hurry," Bessie advised, smoothing a stray curl from Verity's brow. "Your mama will be waiting."

Verity nodded, but her footsteps lagged. Charles Haversham was as kind in his own way as Nicholas Lynton. She knew that with very little encouragement he could be brought to make her an offer—an offer she could not possibly accept without confessing the truth to him.

She smiled wanly at the thought. Sweet Mr. Haversham could easily find himself in a ludicrous predicament. She readily imagined his pudgy face reflecting the revulsion he would naturally feel on learning his intended bride was a thief. Another gentleman might withdraw at once, but Verity suspected Mr. Haversham's kindness and innate sense of honor would compel him to let the offer stand, no matter how abhorrent he found the arrangement.

Nicholas Lynton arrived at the Castle Inn just as the clock struck ten. He had bespoke a private parlor the night before and promised Kate he would join her for breakfast. Nick expected to cool his heels for an hour before his sister came down, but when he opened the door, he found her waiting for him.

"Good morning," she said sweetly from her place at the table. "I have ordered for us, and have coffee waiting. I know you prefer it to tea." She placed a steaming mug before him.

"Thank you." He pulled out the chair opposite, wondering what mischief Kate was brewing. Strong ties of affection bound them together, but his sister was not usually so attentive to his desires. "I'm surprised to find you down so early. The sea air must agree with you."

"Hardly," she answered, watching him closely. "I barely slept at all for listening to the sounds of the waves pounding against the shore. I think Brighton vastly overrated and shall be glad when we can return to London."

Nick added cream to his coffee as he tried to hide his astonishment. The sound of the sea was scarcely sufficient to keep anyone awake, much less Kate, who slept like a baby in Town, though the continuous cries of the night watch and the endless clanking of carriages frequently kept *him* awake. He kept his own counsel, however, and inquired instead of his cousin.

"He seems much recovered and is having breakfast in bed, but I believe he is not enamored of Brighton, either. Really, Nick, I find it hard to understand why you've lingered here so long."

"And posted down to see for yourself? I gather you received my letter?"

Her long lashes hid the confusion in her eyes, but a pale blush betrayed her lack of composure. Kate toyed with her spoon as she searched for words. "I did. I confess it took me by surprise." She glanced up to meet his eyes, and saw his disappointment. She felt decidedly uncomfortable and had to remind herself that Miss Parnel was a thief. A thief out to ensnare her brother.

"I had hoped you would befriend Miss Parnel," Nick said quietly, his gaze never wavering from hers. "But perhaps I misjudged you."

Oh, how unfair, she thought, and replied swiftly, "You certainly misjudged someone! Has this girl so bewitched you that you would ask your own sister to employ her as a companion? A common thief to be forever at my side?" Kate laughed, the sound harsh and grating against the stillness of the morning. "Why, when I think how you censure Bryce, our own cousin, I must wonder if your wits have gone begging."

"I would trust Verity Parnel with my life, which is far more than I can say for Bryce."

"I cannot believe my ears. You would trust this brazen, immoral creature before our own flesh and blood? Indeed, you must be bewitched."

Nick opened his mouth to reply, but the door swung open, admitting a maid with their breakfast. He sat in uncomfortable silence while the girl deftly served them. She was a pretty lass with coal-black hair, laughing blue eyes, and lips the color of ripe strawberries. Setting down a plate of ham and eggs before Nick, she stooped a little, giving him an enticing view of the ample charms beneath the low-cut bodice of her gown. Her lips curved in a warm smile, and her eyes held an invitation many men would find hard to resist.

Kate, sitting across the table, stared in disbelief when Nick took no notice of the girl. Her brother was not like so many gentlemen, always leering after a pretty serving girl, but he was not a monk either. Normally, he would have smiled at the lass and perhaps joked a bit. This morning he seemed oblivious. Apparently, all he could think of was Miss Parnel.

Kate thanked the serving maid herself and, when the door had closed, turned to her brother. She made an effort to speak calmly. "I came to Brighton because I'm worried about you, Nick, and what I've seen of your behavior thus far convinces me that I'm right to be concerned. You are far from rational."

"You make too much of this, Kate. I seek only to help a young lady down on her luck. As for her being a thief, I can only say she must be a most unusual one. She stole nothing from me and I have twice offered her a draft on my bank. She refused my help both times, although I know she's desperately seeking some sort of position. Does that sound like a common thief to you?"

Kate sipped her tea. It wouldn't do to tell Nick the girl was obviously a clever schemer. Why should she settle for a bank draft when she had a chance to marry a rich young man—or if not marry—at least be kept in lavish style? It had been tried before with Nick.

Her brother was a handsome, personable man by any standards. His wealth made him much sought after by matchmaking mamas and young ladies who shamelessly pursued him. She remembered the summer she'd turned sixteen and Lydia Howell arrived in Newbury. Clad in the latest French fashions and elegantly coiffed, Lydia had made all the other girls in the village look frumpish. Every male for miles around had courted Lydia, but she had eyes only for Nicholas Lynton.

Kate and the other girls had despised her, not that Lydia cared. She'd no use for females and, when forced into their company, behaved with maddening condescension and spitefulness. Of course, she took care never to do so when a gentleman was present. Let a man get within hailing distance, and Lydia turned into an angel.

Kate had spent a wretched summer, fearful her adored brother would make Lydia an offer. But Nick saw more than one thought. He'd taken Lydia's measure and had somehow evaded that young lady's attempts to pitch him into a compromising situation. Kate suspected her brother had been secretly amused when Lydia suddenly announced her engagement to James Whitmore.

She stole a glance at Nick, remembering other

summers and other ladies. He was no one's fool, but on the other hand, she feared Verity Parnel was shrewder than most and had somehow managed to pull the wool over his eyes.

Kate set down her cup and spoke quietly. "I do not wish to be disobliging, but I cannot believe Miss Parnel would make a suitable companion. I am surprised you ask it of me."

Nick heard the concern in his sister's voice, saw the troubled look in her eyes. He reached across the table and clasped Kate's hand in his. "All I ask is that you give the lady a chance. Talk to her, my dear. I'm sure that once you come to know her, you will like her a great deal. Just come with me to see her. Then, if you're still of the same mind afterward, I shall say no more."

Kate sighed. "Very well. Since it seems to mean so much to you, I'll call on the girl."

"I knew I could count on you. We could drive over this afternoon if—"

"Nick! Have you forgotten Bryce lies ill above stairs? I must be here when the doctor comes today, and I should think you would wish to be here as well."

"Bryce will manage fine without me. He took a knock, but his head is hard enough to withstand a dozen such blows. Nurse him if you will, but don't let him take advantage of you."

"I might advise you the same," she retorted, but softened her words with a smile. "I gather you intend to call on Miss Parnel today?"

"I want to be certain they arrived home safely. May I tell them you will call tomorrow?"

"Tomorrow or Thursday," Kate replied, her head down. "We must wait to see how Bryce does."

"I shall see him after breakfast. Now, tell me what has been happening in London. Have you any prospective suitors I must warn off?"

Kate amused him with tales of the latest *on-dits* and gossip. By the time they'd finished breakfast, brother and sister were once more on easy terms, and Nick good-naturedly accompanied Kate to visit their cousin.

When Nick left, Kate crossed to the window of Bryce's room. She watched her brother emerge from the hotel and step into the bright sunlight. She wished he did not look quite so handsome. Although Bryce dressed with far more flair, there was a quiet elegance about Nick. His collar might be of only moderate height, and his superfine coat a drab bottle green, but the excellent cut fit his broad shoulders admirably. By most standards, Nick would not be considered at all stylish. But Kate saw two young ladies turn their heads to stare after him.

"Come talk to me, my sweet. You look as though you've lost your best friend," Bryce called from his bed.

"Perhaps I have. Nick is going to see Miss Parnel. He wants to be certain she arrived home safely last evening."

"I see. So your talk with him had little effect," Bryce drawled. "You know, Kate, I do believe a glass of wine with my midday meal would do much to restore me, and it might improve your spirits as well. Would you mind fetching up a bottle of the Bordeaux?"

"On one condition," she said, turning from the window to study her cousin. He sat propped up against several pillows. His silk nightcap was slightly askew, but his dark hair had been artfully combed and he was freshly shaven. The only sign of his mishap was the large white bandage above one eye.

"Have mercy, Kate. You dragged me from London to this godforsaken town, traveling, I might add, at an indecent pace, and then injured me dreadfully. I thought you were fond of me."

"And so I am," she replied, sitting down in the

chair near his bed. "But I need your help, Bryce. How are you feeling?"

"You see before you a sick man. I doubt I have the strength to rise from this bed."

She didn't believe him, but she smiled. "Good. Because, even if you should feel inclined to do so, I want you to promise to remain in bed until tomorrow evening."

"Now what the devil are you up to?"

"Why, I am going to do as Nick asked and have a little chat with Miss Parnel," she said with what he called her sweet-as-cream smile.

"Give over, Kate. What has that to do with me?"

"I do not wish Nick to know. Now, Bryce, if you would ask him to bear you company tomorrow, he couldn't refuse. And while he's occupied, I think I can contrive to have Miss Parnel pay me a visit in my room."

He whistled and shoved his nightcap farther back on his head. "Nicholas won't like it, you know."

"I hope he'll never learn anything about it. I promised Nick I would call on the girl, and I will, but I want a word with her in private first. Bryce, I have never seen Nick so ... so bedazzled by a girl. Why, we nearly came to blows in the dining room over her. He will not listen to a word against her, but I'm convinced she means to entrap him into marriage somehow. I want her to know that I will not stand for it."

"Well, if that's what you intend to say to Miss Parnel, I don't think you'll accomplish much. Like as not, you will put her on the alert, or else she'll run to Nick and tell him how you abused her."

"I have to do *something*," Kate cried as she stood. Pacing the room, she told him, "I will not just stand by and let Nick make a fool of himself."

Bryce watched her for a moment while he considered the situation. A glimmer of an idea came to him and he grinned wickedly. "Kate, my dear, how much money do you have on hand?"

She shrugged. "Two hundred pounds or so, I suppose. I was not certain how long we would be here, or what our expenses would be. Why do you ask?"

"Not enough," he muttered. Then, abruptly, he added, "Toss me my purse, will you?"

She retrieved it from the desk and carried it across to Bryce. Feeling uneasy, she asked, "What are you thinking?"

"You are fortunate I am flush this month," he told her as he counted out notes. "Here's three hundred pounds, if you are of a mind to borrow it."

"But—why?"

"Take my advice and offer the chit five hundred pounds to leave Nick alone."

"Five hundred," she gasped. "Why 'tis a small fortune."

Bryce grinned. "Is Nicholas worth it? Or would you prefer the pretty Miss Parnel as your sister-in-law? A small price to pay, one would think, to protect a beloved brother."

Still, Kate hesitated. "Do you think it likely she would accept? Nick told me he offered her a draft on his bank, but she refused it."

"Playing for higher stakes, I should think. Just make it clear you will do everything in your power to prevent her from marrying your brother, then advise her to take the money. Unless she's a fool, she will."

Kate sat down in the chair, the notes piled in her lap. "I don't know . . . if she refuses and tells Nick— Lord, he would be furious with me."

"She won't refuse, not if you approach her right. But if Miss Parnel proves obstinate, tell her you know about the other burglaries in London, and will lay information with the authorities. That should scare her off."

Kate fingered the money in her hands. Talking with Miss Parnel was one thing. Threatening her, as Bryce suggested, was quite another. She glanced up to meet his amused gaze.

"It's up to you, my sweet, but were I in your shoes, I would not hesitate. Of course, if you prefer to see Nick ruined—"

"Why are you doing this?" Kate demanded. She had few illusions about Bryce, and while she didn't believe him to be as black-hearted as Nick painted him, she knew him to be solely concerned with his own affairs. Her cousin would not lift a finger to help anyone—not without some benefit to himself.

Bryce met her gaze unflinchingly. "Why, Kate, how can you ask? After all Nick has done for me, could I stand idly by and see him trapped into marriage by some designing female? Besides, my dear, were he to marry the girl, I would no longer stand in line for the inheritance. Quite disastrous to my expectations."

His words held the ring of truth, but Kate shook her head. "Nick is still a young man. It's likely he will marry sooner or later."

"I much prefer later, sweetling. It's amazing how much one can borrow against one's expectations. Now, be a darling girl and fetch the wine."

Bryce stared at the closed door when Kate had left, wondering if she would dare threaten Miss Parnel. Much as he wished it, he wouldn't wager a penny on it. Kate was too soft-hearted, and she would bear in mind Nick's anger if he learned of her scheme. A pity, he thought, but there it was.

He had no such scruples himself. And if Kate failed to frighten off the young lady, he would take a hand in the game.

Chapter 10

Nicholas arrived at the Parnel home just as Charles Haversham was leaving. The younger man, head bent, walked slowly down the path toward the gate. Nick saw him idly kick a stone off the pathway, and wondered at his general air of dejection.

Charles looked up when he reached the gate. "Oh, it's you."

" 'Morning, Haversham. The ladies at home?"

"They are, and I wish you better luck than me, but I'm not giving up, Lynton."

Nick stepped back, holding the gate open. So Haversham had proposed and been refused. A buoyancy lifted Nick's spirits even while he commiserated with his friend. "Put your luck to the touch, did you?"

Charles nodded, still dazed by his failure. "She turned me down flat. No reason. Just said she could not possibly consider marriage. What do you make of that?"

Nick could make a great deal of it, but he was not at liberty to betray Verity's confidence. He shrugged helplessly. "Perhaps concern for her mother—"

"No. Told her I'd see her mother properly looked after. I thought it might be because of you—well, you're a handsome fellow and no one can deny you have a way with the ladies—but she said she wouldn't marry anyone. I don't know what to think."

"Perhaps she just needs some time," Nick suggested. "After all, you've known her for only a few weeks."

"Knew from the moment I laid eyes on her that she was the one. Never met a girl I liked as well," he muttered as he stared back at the house. After a few seconds he glanced at Nicholas, then offered his hand. "Well, I have business that takes me back to London. You . . . er . . . staying in Brighton long?"

Nick shook hands with Charles and smiled. "Only for a few more days. I expect I shall see you in Town next week."

"Look forward to it," Charles said, but with the enthusiasm of a man facing the gallows.

Nick, watching Haversham amble down the street, shoulders hunched forward and head bowed, felt a surge of sympathy for him. He also felt relieved. Another lady in Verity's situation might have taken advantage of Haversham. But not her. She was too scrupulous to accept an offer without revealing the truth about her past. Pleased to know he'd judged her right, Nick turned toward the house with a light step.

Wythecombe admitted him. The old butler solemnly informed Nick that Mrs. Parnel had stepped out. "However, if you are wishful for a word with Miss Verity, she is in the garden, and quite alone, sir."

Nick thanked him with equal gravity and quickly crossed the hall to the sitting room, where the terrace doors led out to the small enclosed garden. He saw her at once, sitting on the wrought iron bench, obviously lost in thought. He wondered if she was regretting her refusal of Haversham.

One of the cats brushed against his boot, mouthing a pathetic plea to be allowed outside. Nick pushed open the door and followed the Siamese into the garden. "Good morning. I hope I'm not intruding."

Verity glanced up. She had thought of Nicholas

all morning, had longed for him to come but had not believed he would. Happiness flooded her body like a tidal surge, saturating every particle of her being. She could not prevent the radiant smile that curved her lips, or the glow in her eyes.

Nick drew in a sharp breath. With sunbeams dancing in her hair and a delicate blush suffusing her skin, she reminded him of a wood nymph. She belonged in a garden like this, he thought, with sunlight and shadows and only the warm sea breeze to disturb the tranquility.

Verity broke the spell between them, rising to give him her hand in greeting. "You do not intrude in the least. I confess I am delighted to see you, sir."

He bowed over her hand, paying homage to her beauty. Unable to resist, he dropped the lightest of kisses on the top of her wrist. He straightened, still holding her hand, and drank in the warmth he saw in her eyes. An insane urge possessed him. He wanted nothing more than to sweep her into his arms and cover her lips with kisses, to hold that slender body next to his. . . .

"Nicholas?"

Her voice, hesitant and unsure, yet so trusting, acted like a splash of cold water. He dropped her hand at once. Glancing away from her compelling eyes, he even managed a smile. "You should always sit in a garden. It is vastly becoming to you."

"Thank you, but I fear my maid would disagree. She complains I spend far too much time in the sun, and is forever rushing out here with a hat to protect my complexion."

"It has done no harm that I can see," Nick assured her. "Do you dare risk a few moments more, or would you prefer to sit inside?"

"I am a country girl at heart, sir, and must always prefer to be out in the fresh air on a day like this," she said, and gestured toward the bench. As she took her seat, a shadow crossed her eyes. Soon she would be at the beck and call of an employer and would not be at liberty to make such choices.

"What is troubling you, my dear?" Nick asked, instantly aware of her distress.

"Mere foolishness not worth remarking. Tell me instead, how does your cousin? Has he recovered from the blow he received?"

"More or less. Bryce remains abed and will likely do so for a day or two—or as long as my sister is content to nurse him."

"You sound disapproving, Nicholas. Do you suspect him of malingering?"

"At every opportunity," he replied dryly. "However, Kate has a fondness for the rogue, and I will own that at times he can be excellent company."

Verity glanced down at her hands. "Your sister is quite beautiful. I'm sorry we met under such trying circumstances."

"Not the most auspicious beginning, I agree, but you shall have the chance to know her better. She wishes to call on you and your mother either tomorrow or Thursday—much depends on Bryce—but Kate asked me to convey her regards."

"I . . . I am surprised."

"What? That my sister wishes to call? It is the sole reason she journeyed to Brighton. I wrote her about you, my dear, and she is eager to meet you."

Verity's heart raced uncontrollably. She watched Cleo chase a leaf across the garden for a moment before asking, "Does she know about . . . about me?"

Nick reached out a hand to clasp hers. "She knows everything. She was at the house in London that night, and my cousin as well. But you must not let that concern you. Kate is extremely kind, and I'm certain, once she becomes acquainted with you, she will stand your friend. In fact, she may even be able to help you find the position you want."

"I pray you're right," she murmured, but silently

doubted it. She'd seen the contempt in Katherine Delacourt's eyes, and remembered too well the lady's coolness. She said nothing, however, and they passed a pleasant half hour before Lavinia arrived home and urged Nick to come inside for tea.

He glanced at his watch, then regretfully declined. "I promised my sister I would return to the hotel, but Kate and I shall see you both tomorrow or Thursday."

Lavinia desired him to carry numerous messages to his sister and, with a triumphant look at her daughter, added, "I am so looking forward to seeing her again. She's a delightful girl."

The moment Nick left, Lavinia turned to Verity. "There! What did I tell you? His sister is coming to call just as I said she would."

"Yes, Mama."

"One of these fine days you'll learn your mother knows a thing or two."

"Yes, Mama."

Lavinia peered closely at her daughter. She saw the strain about her eyes and the pinched look of her mouth. "Good heavens, I hope you're not becoming ill. You look extremely tired, Verity."

"It is nothing, just a slight headache. Would you excuse me, Mama? I think I should like to lie down for a bit."

"Of course, darling. You rest and have Emma cut some cucumbers to put over your eyes, and perhaps rub a bit of lemon juice on your cheeks. Really, dearest, one should not sit in the sun so long without a hat. But, there, I don't mean to scold. I know it's hard for a young girl to think of such things when she's sitting in a garden with a handsome man like Lynton."

Verity thankfully escaped. Nicholas, and his promise to call with his sister, had, for the moment, driven all thoughts of Charles Haversham from her mother's mind. Lavinia would not be pleased when she learned her daughter had turned down an eligible suitor like Haversham—especially when she discovered Nicholas Lynton intended only friendship.

A light tap on the door aroused Verity, and she called permission to come in. Emma entered, bearing a folded letter. "This just came for you, Miss Verity," she explained as she crossed the room and handed over the sealed billet.

"Thank you, Emma." Verity noted the elegant handwriting on the front and felt a twinge of uneasiness. She waited until the maid left, then slit open the folded sheet. Her eyes caught the signature at the bottom and her uneasiness increased. Why would Katherine Delacourt write to her when they were to meet soon?

She quickly scanned the neatly written lines, then read the note through again more slowly. "My brother has asked that I call on you and your mother, and while I am wishful of pleasing him, I would appreciate a word alone with you first. Would you grant me the courtesy of calling on me in my room at the Castle Inn at eleven tomorrow morning? Nicholas will be occupied with his cousin, and we may speak in private."

Verity dressed carefully the next day. She knew she looked as good as possible, but she was still beset with nervousness when she tapped on the door of Katherine Delacourt's room.

She heard a rustle of silk and then the door opened. For a moment neither lady spoke, each taking measure of the other.

Kate saw before her a pretty girl a few years younger than she, neatly dressed in an outmoded gown with a high neck and long sleeves. Hardly the sort of dress designed to seduce a gentleman, she thought fleetingly. The girl's eyes beneath the wide brim of her hat were wide and somehow looked vulnerable, although she met Kate's gaze boldly enough.

Verity clasped her hands tightly to hide their trembling as she stood before Nick's sister. The lady was elegantly clad in a blue silk gown of the latest mode. She carried herself proudly, with all the natural assurance that comes with inherited wealth. Verity thought her cold and proud, and were it not for the blue eyes, so like Nick's, she would have turned and fled.

"You are very prompt, Miss Parnel. Do come in," Kate said as she stepped back and gestured toward two chairs drawn up by the window. She regretted for a moment that she had not ordered tea. She had not wished to show this girl any undue civility, but fussing with the cups would have given her something to do with her hands. Hiding her own nervousness, she watched Miss Parnel cross the room and sit, her back stiff and her head held high.

Verity, feeling much like a prisoner on trial, waited for her hostess to speak.

The silence stretched between them, heightening the tension in the room. Kate was uncomfortable. She'd thought this would be easier, that the girl would try to ingratiate herself with a conciliatory manner. Instead, she just sat there. Too proud by half, Kate decided.

She sat down opposite her visitor and smoothed her skirts. "My brother wrote to me about you, Miss Parnel. He is a kind, generous man, and is much moved by your ... unfortunate experiences. Nicholas even feels himself in some way responsible for your troubles, though I have told him that is nonsensical."

"I agree, Mrs. Delacourt. I told him much the same," Verity answered, unconsciously lifting her chin a fraction.

It was not the sort of reply Kate expected. Disconcerted, she tried a different tactic. "Tell me, Miss Parnel, what do you intend to do when Nicholas returns to London with me?"

"I beg your pardon?"

139

"Have you plans to return to Town yourself?"

"I have thought of it," Verity replied truthfully. She saw no need to mention her half-formed plan to seek a position in London, a very menial position, far removed from the circles in which Nicholas Lynton traveled.

"I should not advise it," Kate said abruptly. She rose, moving restlessly about the room. "Let us not fence. I believe in plain speaking and I asked you here to make certain matters perfectly clear. You are grievously mistaken if you think I shall stand quietly aside and allow you to presume on my brother's kindness. In short, Miss Parnel, you will find yourself extremely unwelcome in London."

When Verity remained silent, Kate turned to face her. "Well? Have you nothing to say?"

"Not much, Mrs. Delacourt, though I now see why you requested we meet privately. It's true I don't know your brother well, but I suspect he would not approve of this discussion."

Kate flushed. "Nicholas would be furious, I grant you that. However, we are extremely close and he would readily forgive me. He knows I care only for his happiness."

Verity stood. "It may surprise you to learn that I care for his happiness, too. I shall not mention this morning to him. Good day, Mrs. Delacourt."

"Wait! I have a proposition to put before you."

Verity lifted her brows. She watched warily as Kate crossed the room and lifted a bulging purse from the table.

"I have five hundred pounds here, Miss Parnel. If you give me your word that you will not follow Nicholas to Town, it is all yours."

The color drained from Verity's face. She felt as though the woman had slapped her. Searching in her reticule for a handkerchief, she kept her face averted until she regained a little self-control. When she finally looked up, there was no trace of the deep hurt she'd felt. Her voice full of mockery, she said, "How very trusting of you to accept my word."

Kate had not considered the possibility that Miss Parnel might take the money and still follow Nick to Town. She stared at the girl, not knowing what to say.

"Should you like to reconsider your offer?" Verity asked, and very nearly smiled at the older woman's confusion.

"The offer stands. I shall have to trust you to keep your word," Kate replied stiffly, even while silently acknowledging that Miss Parnel was not the sort to break a promise.

"And if I refuse?"

"I warn you I shall do everything possible to keep you away from my brother. He will never marry you. Take the money, Miss Parnel, and consider it a gift from me. If you are careful, it will last you a long time, and it is more than you can expect from Nicholas."

"I see." Verity reached out a hand and accepted the heavy purse. "Five hundred pounds is a small fortune. It would see my mother cared for and pay all our bills." Then she opened the bag and emptied it on the floor.

"What—what are you doing?"

Ignoring her, Verity deliberately trod on the folded notes as she crossed to the door. She paused there, her hand on the knob. "I am much in need of funds, Mrs. Delacourt, but I would starve before taking a penny from you."

"But you—"

"I do not accept charity."

"Oh, very laudable, but I'm not deceived. I know about the robberies you committed in London. Of course, that was not exactly charity, was it?"

Verity swung around. "No, it wasn't. The money I took was stolen from my father. No matter what you think, I claimed only what was rightfully

141

mine." Her eyes glistened with angry tears, but she managed to keep her voice steady.

"Perhaps, but that does not alter—" Kate broke off, startled by a rap on the door.

"Kate? Are you there, Kate?"

Verity recognized Nick's voice instantly and moved away from the door. She glanced at Katherine, who suddenly looked very frightened.

A second later the door swung open and Nick stepped in. "Kate, I just came—why, Verity, what are you doing here?" He looked from her to his sister, his eyes questioning.

"Good morning, Nicholas," Verity greeted him, stepping in front of Kate as she extended her hand. "I needed a few things from town and chanced to meet your sister. I promised to show her the better shops, but she discovered she'd left her purse here. When we returned to fetch it, the stupid clasp broke." She turned to Kate. "Could anything be more vexing? It is ever so when one is in a hurry."

Kate quickly stooped to gather up the scattered notes.

Nick watched her for a moment. "You are carrying a large amount of money, Kate. Do you think it wise?"

Verity laughed, taking his arm. "Spoken like a true male. You men never understand such things, but it is far better to have too much money when one shops than not enough. But how came you to be here, Nick? Your sister told me you were sitting with Mr. Gyffard this morning. He is well, I hope?"

"Bored to death if he would but admit it," Nick replied with a wry smile. "We were playing chess, and while I mulled over a move, poor Bryce fell asleep. I left him to rest a bit and came to see if Kate wanted to go down for luncheon. We would both be pleased if you cared to join us?"

Verity shook her head. "Thank you, but I must do some shopping and Mama is waiting for me."

"Then I suppose I'd best not keep you. I shall

contrive to make do with Bryce's company, though it will not be nearly so pleasant. Kate, dearest, do come rescue me as soon as you return."

He left them and Verity gently shut the door.

"Why didn't you tell him the truth?" Kate asked.

Verity glanced around. "I told you, Mrs. Delacourt, that I, too, care about his happiness. Nicholas holds you in high regard. He has the notion that you are kindhearted and compassionate. I don't wish to be the one to disillusion him. Now, if you will excuse me, I shall bid you good day."

"But Nick expects us to go shopping. What shall I tell him?"

"Why, whatever you please. It would appear you are adept at lying to your brother."

Kate flushed, but she knew the words were deserved. "You are not at all what I expected, Miss Parnel."

Verity smiled sadly. "No, Mrs. Delacourt, I fear I am exactly what you expected. I'm a thief who cares very much for your brother. However, you may rest easy. I know I'm not fit to be his bride, and do not aspire to such a position. Had you asked me, I would've told you as much."

Verity opened the door and left before the tears gathering in her eyes spilled over.

Kate spent the rest of the morning shopping, her footsteps dragging and her conscience bothering her. She felt guilty for approaching Miss Parnel and, despite her words earlier, she knew full well that if Nick ever learned what she'd done, he would not easily forgive her.

She reluctantly returned to the Castle Inn, her arms laden with purchases to deceive her brother, and went at once to Bryce's room. Her cousin appeared nearly as miserable as she felt, and Nick looked distinctly unhappy. She suspected they'd quarreled again.

Smiling brightly, she inquired about Bryce's

143

health, then presented him with a new nightcap. For Nick, she'd chosen an elegant snuffbox, replete with a tiny silver ladle. After exclaiming over the bargains she'd found—with little encouragement from either gentleman—she offered to sit with her cousin, who had watched her display with puzzled eyes.

When the door closed after Nick, Bryce drawled lazily, "Shopping, my dear, and with Miss Parnel? Surely, that was not part of our plan?"

She turned on him furiously. "Indeed, it was not. You were supposed to keep Nick occupied this morning, and instead he barged into my room while I was with that girl."

He shrugged. "Sorry, dear heart. I did try, but Nicholas can be frightfully boring and he took forever to make a move. I never knew a bloody chess game could take so long. But what happened? He told me only that you had met Miss Parnel and gone off shopping with her. I gather he does not know the true purpose of your meeting?"

"No, and for that I'm indebted to Miss Parnel." She quickly told him of the scene in her room when Nick had entered. "I could not think, Bryce, and knew not what to say."

"The girl refused the money? Perhaps she is more clever than we gave her credit for."

"Or perhaps not as black as we feared. Bryce, she's not in the least what I had imagined. I don't think she intends to marry Nick at all. I felt the worst sort of beast for accusing her, and *she* behaved most nobly. And now I must call on her tomorrow! What in heaven's name am I to say to her?"

He studied his cousin for a moment. He'd hoped Kate would be able to pay off the blasted girl, but it appeared Miss Parnel was not to be gotten rid of so easily. "I think there is only one thing to be done."

"What?" she cried eagerly, sinking down in the chair near his bed.

"Offer to employ her as your companion."

"Have you lost your mind? I believe that cut on your head has addled your senses."

"Think about it, Kate. Nicholas has decided he's responsible for this girl. As long as she's struggling, he will constitute himself her champion. But if she has a secure position, light duties, and a delightful home—he won't worry about her. And you, my lovely, can keep her so busy she won't have any time to spend in your brother's company."

Kate considered the idea. It made sense, in an odd sort of way. "I suppose it's possible, but she might not accept the position. She may be penniless, but she has a great deal of pride."

"Then you must convince her she'd be doing you a favor—which is quite true. Nicholas will be pleased and we shall have the girl where we can keep an eye on her."

"It will be difficult. I doubt she will trust me—"

"Come now, Kate. You can be utterly charming when you wish. Tell Nick at dinner this evening that you've had a change of heart. *He* will help persuade the girl."

"Dinner! Lord, Bryce, I don't know if I can face Nick alone. I'm certain he suspects that I didn't just meet Miss Parnel accidentally."

"You worry too much, my dear."

"Easy for you to say, lying in bed guzzling your wine."

Bryce looked offended. "Tut-tut. Bordeaux is never guzzled, my dear Kate. But I can see you have worked yourself into a frenzy, and shall make allowances for you. Would it help if I joined you for dinner?"

"Oh, Bryce, could you? Are you feeling well enough?"

"It will require an effort, but for you, sweet Kate, I will make the attempt. I may even come with you tomorrow to call on Miss Parnel. I'm of a mind to see this enchantress myself."

"She's not the kind of girl you imagine, Bryce," Kate warned. "I think, had we met under different circumstances, I would like her very well."

"I'm not surprised. She would have to be exceptional to have Nick behaving like a besotted fool." He yawned. "I think it would be best if you leave me now, Kate. If I'm to join you for dinner, I must rest a bit."

"Of course you must. How thoughtless of me." She rose swiftly, kissed his brow, and straightened the covers. "Is there anything I can do for you before I leave?"

"Nothing, my dear." He yawned again, snuggled against the cushions, and closed his eyes as Kate softly shut the door.

A moment later Bryce threw off the covers and rose, stretching languidly. He poured another glass of wine, carried it to the window, and sipped it slowly as he stared out at the empty street. Brighton might be a bustling town when the regent was in residence, but this time of year it was devastatingly dull. He'd be glad to return to London.

Once in Town, if it looked to be necessary, he'd take care of Miss Parnel. He smiled, remembering the letter that she'd left in Nick's rooms. Bryce had pocketed the note, thinking it might be useful one day. It reposed now in his jeweled dressing case in London—just the thing to ruin Miss Parnel.

Chapter 11

Verity, who had not expected Katherine Delacourt to call, greeted her arrival with astonishment. She stood numbly while Nicholas, his cousin Bryce Gyffard, and Katherine were ushered into the drawing room. She knew she stared rudely, but the lady gave no indication that anything was amiss. She greeted her hostess warmly and was fulsome in her praise of the house. Delighted, Lavinia immediately offered to take her guests on a tour. Only Mr. Gyffard declined, pleading that he'd seen sufficient antiquities to last him a lifetime.

Verity politely remained with him in the drawing room, covering her confusion with the mechanics of serving tea and cake. She felt awkward alone with him, but the door stood open and Wythecombe waited in the hall.

"Daydreaming, Miss Parnel?"

"I beg your pardon?" she asked, abruptly recalled to attention.

"I would offer a penny for your thoughts, but I suspect they are much more valuable."

"Then 'tis a poor bargain you would strike, sir. I was merely wondering if I should ring for more tea."

"Oh?" Bryce grinned at her, a knowing smile that made mockery of her answer. "Well, it is precisely the sort of reply I deserve for offering you a paltry sum. My uncle always said one gets what one pays for—depressing thought—but perhaps there is some vestige of truth in his words."

"Perhaps, but from what little I know of your uncle, he did not live by such a maxim."

"Egad, but I'm a clumsy fellow. I forgot you were . . . acquainted, with my uncle."

"Did you, indeed?" Verity asked. She took a deep breath, and presented a façade of cool serenity as she filled his cup and passed it to him. Her clear gaze met his directly. "I rather thought you mentioned him deliberately."

Deviltry danced in Bryce's eyes as he mentally revised his opinion of Miss Parnel. She was not only beautiful in her outmoded gown, but possessed of a cool intelligence. The lady would require careful handling. He accepted the cup she proffered and thanked her with a dazzling smile. "It was a mere slip of the tongue, I assure you. No offense intended, and none taken, I hope?"

"Indeed not, sir, and it is I who should apologize for referring to your uncle's reprehensible behavior."

"Touché. You have a quick mind, Miss Parnel. I begin to look forward to knowing you better. Shall we cry friends? I promise you I am nothing like my cousins."

"Is that meant to be a recommendation, sir?"

He shrugged. "The Lyntons have not treated you well. Certainly, one could not blame you if you harbored some resentment. First, my uncle robs your father, then Nick shoots you, and, finally, dear misguided Kate offers you a bribe."

Verity stiffened. She had not thought Mrs. Delacourt would confide in anyone about the meeting between them.

"Kate tells me everything," Bryce added, accurately reading her expression. "I warned her you'd likely consider her proposal an insult, but, alas, she does not always heed my advice."

"And what advice did you give?"

Taken aback, Bryce chuckled. "You're very direct, Miss Parnel. I do admire that in a lady."

"As I do in a gentleman." She studied him for a moment. He sat at ease in his chair, occasionally adjusting the fall of ruffled lace at his wrist. One could not deny Bryce Gyffard was a handsome man, even with the white bandage taped over his eye. It gave him a dangerous look, Verity thought, and deemed it appropriate. For all that Mr. Gyffard cultivated an air of lazy charm, she suspected there were muscles beneath the smooth lines of his coat, and a strength few would guess. He might disguise it with fine lace, diamond pins, and the air of a dandy, but one did not acquire broad shoulders, a narrow waist, and lean hips by living a life of ease. She wondered if he fenced, then smiled at the thought. He was certainly adept at verbal fencing.

"I am pleased to afford you amusement."

The words were mocking, and though a smile curved Bryce's lips, Verity saw the flash of irritation in his eyes. He was used to being admired and would not take ridicule lightly. "Forgive me, sir. I fear I was distracted. Would you care for more cake?"

"No, I still have—" He broke off his words, glancing sharply at his plate on the table. He'd not touched a bite, but only crumbs remained.

Verity hid a smile. She'd seen Antony's velvet paw flash out and snare the slice of almond torte. Paw and cake had disappeared beneath the sofa. Bryce was still puzzling over the matter when the others returned. He rose at once in deference to the ladies and, somehow, when they were all seated again, it was Nicholas who claimed the chair next to Verity.

Lavinia took charge. She might be incapable of balancing her household accounts, but she was a skillful hostess and knew to a nicety how to direct a conversation. She encouraged Nicholas and Katherine to speak of their home in Newbury, and its splendid situation on the River Kennet. Then, when Bryce seemed to be left out, she turned the talk to horses and had the satisfaction of seeing him and Nick engage in a spirited discussion of their respective teams.

The afternoon passed pleasantly, and Verity would have enjoyed it if she were not so worried. The others seemed to, and she was not surprised when they stayed for dinner. It was a superb meal. Bryce was completely won over when he tasted the white Chablis served with the fish. Lavinia, with childlike innocence, told him the wine had been smuggled in from France. She explained that there was a small shop near the library where one might purchase incredible bargains, and, in anticipation of their visit, she'd bought a bottle of brandy rumored to be from Napoleon's private stock.

Verity nearly choked on her wine. Appalled, she glanced across the table at Katherine, expecting shock or dismay. One might purchase contraband goods, but one did not discuss it in polite company. Katherine, however, appeared amused, and Bryce was too eager to sample the brandy to care whether it was contraband or not. Verity met Nick's gaze and saw the warm reassurance in his eyes. He smiled, then lifted his glass in a toast to his hostess.

Lavinia thanked him and then rose. Suggesting they leave the gentlemen to their cigars and brandy, she led the way to the drawing room. As they neared the door, the ladies heard a fearful, screeching cry. The cats, shut in to keep them from begging at the table, were demanding their freedom with piercing Siamese yowls.

Verity opened the door and looked down at the pair with a sigh. "They are accustomed to a romp in the garden after dinner, and if I don't let them out, we will have no peace. Please, excuse me for a moment."

It was the opportunity Katherine sought. "Certainly, but if you do not object, I would be pleased to bear you company."

"Now, that is a wonderful notion," Lavinia declared before Verity could reply. "You girls run along and enjoy a stroll in the garden while I just step into the kitchen and have a word with Tobias. Our chef, you know," she explained to Katherine. "A marvelous man, and I'm perfectly certain he's prepared something delicious for us to sample later."

"Oh, not for me," Katherine protested. "Really, Mrs. Parnel, I could not eat another bite."

"Nonsense, child. You're much too thin. Now, you go ahead with Verity and I shall see what may be contrived."

"I'm afraid there's no use arguing," Verity said, leading the way through the sitting room and out the terrace door. "Mama believes having some sort of sweet is the only healthy way to end an evening. She claims it ensures pleasant dreams."

"She's a dear lady, but however do you manage to keep your figure? I fear I would grow enormous were I to live here."

"We don't often enjoy such a large meal, and rarely do we partake of wine. The dinner tonight was a feast in your honor."

Verity paused, glancing around the secluded little garden. She gestured toward the bench where she'd so often sat with Nicholas. When they were seated, she spoke softly. "I am glad you didn't disappoint my mother, Mrs. Delacourt, but I confess I am puzzled to know why."

"I owe you an apology," Kate replied, her eyes focused on one of the cats determinedly pursuing a firefly. After a moment she faced Verity. "I misjudged you, Miss Parnel, and I hope you will be generous enough to forgive me, though I know my behavior was inexcusable."

Verity stared at her. "I am not certain I understand. Yesterday you considered me beneath contempt."

"I judged you most unfairly. I quite expected you

to either take the bribe I offered or to betray our conversation to Nick. I told you he would readily forgive my interference, but I suspect you know him well enough to realize that is not precisely true. He'd be furious to know the way I insulted you. Why, I'd not put it past him to marry you merely to teach me a lesson."

"I see. You wish to apologize so your brother will not wed me out of anger—"

"No! Good heavens, I'm making a mull of this. I don't say such a match would have my blessing, but I do know now that you are not the sort of scheming female I envisioned. Indeed, you went out of your way to protect me, and I feel the veriest wretch for treating you so shabbily."

"I fear you mistake my intent," Verity said, leaning down to scoop one of the cats up into her lap. "I was not protecting you. I tried only to spare Nicholas a bit of unpleasantness. He has been most kind to my mother and me."

"I know. We had a long talk last night and he told me something of your unfortunate situation. He also said you will not accept any financial assistance from him, though he wishes very much to help."

"It is not his responsibility to provide for us."

Katherine laughed, a musical trill that did much to ease the tension. "My brother considers everyone in the world his personal responsibility. I think he was meant to be the patriarch of a large family. You would not credit the number of persons he's helped on our estate at home. Every homeless waif, every struggling farmer, and any and all who come to him with a problem—even my cousin."

"Mr. Gyffard?"

Katherine nodded. "Poor Bryce thought he would inherit from our uncle, and when Nick did instead—well, my cousin has made his home with us ever since. I find him amusing company, but

Nick does not quite approve of him, or of Bryce's influence on me."

"He's mentioned something to that effect," Verity agreed.

"I'm not surprised. It's all he talks about of late. He's forever telling me I should engage a companion—" She gasped as though much struck. "Why, it is a perfect solution—I shall engage you!"

Verity laughed. "You cannot be serious."

"Oh, indeed I am. You are in need of a position—Nick told me you were seeking a post—and I need a companion, one whom my brother approves of. What could be simpler? That is . . . unless you're still angry with me?"

"No, but—"

"Then, there's nothing more to be said. You'll find me a generous employer, well, Nick actually since he pays all my bills—"

"Mrs. Delacourt, I could not possibly accept such an offer."

"Oh. You *are* still angry with me."

Verity shook her head. "Setting aside the exceptional circumstances of our meeting, I'm not the sort of person you should engage. You need someone older, someone to lend you proper countenance and who knows her way about in Society."

"Nonsense. The sort of person you describe would bore me to tears. I'm not a green girl, my dear, and you must admit you're far more suitable than Bryce. I know Nick will think it a splendid idea. Now, can you return to Town with me next week?"

"I could not possibly—my mother, the cats . . ." Verity caressed the Siamese in her lap.

Katherine stretched out a hand and scratched Antony behind his ears. He purred contentedly. "There, you see? He approves, and of course you may bring your cats with you. I do adore the creatures. As for your mother, do you think she would be content to remain here? I can advance you half your salary, so you may see to her expenses. Let us go in and ask her."

A week passed in a flurry of packing and plans. Verity, feeling much as though she had stepped into one of her mother's daydreams, closed the valise and placed it on the floor. She glanced around the candlelit room, stripped now of all her personal belongings. She still found it difficult to believe that in the morning she'd be on her way to London as Kate Delacourt's companion.

And living in the same house as Nicholas Lynton.

The arrangements had been completed with remarkable speed, and though Verity had continued to protest, her every objection was swiftly countered by either Kate or Nicholas. Even Lavinia had conspired against her daughter. When Verity had said she could not leave her mother alone, Lavinia had pointed out that she must if she were to accept any position.

Verity was not deceived. She knew her mother. While disappointed that Nicholas had not offered marriage, Lavinia had not given up hope. She felt certain it was a mere matter of time before he proposed. Until then, she told Verity, it could be only to her advantage to live with his sister.

Arguing was futile, and Verity had finally accepted the inevitable. In truth, she was not unduly worried about her mother. Lord Lewes had driven to Brighton twice in the last week to call on them. When he'd learned Verity planned to go to London, he'd spoken with her privately. She smiled, remembering the gentle concern in his eyes. He had guessed the true reason for her reluctance. With exquisite tact, the earl had made certain she had his direction, and made her promise she would write him if she found her position in London to be an unhappy one. He would come at once, he said, and bring her home.

Verity brushed out her hair and, after shooing

154

the cats from the bed, slipped between the covers. Cleo protested with a soft mew, immediately reclaiming her place on the bed. Antony kneaded the pillow on her other side, purring loudly as he curled up next to her. Even the cats had not posed a problem. Kate insisted the pets would be welcome, but Verity refused to take them. Cleo and Antony would be happier in the country. As she herself would be, she thought, if only she could have found another position—a position where she might find some peace of mind instead of recklessly risking her heart.

Before Kate's tumultuous arrival, Verity had known the time would come when Nicholas would disappear from her life. She'd anticipated it and savored their moments together, locking the precious memories away in her heart. But now she was to be part of his life. Perhaps only a small part, but she would probably see him most days, and it was that she feared. She did not aspire to wed Nicholas—she knew she was not fit to be his wife. But she couldn't help loving him. It was foolish beyond belief, yet her heart wouldn't listen to reason.

Tears rolled silently from her eyes, dampening the pillow beneath her cheek. Kate, under the illusion that it would be a treat for Verity, told her they would go to all the balls, routs, and theater parties that were so much a part of the London Season. Verity dreaded it. She knew she'd have to watch Nicholas escort one young lady after another, watch him dance with some nameless dark-haired beauty in his arms . . . and surely, it would be only a matter of time before he announced his betrothal.

Verity felt the rough edge of Cleo's tongue licking the salty tears from her cheek. She pulled the cat into her arms and gently stroked the silky fur. Foolish creature, she thought, then realized she was just as bad. She should be counting her blessings instead of thinking of Nicholas. Mama was rapidly recovering her health and would be well taken care of. The generous salary Nick insisted on would solve most of her financial worries, and Kate had even promised her a new wardrobe. Clothes . . . it had been ages since she'd had a new gown. She pictured herself clad in the latest style. Just as she drifted off to sleep, she wondered if Nicholas would admire her once she was fashionably dressed.

Bryce, Kate, and Nick lingered over dinner in their private parlor at the Ship's Inn. It was their last night in Brighton—reason alone in Bryce's opinion to celebrate—but Nick was rejoicing in Verity's decision to return to Town with them. Feeling festive, he ignored Kate's protest and refilled their wineglasses for a final toast.

"To the finest sister a man could have—"

"Really, Nick, I have done nothing to deserve such praise."

"Do not declaim, Kate. You've behaved like an angel this week, and I'm much indebted to you for your compassion, and your understanding."

A tap on the door interrupted Nick. The warm smile of approval he bestowed on his sister turned into a wide grin. "That will be Crimstock. Excuse me a moment."

"How very touching," Bryce murmured when Nick left them. "Do you still doubt his feelings for this girl?"

Kate hesitated. "I know he's gone to extraordinary lengths to see her settled comfortably, but that's his nature. He considers all the tenants at home as sort of an extended family. He takes his responsibilities—"

"Oh, spare me the canonization of Saint Nick. Frankly, my dear, I'm fed up to the teeth with all this talk of how good, how kind, how charitable dear Nick is." His voice mimicked hers and he drained his glass, missing the flash of anger in Kate's eyes.

"Very pretty talk for a man who lives off my brother's charity," she retorted.

Bryce's eyes narrowed. He stared at her for an uncomfortable moment. "I shall contrive to forget you said that, unless, of course, you no longer desire my assistance?"

Kate flushed at the subtle reminder of their conspiracy. She knew it behooved her not to anger Bryce, though she devoutly wished she'd never taken him into her confidence. At first, she'd willingly told him everything Verity said, and even laughed when he'd ridiculed the girl. But during the last week she had come to know Verity Parnel better. Now Kate found it difficult to believe her a villainess.

"Having second thoughts, my dear?"

"No . . . not really. It's just that I feel so wretched about deceiving Nick."

"Remember, it's for his own good, my sweet, and you *are* doing him a favor employing Miss Parnel."

She nodded, then glanced up as Nick returned to the table carrying two wrapped packages. "What is this?"

Her brother grinned. "Just a token to express my gratitude. I know the pair of you spent a miserable week here, and would not have stayed except for my sake."

Kate took the small, elegant box and slowly undid the wrappings. She lifted the lid. Inside, nestled against a bed of black velvet, reposed an intricately fashioned gold locket in the shape of a heart. She gingerly picked it up, and heard her brother urging her to open it. The locket was cunningly worked and snapped apart to reveal two miniatures. Tears threatened as she stared down at the tiny hand-painted faces of her parents.

Nick dropped a kiss on her brow. "Pleased, my dear? I rather thought a heart of gold appropriate for you."

"How did you manage—" She broke off, biting her lips to control her tears.

"I commissioned a portrait painter to do the miniatures some time ago. He copied them from the paintings in the hall at home. Remarkable bit of work, do you not think?"

"I shall treasure it always. Thank you, Nick."

He grinned, then turned to his cousin, handing him a larger, heavier box. "And this is for you. Go ahead, open it up."

Bryce hid his surprise and quickly stripped off the paper. He lifted out a bottle of fine aged brandy—the same he'd enjoyed at Mrs. Parnel's. He glanced up at his cousin, his brows slanted in mock astonishment. "Smuggled brandy? I'm shocked, Nick, to think that you would buy contraband goods—and entirely grateful for your excellent taste."

"All I ask is that you don't tell anyone from where you had it! There's a dozen bottles of the stuff in your carriage, and I hope you may drink it in good health. Now I shall bid you a good night. Remember, we leave early in the morning."

"Perhaps he should be canonized," Bryce muttered a moment later, watching Nick stride from the room. "He's much too kind. Someone is sure to take advantage of him."

"Just be certain that it's not you," Kate replied, caressing the gold locket between her fingers.

Chapter 12

Verity softly closed the door of her bedchamber and tiptoed down the long hall, now dimly lit by a candle sconce at the top of the stairs. Both Bryce and Kate had their doors firmly shut, but Nick's stood slightly ajar. She held her breath as she edged past his room, then paused and listened intently. The house remained silent save for the ticking of the grandfather clock.

Carrying her shoes in one hand while holding to the banister for support with the other, Verity crept down the stairs and through the maze of hallways to the small sitting room at the rear. She risked lighting a candle, and by its flickering light managed to unlock the French doors leading to the garden. Then she pulled on her silk slippers, placed the taper carefully on top of the spinet, and stepped out into the cool night air.

Shivering within her thin wrapper, Verity looked up at the heavens. The thin crescent moon was barely visible behind the banks of dark, ominous clouds. A thunderstorm was brewing. One could almost smell it, she thought, sniffing at the dampness in the air. And not a star to be seen, not one star to wish upon.

She drew her wrapper tighter, and briskly rubbed her chilled hands as she watched the swift movement of clouds snaking across the sky. Her first night in London seemed as unsettled as the turbulent emotions that kept her from sleep.

She knew she should be thankful for her present

position. Besides paying her an exceedingly generous salary, both Kate and Nick treated her as though she were a member of the family. Still, a feeling of ill-boding haunted her tonight, a premonition that she'd made a dreadful mistake in accepting Kate's offer. Something terrible loomed ahead of her, and she was alone here, as lost in the sprawling city as one tiny star in the vast sky.

"Verity?"

Nick's deep voice came to her out of the night. Had she willed him to appear? She turned slowly and gazed up at him. He looked endearingly disheveled, his curls tousled from sleep, and his white cambric shirt open at the neck. Her eyes were immediately drawn to the dark, curling hair visible on his chest. Immoral thoughts chased through her mind as quickly as the clouds across the moon.

"Verity, my dear, are you ill?"

She shook her head. The concern in his voice both warmed and shamed her. She hastened to apologize. "I'm sorry if I woke you, Nicholas. I had trouble sleeping and felt too restless to remain inside, but I never meant to disturb you."

His mouth turned up at the corners. "Have you forgotten that I'm a light sleeper?"

Blushing furiously, Verity turned away. He would never forget the manner in which they'd met. Both he and Kate had said to put the past behind her, that it mattered not. They said what counted was the future, but Verity knew that whatever she did in the months and years ahead, Nicholas Lynton would always remember that she was a thief.

It might have been the lateness of the hour, or her weariness from the long journey, but for once Verity could not show a brave face. Tears welled in her eyes, and her throat closed so she could not speak.

Nick cursed beneath his breath. He hadn't meant to embarrass her. He saw her shoulders shaking and took a step toward her. "Verity, forgive me. I did not mean—it's only that when I saw you in the hall, it reminded me . . ."

She whirled around, choking back tears. "I know what it reminded you of, Nicholas. Were you afraid I was sneaking out to rob someone else?"

She saw the truth reflected in his eyes and flinched. She'd hurled the words at him without thinking, not really believing he would think so ill of her. She lifted her chin. "I shall leave in the morning."

"You will do nothing of the kind!" He reached her side in an instant and grasped her shoulders. "Look at me, Verity," he ordered, and waited until she tilted up her head.

Tears stained her cheeks and her eyes glistened in the pale light, but she was still beautiful. With an effort Nick controlled his desire to lower his head and kiss away her tears, kiss her until her lips yielded to him.

"Why do you wish me to stay?" she demanded. "Are you not afraid I'll steal the silver?"

"Not in the least," he murmured. Then, realizing how much he'd hurt her, he smiled tenderly. "If the silver disappeared, I would look at once for Bryce."

Verity was in no mood for his jests. She struggled to be free of his arms, but his hands were like iron traps. "Let me go," she demanded.

"Not until you listen to me. I did think when I saw you slip past my door that perhaps you meant to settle the score with Lord Ashford—but it was only a fleeting notion, gone in an instant. Then I became concerned that you might be ill, or troubled. I thought maybe you missed Brighton, and I came down to see if I could help."

This, too, was the truth. She couldn't doubt the sincerity in his voice, but his words changed nothing. She gazed helplessly up at him. "I don't belong here, Nicholas. You will always recall how we met."

"I hope so. It's one of my fondest memories," he

replied softly, and because there was still so much sorrow in her eyes, he bent his head to drop a light kiss on her brow. He meant only to comfort her, to ease her heartache a bit, but she looked up at the same time, and his lips naturally found her mouth. Like coming home, he thought, and deepened the kiss. He forgot the words he meant to say, forgot the proprieties, forgot everything except for the sweet taste of her lips.

Verity tried to speak, but when her mouth opened, his tongue slipped inside and stole her breath. She quit struggling and leaned against him, wanting only to be closer, wanting the moment to never end.

Nick released her arms and slid his hands around her shoulders and back. He felt the curve of her waist beneath the silk wrapper, and the swell of her hips as she pressed against him.

A thunderclap shattered the stillness, and lightning rippled over their heads, but neither noticed. Then the heavens opened and the rain poured down in torrents.

The cold, stinging water brought Nick back to his senses. He grabbed Verity's hand and ran for the safety of the house. Both of them laughed with the exhilaration of the moment. Once inside the sitting room, he tried to dash some of the water from his shirt and breeches, but he was drenched. As was Verity. The laughter died on his lips as he gazed at her. Did she realize how transparent her wrapper was . . . that the enticing curves of her body showed clearly beneath the thin, wet material? Not wanting her to see his growing desire, Nick turned away.

Good Lord, what was the matter with him? Kissing Verity as if she were some street doxy instead of a member of his household, a young, gently bred girl under his protection. No wonder the storm had broken over his head—he deserved the wrath of God. Had he been without a woman so long that he could no longer control his instincts, behaving like a rutting stallion?

He crossed to the sideboard and poured himself a generous portion of Bryce's brandy, wondering if he should offer Verity a drink as well. The warmth would do much to ward off a chill, but after his barbarous display in the garden, she might think he was merely trying to seduce her. He downed part of his drink. The brandy helped to restore a measure of his control, enough so that he risked looking at her.

She stood near the door, a bedraggled angel. Her blond hair, wet from the storm, curled in tiny tendrils about her face and shoulders. The sodden wrapper clung to the contours of her body, and droplets of water puddled on the floor at her feet. Her eyes, always expressive, did not reproach him but watched him warily.

"Come here, Verity," he said, trying to keep his voice gentle. "I think a drop of brandy will do us both good."

He wondered if it was raindrops or tears that made her eyes seem so luminous. "Are you angry with me?"

She shook her head.

"Afraid?"

That brought a tremulous smile to her lips. "No, Nicholas, but it is wrong for me to be here alone with you."

"You are right, of course, and I deserve that you don't trust me."

I don't trust myself, she thought, gazing with longing at his muscular body. In his arms she'd found what she'd been missing most of her life. Someone who cared for her, someone who wanted to be with her. And even though it was wrong, she had felt safe in his embrace. She suddenly understood how easily a woman could be tempted into a life of sin. If Nicholas asked it of her, she doubted she would have the will to refuse him.

"Are you still thinking of leaving in the morning?"

"I believe it would be best."

He drained his glass. "If I apologize—give you my word of honor that such a scene will not happen again, would you reconsider?"

He looked so unhappy, Verity yearned to comfort him. She controlled the impulse, wrapping her arms tightly about her body. "That ... that had nothing to do with my decision. It was kind of you and Kate to arrange a position for me, but I should not have agreed. Nicholas, you must see that I don't belong here."

"So you said, but I'm at a loss to understand why." Forgetting his resolution to stay away from her, he crossed to her side. "Verity, my dear, I brought you here because I wanted you to have the opportunity to enjoy the sort of life you were meant to—I want you to attend all the balls and parties, and to have young men courting you. They'll be writing sonnets to the beauty of your eyes and bringing you flowers, and that is as it should be."

"But you are not responsible for me. You cannot just decide I should have the world and provide me with it."

"I can, and I claim the right to do so. If my uncle and his friends hadn't robbed your father, you would now be living much as Kate does. Give me the chance to rectify what my uncle did. Don't deny me that."

She looked into the depths of his imploring blue eyes and lost the battle. She could refuse him nothing.

"You must allow me to make amends, Verity. Promise me you will stay here for the rest of the Season. Then, if you're still determined, I will escort you back to Brighton."

It would be wrong of her to stay. Foolish beyond belief. She met his gaze. "If it means so much to you ..."

"It does. Have I your word?"

She nodded, unable to speak, then turned to go, struggling blindly with the door for a moment.

Nicholas rose early the following morning, well before the rest of the house was stirring. He had slept but little, too troubled by thoughts of Verity to rest easy. He considered his conduct reprehensible. If any man dared to kiss Kate so, Nick would see to it that the banns were posted, or meet the man on the dueling field.

"Good morning, sir." Crimstock backed into the room with a heavy tray bearing tea and toast. "I heard you moving about and brought you breakfast, sir."

"Thank you," Nick replied. He had no appetite, but the tea would be welcome. "Just set the tray down over there." He turned his back on the valet and continued to haphazardly toss shirts and stocks into the open valise on his bed.

"Are we going traveling again, sir?"

"I am," Nick answered abruptly.

"If you will allow me," Crimstock murmured, taking a shirt from his hands and folding it neatly. He removed the other shirts and deftly began replacing them in perfect order. "May I inquire how long you intend to be gone, sir?"

"A fortnight, perhaps longer."

"I see."

Nick helped himself to the tea, and then a bit of toast. Feeling somewhat better, he watched Crimstock for a moment. He'd been curt with the old man, who deserved better. Nick made an effort to explain. "I decided late last night to visit my home in Newbury."

"The Kennet Valley? 'Tis pleasing country."

"Have you been there, then?"

"Not in many years, sir, but once long ago with your uncle. We were on our way to Lambourn and stopped a bit at Falkland Garth. I believe your uncle mentioned your father lived nearby, but he was away from home at the time."

"A pity you did not have the opportunity to visit our estate. I know of no place lovelier."

"Perhaps it's still not too late," the elderly valet suggested with a twinkle in his eye.

Nick smiled. "In truth, I should be glad of your company. I fear I've become accustomed to your pampering, Crimstock, but I hesitated to ask it of you as we've just returned. Are you certain you wish to go on the road again?"

"My place is with you, sir, unless, of course, you think I am too old to be of use."

"I hope I'm not so foolish as to believe that. If you're of a mind to come, pack your bags. I leave within the hour."

"Very good, sir."

He made no other comment, but Nick watched him move quickly and efficiently about the room. He envied the older man his stamina. He himself felt as though a wagon had rolled over his body—several times. His head ached with a dull, persistent throb, no doubt the result of finishing off the brandy the previous night. Rubbing his brow, he wondered how his cousin managed to consume copious amounts of the stuff without feeling the effects.

Leaving Crimstock to his packing, Nick went down to send a footman to the mews to order his carriage brought around. Then he stepped into the garden. The storm during the night had cleared the air, and the morning promised to be a fine one. Nick lingered outside, recalling the kisses he'd shared there with Verity the night before. Despite his headache, despite the early hour, desire flared within him.

He wanted her. Heaven help him, how he wanted her. But the capricious winds of fate blew with exquisite irony. Until the night before, he had not realized how much he loved the girl. Not until the

166

moment she'd stepped into his arms. He'd believed his own words to Bryce and Kate, believed he was merely doing his duty, believed he had a responsibility to see Verity properly settled. But somewhere along the way he'd fallen in love with her . . . or had he loved her all along and been too blind to see it?

It was almost laughable. He had finally found the one girl in the world destined to be his, and he could not offer for her—though he'd been sorely tempted to do so the night before, when she had stood there looking so forlorn and lost. The trouble was, he knew Verity would not consider a proposal from him. Not now. No matter what he said or did, she would think he sought only to do the honorable thing. One word of marriage, and she would disappear. He smiled, remembering the chase she had led him on before. He couldn't chance losing her again.

Nick paced the garden, oblivious of its beauty, while he considered his dilemma. He not only had to persuade Verity that he truly cared for her, but he must convince her that she was worthy of being his bride. She seemed obsessed with this notion that she was a thief, and therefore unfit to enter Society. Absurd, when one considered that half the lords and ladies of the ton had not one tenth Verity's integrity.

He glanced up at the house, wishing he could speak with her this morning. But it would be wiser to leave without seeing her. He meant to give her a chance to become adjusted to living in his house, to taking her rightful place in Society. Then, when he returned in two or three weeks, he could begin courting her as she deserved.

Nick plucked a rose, a yellow rose still wet with dew, and carried it carefully into the house. He sat down at his desk in the library and dipped his quill into the ink. He must leave her some sort of message. There was not much time. The clock had chimed six, and the servants were already bustling about. Nick wrote quickly.

"My dear, may this one poor rose serve to remind you of your promise to me. I hope to return within a fortnight and shall send you a proper bouquet then. Though I shall miss you, little one, it will give me pleasure to know you are here in my house—where you belong."

He read it through quickly and rose before he could change his mind. After folding and sealing the missive, he rang for Dulcie. When she appeared, he instructed her to put the rose in water and place it on Miss Parnel's breakfast tray, along with his note. Verity would find it when she drank her morning cup of chocolate.

He scrawled another quick note for Kate and left it propped on the desk. Then he hurried out front. The carriage and Crimstock were waiting. Nick took the reins himself, and set the horses cantering down the lane. He glanced back once, a wistful look in his eyes.

Chapter 13

"Well, if you were bored to tears, it's your own fault," Kate scolded. "I don't know why you feel obliged to sit with the dowagers and chaperones."

Verity, in the seclusion of their carriage, slipped off her shoes and rubbed one aching foot against the other. She smiled fondly at Kate. "I was not in the least bored. Mrs. Bonaby is a fascinating woman."

"If you say so, my dear." The carriage came to a rolling halt, and as the postillion came around to open the door and let down the steps, Kate glanced at her companion. She hesitated a moment, then asked softly, "You are not unhappy here, are you, Verity?"

"How could I be when you've been so kind?"

She spoke the truth. During the last few weeks the two had become close friends. Their tastes were much the same, as both were inclined to view the London Season with amusement bordering on disrespect. Verity thought it laughable the way the younger girls postured for the benefit of eligible bachelors, and Kate frequently offered wagers on a lady's chances with a certain gentleman.

Conscious of her role as companion, Verity had tried at first to discourage such improper conduct, but Kate had quickly seen through her. Now if Verity dared utter some prim stricture, Kate made faces until both of them dissolved into an unseemly fit of the giggles.

Far from the agony Verity had once imagined,

she found living with Kate to be a delightful if unpredictable experience. And although Verity missed her mother, her letters home were filled with vivacious accounts of all the parties she attended and the gay life they led. If any mention of Nicholas Lynton was conspicuously absent from her letters, other gentlemen's names appeared in profusion. One might even conclude, after reading of the dizzying round of morning calls, shopping, dinners, and dances, that Verity had no time to think of Nicholas. But he was seldom out of her thoughts, though she had not seen him in weeks.

Thinking of him now, Verity quickened her steps as she and Kate entered the house. She'd heard Nicholas was expected to return from Newbury today. Despite herself, she couldn't suppress the rising tide of anticipation that set her heart beating erratically. Once, she'd thought that seeing him every day would prove unbearable, but she'd quickly learned his absence was far worse. Her soul yearned for just a glimpse of him. She would have willingly given all she possessed to remain at home tonight. But Kate had accepted Lady Caroline Green's invitation to attend a small dinner party with dancing afterward. It was precisely the sort of affair Nick scorned, so there was little hope he would provide them escort. But, with luck, she might see him for a few moments this afternoon.

Kate led the way down the hall, and Verity followed eagerly. Unfortunately, it was Bryce who greeted them as they entered the drawing room.

"Ah, at last the wanderers have returned. I trust you two had a pleasant afternoon?"

"We did, indeed," Kate told him, dropping into one of the tall wing chairs. "But fatiguing, vastly fatiguing. Be a lamb and ring for tea, will you?"

"I anticipated your wishes, dear heart. The tray was brought in not five moments past." He waved a hand toward the ornate silver teapot but kept his gaze on Verity. "Well, well. Our little wren is looking more like a peacock these days. Very becoming, my dear. Dare I imagine the roses in your cheeks are due to the attentions of some discriminating gentleman? Charles Haversham, perhaps?"

Verity flushed. "More likely from the drive."

"Kate, my sweet, do observe how prettily our little bird declaims. Such a charming air of modesty—precisely the sort of manner a well-bred young lady should strive to adopt. Kate? Kate, you are not paying attention."

"You *are* observant," she agreed, but continued to ignore him while she fussed with the teacups. She filled one, then passed it to Verity along with a bit of advice. "Pay my cousin no heed. If you once allow him to disconcert you, he will tease you forever."

"Thank you," Verity murmured, wishing she could accept Kate's advice, but she was still not entirely comfortable with Bryce Gyffard's easy manners and teasing banter.

For his part, he grinned, totally unrepentent and not in the least disturbed by Kate's remark. "But think how dreadfully tedious you'd find life without my diverting chatter. Besides, I was merely curious to know who sent all the flowers."

Both ladies looked at him.

"I rather thought that would gain your attention. Dulcie took them up to your rooms—several posies for each of you."

"Who sent them?" Kate demanded.

"I cannot say for certain, but I thought I glimpsed Haversham's scrawl—"

"Never tell me you didn't read the cards," Kate interrupted, her voice heavy with skepticism.

Bryce shrugged. "Crimstock was in the hall when the flowers arrived. Somehow I had the impression he would take it amiss were I to satisfy my natural curiosity. Sanctimonious old man—reminds me of my grandfather. I cannot understand why Nick insists on keeping him about."

"Perhaps to keep you in line," Kate replied,

laughing. "I gather Nick is home, then? Where is he?"

"Out visiting his man of business, of course. The chap is a glutton for punishment."

Kate glanced at Verity. "Shall we go up and discover which gentlemen have the excellent taste to admire us?"

Verity smiled and stood at once. All she could think of was that Nick was home, but she replied calmly, "I am agreeable, and would be glad to change and rest a bit before dinner."

Kate set down her cup and started to rise, but Bryce protested.

"Stay a bit, cousin. Why, I've scarce had a word alone with you since we returned to Town."

Kate hesitated, but Verity had seen her indecision and caught the hint from Bryce. She fabricated a yawn and then laughed. "Heavens, I really must rest or I will likely fall asleep at dinner tonight. Kate, do stay here if you wish—we may talk later."

When Kate took her at her word, settling back comfortably in her chair, Verity hurried up to her bedchamber. The apartment, decorated in pale blue and gold, was one normally occupied by distinguished visitors and adjoined Kate's own. In addition to the enormous four-poster, the room held a delicate rosewood writing table, a double chest of drawers, several comfortable armchairs and center tables, and a small but pretty settee. Rosewood bookshelves lined the walls on either side of the huge old fireplace. There had been several nights when Verity read herself to sleep with one of the beautifully bound volumes.

That afternoon her attention went immediately to two posies, both artfully arranged. The violets on the center table were almost certainly from Charles Haversham. She'd once mentioned how much she liked the tiny purple flowers, and he had sent a similar bouquet last week.

The other flowers, a dozen pale yellow roses just opening their buds, were on the writing table, where they caught the late afternoon sun. Ignoring the violets, Verity swiftly crossed the room and removed the card from the roses. Bold black letters greeted her eyes. Even before she read the signature, she knew the roses were from Nicholas.

Kate sipped her tea, eyeing Bryce warily over the rim of the cup. She suspected he wanted to discuss Verity and wished it were possible to avoid the conversation. During the last few weeks, Kate had been much in Verity's company, and she had come to admire and like her new companion. No matter what Bryce said, Kate no longer believed Verity posed any sort of threat to Nick. But her cousin did not share her feelings, and he had a silvery tongue capable of making her reasoning seem foolish and naive.

"Your brother astonishes me," Bryce said, breaking the silence between them.

"Nick? In what way?"

He did not answer immediately, but strode to the sideboard and helped himself to a generous portion of brandy. Cradling the glass in his hand, he leaned against the mantel of the fireplace. "He seems, at first glance, such an unassuming, affable fellow. Quite deceptive, really, when one considers the matter."

"You speak in riddles, cousin—that is, if you are still speaking of my brother. I've known him all my life and he is unassuming and affable. No one is as kind, as nice, or more generous than Nick. You, of all people, should know that."

"I do not dispute his generosity or tolerance, and will grant you that he is the most agreeable of gentlemen—as long as he has his own way. But your brother, my dear heart, possesses a will of iron."

Kate laughed outright. "You've been imbibing too

much brandy, Bryce. I doubt anyone who knows him would describe Nick in that manner."

"Ah, that's the irony of it. I find it incredible how he manages to get his own way without anyone ever being aware of the iron hand beneath the velvet glove."

"I find it incredible that you could utter such nonsense. If this is what you wished to discuss, I shall leave you to your musing. Iron hand, indeed!"

"It pleases me to afford you amusement, my dear, but if you will set aside your natural fondness and consider Nicholas in a rational manner, you'll see I'm correct. Think of it, my sweet. Your sainted brother objected to the amount of time you were spending in my company. He also desired to have his little wren in London with him. Did he not achieve both those aims—and with single-minded determination?"

Kate laughed. "But bringing Verity to London was our idea!"

"Was it? Think again."

"Regardless, one has nothing to do with the other. I admit that at first Nick pursued Verity to the exclusion of all else, but you must remember his exaggerated sense of responsibility. And he's barely seen her since our return."

She hesitated. Bryce's smile, a superior, smug sort of smirk, made her uneasy. "What is it?"

"He sent her flowers today—a dozen yellow roses."

Kate's brows rose. "I thought you didn't have an opportunity to read the cards. How do you know they were from Nick?"

"As it chanced, I happened to stroll by Miss Parnel's room and found the door ajar."

"You're incorrigible, Bryce. But even if Nick did send Verity flowers, it means nothing. He would do the same for any lady staying in the house."

He shrugged. "If you are of a mind to have the

little wren as a sister-in-law, I suppose it's no concern of mine."

Kate sipped her tea, considering the idea. She liked Verity well enough and, except for her unfortunate past, there was nothing about the girl to make her ineligible. The more she thought about it, the more Kate was inclined to believe that Verity might make an ideal bride for Nick. But the unease she'd felt before kept her from saying so to Bryce.

She had few illusions about her cousin. He'd told her bluntly he did not wish to see Nick wed—but how far would he go to prevent such a marriage? Surely, she thought, he would not actually *do* anything. Still, her uneasiness increased.

She managed a smile for his benefit. "I suspect the brandy has muddled your thinking, cousin. I'm convinced Nick is merely being a thoughtful host."

"Is he? I wonder."

The door opened before Kate could reply.

"Speak of the devil," Bryce muttered, then raised his glass in greeting to his cousin.

Kate glanced around and rose with a glad cry. "Nick! Oh, it's so good to see you. Did you have a pleasant trip? How are Matilda and Emily? Did you see Mrs. Crispin?"

He hugged her warmly, kissed her cheek, then set her from him. "Everyone at home is fine. I'm charged to convey dozens of messages. You are sorely missed, Kate."

"I miss our people, too," she replied, taking her seat once more. "Just thinking of all of them makes me a trifle homesick."

"We could go back tomorrow if you wished."

"Impossible. You must know we have engagements."

"Engagements are made to be broken."

She looked up at him and realized he was teasing. "Beast. Will you have tea?"

He nodded, but his eyes were busy searching the room. "Where is your companion?"

Kate, carefully avoiding her cousin's eyes, passed her brother a teacup. "Verity's resting. We had an exhausting morning, and there's a long evening ahead."

"You've no idea of the pleasures you've missed," Bryce said, crossing the room to sprawl in the chair next to Kate's.

"Indeed I do, which is why I dallied in Newbury. But what momentous event is scheduled for tonight?"

"We dine at Lady Caroline's," Kate told him. "She's engaged an orchestra to play afterward for an impromptu dance. I think Caroline has a tendre for you, Nick. She said if you returned to Town in time, she'd be pleased to have you join us."

"Perhaps I will."

Kate nearly dropped her cup. "Are you serious?"

"Unless you have no wish for my company?"

"Don't be foolish, Nick. Or course I would be pleased, only—well, it will be just the sort of evening you have always disliked."

"Why so surprised, Kate?" Bryce asked. "I'm not. It must be thought only natural for Nick to wish to accompany us after so long a time away from his . . . sister."

Kate hastily changed the subject, but Bryce's innuendo disturbed her. She found herself suddenly wishing that Nick had remained safe in Newbury, then immediately thought how absurd to imagine Bryce intended her brother any harm. Or harm to Verity, either.

She refilled her brother's cup and plied him with questions about Newbury. Bryce, who'd never visited the estate there and knew none of the people they spoke of, soon grew bored and left them alone. Kate continued to chatter, but she only half listened to her brother's replies. When she asked him for the second time about Mrs. Crispin's health, he stared at her for a moment, his blue eyes troubled.

"Is something amiss, Kate?"

It seemed the perfect opportunity to confide in Nick, to tell him she suspected Bryce of some sort of mischief. But her loyalties were divided. She was fond of her cousin, and believed he cared for her, too. And until Verity's arrival, he'd been her constant companion. If she voiced her concern now, Nick might very well order Bryce from the house. And he had nowhere else to go, no other family.

Easing her conscience with the thought that she had no real evidence Bryce meant any harm, Kate sighed and shook her head. "I'm just rather tired. I think I should join Verity and rest awhile before this evening."

Nick stood as she rose. "You do look worn to a frazzle. Must we go out tonight? We could have a quiet evening at home—"

"And spoil Caroline's seating arrangements? I would not dare." She laughed lightly and stood on her toes to kiss her brother's cheek. "I shall be fine with a little rest. Do you truly mean to come with us?"

Nick smiled. "I think I must, if only to keep an eye on you."

"Then I shall see you later."

Kate left him and walked slowly up the stairs. She could not warn her brother, but perhaps there was a way to persuade Verity it would be unwise to show a preference for Nick.

"Bryce, I think we shall be the envy of every gentleman present tonight," Nick said as he watched his sister and Verity descend the curved staircase in the hall.

"Undoubtedly," Bryce agreed, but his attention was on Nick. He didn't miss the way his cousin's gaze followed the graceful figure of Verity Parnel, or the admiration in his eyes.

"I hope we've not kept you waiting," Kate said, coming down the last step. She was elegantly gowned in a blush-colored satin slip with a patent

177

net overdress. Her dark curls were drawn back and a spray of white flowers held the ringlets in place.

"Of course you have," he replied with a laugh. "But the pleasure of escorting two such beauties makes the wait well worthwhile."

"Prettily said, Nick, but save your flummery for those who will believe it," Kate retorted for Verity's benefit. She'd spoken to her while they were dressing, and dropped a hint that her companion shouldn't take Nick's praise to heart. Verity had seemed startled, and then hurt, which was not at all what Kate wished. She'd tried to make amends, but suspected she'd only made matters worse.

Verity, following a step behind Kate, paused, and then shyly lifted her eyes to meet Nick's gaze.

He drew in his breath. She looked like an angel descending from the skies in her celestial blue gown. The silk clung to her body and the low-cut bodice emphasized the beguiling swell of her breasts. The wisps of blond curls framing her heart-shaped face might have been a halo, and the depths of her dark eyes held all the promise of Eden. The words he'd intended to utter died on his lips. Nick simply stared at her.

Verity returned his look, spellbound. She saw the growing desire in his eyes and knew it was mirrored in her own. Her lips parted slightly as she found it difficult to catch her breath. Kate and her warning were banished from her mind. Bryce no longer existed. She saw no one except Nicholas and, at that moment, she would have followed him anywhere.

Dressed formally, Nick appeared every inch the gentleman. But she knew the clean lines of his black dress coat concealed a set of broad shoulders and powerful arms. She remembered the strength of those arms from that fateful night when he'd carried her to his bed. She fought down an irrational, immoral desire to repeat the experience.

Still, it flamed within her, burning strongly until she ached with her need of him.

Appalled, Kate watched the scene. If Bryce had any doubt of his cousin's infatuation, it was surely destroyed in that instant when Verity and Nick stared speechlessly at each other. Kate was both embarrassed and envious. Roland had never looked at her with such obvious, naked longing, not even in those first weeks of her marriage. She felt like a voyeur, witnessing a moment of deep intimacy, and blushed at her scandalous thoughts.

Beside her, Bryce whispered in her ear. "Do you believe me now, sweetling?"

Kate spoke sharply to her brother. "Nick, we must hurry or we shall be late."

Abruptly recalled to his senses, Nick mounted the step to offer Verity his escort. "You look enchanting tonight."

Verity placed her gloved hand on his arm, averting her gaze. She'd heard Kate, and could not blame her friend for her anger. Verity had admitted she was not a proper bride for Nick. She'd said the words, had known the truth of them, and knew it still. But though she could never hope to wed him, she couldn't help loving him any more than the river could cease flowing.

The drive seemed endless. When they arrived, they found a long line of carriages waiting their turn in the square. Verity sat quietly next to Kate, responding in monosyllables when addressed. It was ill bred of her to show her feelings in such a manner, but grief lay heavy on her heart. She should not be there, she thought. She didn't belong in this glittering world of London's elite.

"Verity, do look at all the carriages. I declare, Caroline must be sitting thirty or forty down to dinner."

"I thought this was a small party," Nick complained.

"I never said so," Kate returned. "You know Caroline never does anything by half."

"Most of London must be here," Bryce observed. "Well, at least we may be sure of a tolerable dinner. Lady Caroline dresses an elegant table."

Their carriage rolled to a stop in front of the town house. The footman opened the door and let down the steps. Verity, glancing out the window, saw the guests crowded around the entrance. She glimpsed the hundreds of candles lighting the tall house in a festive aura. She could hear the soft strains of music beneath the rising tide of conversation and gay laughter. But none of it made much of an impression, for Nicholas stood before her, waiting to hand her from the carriage.

She must compose herself. She must behave sensibly and put as much distance between them as possible. She accepted his hand and stepped down, much too aware of him.

He tilted his head so only she could hear his words. "The evening will be interminable, but I shall bear it well if you promise me the first waltz."

She glanced up and was lost in the blue of his eyes and the warmth of his smile. Her lips curved upward in answer. It was wrong of her, but she couldn't refuse him.

Lady Caroline saw them at once and crossed the room to greet Nicholas. She was a slender, dark-haired woman, driven almost to obsession to become one of the ton's leaders. She'd married the older, immensely wealthy Lord Green to improve her position, but among the ton it was rumored that she had a yen for handsome young men. She had one in tow, and introduced him as Giles Calvert.

When Bryce greeted him as an old friend, Verity looked at the man curiously. This was Mr. Donahue's cousin—the one from America—that they'd heard so much about. Tall and lean, he had a deeply bronzed face with a rugged look that bespoke hard living. He seemed uncomfortable in his dress coat, though it suited him well. She glanced from him to Bryce. No two gentlemen could be more different, but the American spoke warmly to Gyffard and Verity listened, liking the sound of the stranger's voice with its odd pronunciation.

Kate, too, found much to admire in Calvert and drew him away from the others. "I have been dying to hear about America, sir. Is it true that there are savages there and that men never go out unarmed?"

Verity smiled at the look of chagrin on Lady Caroline's face as Kate drew Mr. Calvert away. Caroline, however, was an accomplished hostess. She summoned a smooth smile as an elderly, corpulent gentleman joined them.

After greeting the man warmly, Caroline turned to Nick. "You remember Lord Dinsmore, I am sure."

Verity paled and would have fled were it not for Nick's reassuring hand at her elbow.

Chapter 14

"Parnel?" Lord Dinsmore muttered, staring intently at Verity. "I know a George Parnel—play cards with him now and again at Whites—are you any relation, my dear?"

"His daughter, sir," Verity replied, wishing she could escape the man's inquisitive eyes.

"Well, by all that's wonderful, 'tis a small world. Is your papa in Town? Tell him to send me word and we'll set up a game."

"My father died a few months ago," Verity said. Unable to avoid it, she met his gaze directly. "He was on his way home from Whites when his heart gave out."

The color drained from Dinsmore's ruddy cheeks. His face turned a sickening gray as his mouth hung open. "George . . . dead? I'd no idea . . ."

He teetered on the heels of his jeweled black patent pumps. Verity feared he was going to faint, but Nicholas moved quickly to the man's side and unobtrusively slipped an arm beneath his shoulders.

Lady Caroline hastily signaled a footman circulating with a tray of champagne. She removed a glass and handed it to Dinsmore. "Drink this, my lord. It will help ease the shock."

He accepted the champagne and drained the glass, but his eyes remained fixed on Verity. When he'd regained a measure of composure, he waved Nick aside and spoke gently to her. "Allow me to offer my deepest condolences, Miss Parnel. I liked

George—not a more amiable soul in London. He will be sorely missed by all of us at the club."

"Thank you, my lord," Verity murmured, her eyes downcast. Shaken by Dinsmore's sincerity, she had not the heart to tell him she thought he was partially responsible for her father's death. She turned to Nick. "I believe I should find Kate."

He nodded, spoke briefly to Dinsmore and Caroline, then escorted Verity across the room.

They found Kate seated beside Giles Calvert on a small serpentine sofa. She'd succeeded in persuading the gentleman to tell her something of the country called America—a wild and wonderful place to hear him speak of it—and a small group of men had gathered around to listen.

Nicholas glanced down at Verity. He thought she seemed a trifle pale, and though she kept her face turned toward the American, Nick doubted she heard a word the man said. He placed a gloved hand beneath her elbow. "Shall we find a quiet corner?"

She gazed up at him, a confused look in her eyes. But before she could reply, Charles Haversham hailed her.

"There you are, Miss Parnel. Lady Caroline told me you were here and I've been searching for you. Dreadful crush, is it not? Evening, Lynton. Ravenscar mentioned he saw you in Town. Bought his grays, did you? I wouldn't have thought they were your sort. Showy brutes, but not much stamina."

Nicholas, very much wishing the young man to the devil, nodded pleasantly. "I intend the pair as a surprise for my sister."

"Ah, that explains it. A surprise, eh?" He glanced at Kate sitting beside the American, and grinned. "They should suit her. Well, you may trust I won't say a word."

A trifle late for that, Nick thought. He'd felt Verity stiffen beside him when she'd heard Ravenscar's name. Coming on top of her unexpected encounter with Dinsmore, the mention of her second victim must have shaken her badly. Still, she spoke to Haversham with remarkable composure. Indeed, he thought it hardly necessary for her to smile so brightly at the gentleman.

"Miss Parnel, my mother is here this evening—in the adjoining salon—and she asked that I bring you to her. She is most eager to meet you."

"I'd be pleased to make her acquaintance," Verity replied, and with only a fleeting glance at Nick, allowed Haversham to guide her through the crowded room.

Nicholas had little choice but to let her go. He wanted to assure her that she had nothing to fear from either Dinsmore or Ravenscar, but private conversation would be impossible until later in the evening. Unaware of the yearning in his eyes, Nick watched her graceful exit from the room. Her back held perfectly straight, her head lifted regally, Verity drew admiring glances from dozens of gentlemen.

Bryce, standing just behind him, chuckled suddenly.

Nick turned at the sound, wondering how long his cousin had been there.

"Well, it does look as if your little bird has found the perfect way to feather her nest. Haversham is rumored to be pretty plump in the pocket."

Nick concealed his displeasure well. His facial expression sanguine, he glanced at Bryce, managing a small smile as he withdrew his snuffbox. He offered it courteously, along with a bit of advice. "I would not wager on the outcome just yet, cousin. I fancy you're a trifle premature in your conjectures."

Bryce declined the snuff. He'd never perfected the art of taking it in the polished manner of his cousin. He lifted his glass of champagne instead and, after a sip, remarked, "Perhaps, but I've been observing our little friend these past weeks. Did she not tell you that Haversham has called frequently? He practically dogs her footsteps—and I do not believe she's indifferent to him."

Nick shrugged. "It would be an unexceptional match. I like Haversham, but at the moment I'm more concerned with Kate. She seems rather taken with the American. What do you know of him?"

Bryce glanced toward the sofa where Katherine was still sitting with Calvert. She leaned toward the gentleman, her gaze intent on his face. She did seem captivated, and Bryce wondered if there was any way to turn her interest to his advantage.

Nick saw the speculation in his cousin's eyes and took the opportunity to move away. He knew Kate stood in no danger. Leery of most men since her marriage, it would take someone exceptional to cause her to lose her head. Verity, however, lacked such experience. He felt protective toward her, and were it not for the dozens of eyes watching him, he would have followed her directly to the salon and whisked her away from Haversham. Instead, he wove his way across the room, stopping to speak politely to various acquaintances as he edged nearer and nearer the door. But before he could escape, Lady Caroline announced dinner.

After dancing the opening minuet with Charles Haversham, Verity sought refuge in the ladies' retiring room. She needed a few moments alone to compose herself. Thankfully, she discovered a love seat in the far corner of the room, hidden from prying eyes by an elaborate Oriental screen. She sank down on the embroidered cushions and rubbed her aching head.

She wished she could return home—not to the house in London—but home to her mother and her cats. She wished she'd never met Nicholas, for then she wouldn't have this aching void in her heart at the knowledge that she must leave him. And leave him she must. That much had been made clear tonight.

She shuddered, remembering her encounter with Lord Dinsmore. That kind old man had been genuinely distressed to hear of her father's death. It was obvious he'd not known George Parnel was playing for stakes above his means. To Dinsmore, it had been just a friendly game. If he learned the truth, would he realize Verity might be responsible for his burglary? She'd left him that foolish note . . . and Nicholas had pieced together the clues easily enough.

Nicholas. Why had he visited Ravenscar? Once, when she'd been talking of the robberies, Nicholas had mentioned he knew the man but did not stand on terms with him. Why, then, had he suddenly paid him a call? Was it only to buy a team for Kate as he said, or did he have some scheme in mind? She half suspected Nicholas had visited Ravenscar with some notion of bribing him—but that would never succeed. Not in London, where gossip reigned supreme. Whatever Nicholas planned, Verity knew she could not allow it. If the scandal ever broke, he would be ruined.

She remembered the odd way Bryce had gazed at her during dinner, like a fly he wished to swat. If no one else circulated the tale about her, Bryce would. She wagered that only fear of Nicholas had kept him quiet so far. Bryce clearly disliked her, though she was at a loss to know why.

The door opened and Verity sat still. The sound of rustling skirts and high-pitched giggles floated over the screen.

"La, that Mr. Gyffard is a handsome devil."

"Stay away from him, Lydia. You heard Mama. He hasn't a penny to his name."

"Maybe not now," the saucy voice retorted, "but he's Mr. Lynton's heir, and who's to say what might happen?"

"Mr. Lynton is a young man. He'll marry soon, and that will leave your handsome devil out in the cold."

"I'd not be so certain. Sarah Brown told me dozens of girls have set their caps for Mr. Lynton, but to no avail. Maybe he doesn't mean to marry."

"Don't be a goose—"

The sound of the door closing again cut off the rest of the ladies' conversation, but Verity had heard enough. She rose reluctantly, knowing she must return to the ballroom.

She slipped in unnoticed behind a group of elderly dowagers, and trailed in their wake to a secluded corner where Cordelia Harrington sat alone on a settee, shielded from most of the room by enormous brass containers of decorative ferns. Verity had spoken to the homely spinster on several occasions, and liked her. She greeted the lady warmly now, asking permission to join her.

"If you wish, of course, but if you are desirous of dancing, I would suggest the other side of the room. We are rather hidden here."

"This suits me, thank you," Verity said, taking the place beside her. They spoke quietly for a few moments of acquaintances they had in common, then Verity glanced about. She saw Charles Haversham leading a pretty, young girl out on the floor and Mrs. Haversham nodding her white head in approval. Nicholas was across the way talking to Lady Caroline. Kate was dancing with the American, but Bryce was nowhere in sight. Probably in the card room, Verity thought.

She answered a question from Cordelia absently while listening to the beginning notes of a waltz. She dared not look across the room at Nicholas. Would he ask his hostess to dance, or would he remember Verity's promise of the first waltz? Torn between desire and common sense, she half hoped he would remain with Lady Caroline. Better for everyone if he did, she told herself, fighting to keep her gaze focused on Cordelia.

A shadow blocked the flickering candlelight. She glanced up into Nicholas's commanding blue eyes.

He bowed smoothly. "I believe this is our dance, Miss Parnel."

Verity stepped into his arms as naturally as spring turns into summer. Although intensely aware of his gloved hand on the small of her back, she followed his lead easily as he swept her in a wide circle of the room.

"I knew you would dance like an angel," he whispered, his breath warm against her cheek.

His words, the music, and the intoxicating closeness of him sent shivers down her back. She missed a step, but his strong arm caught her up. She breathed deeply, inhaling the unique scent that was so essentially Nicholas.

"Thank you," she managed to say at last.

He laughed gently. "Do you think you might look at me, or do the buttons on my coat hold some particular fascination?"

She smiled at his nonsense, tilting her head back to stare up at him. "They are extremely handsome buttons, sir."

"I am glad something about me meets with your approval. I was beginning to think you were avoiding me."

The sweep of her lashes hid her eyes, but he felt her body tense in his arms. "Verity? What is it, my dear?"

She shook her head. "Nothing—you are imagining things." She caught a glimpse of Penelope Pymm staring at her, the lady's thin lips pursed in disapproval. Bryce stood next to her.

The tempo increased. Nicholas whirled them in a series of dizzying turns that took her breath away. She wished they could dance forever, right across the ballroom, out the terrace doors, and on and on until they were far from London. But the music slowed, then stopped, and she knew she must face all the watching eyes again.

Nicholas did not release her hand, but placed it on his arm. "Let us take a stroll on the balcony."

"I . . . I cannot. People will talk."

His brows rose. "If you're thinking of the proprieties, you need not be concerned. The terrace is
well lit, patrolled by a number of chaperons, and
there are at least half a dozen other couples taking
the air."

Verity shook her head and tried to draw away
from him. "Please don't ask it of me."

Ignoring her plea, Nick tightened his hand on
hers and led her toward the terrace. Short of creat-
ing a scene, she had little choice but to go with
him.

They passed the chaperons sitting near the
door. Nick nodded pleasantly, but did not slow his
steps. He guided her toward the far end of the balcony, which was temporarily deserted. "Now, my
dear, explain this sudden aversion for my company. Have I done something to offend you?"

"You must know you have not," she said softly,
but kept her head turned. She couldn't bear to look
at him.

He regarded her for a moment in silence. "Is it
Dinsmore who troubles you? You need have no fear
of him, or Ravenscar, either."

"I wish that were true," she said. She stood near
the railing, gazing up at the heavens, her gloved
hands clenched tightly together. "I think you cannot have considered the matter. If either of those
gentlemen ever come to realize that it was I who
robbed them—oh, Nicholas, don't you see? The
scandal would be such that—"

"Verity, look at me," he interrupted, then waited
till she turned to him. "Neither of those men are
out of pocket. I repaid the money you . . . er . . . borrowed. With interest."

"You repaid them?" she repeated, stunned. "But
how?"

"I employed a most discreet gentleman to deliver
a purse to each of them, along with a message that
it had been stolen on a dare by a very foolish young

189

person. They will undoubtedly believe it was some young man playing off his tricks, but as long as the money is recovered, neither will care."

"I will repay you," she promised in a low voice. "It will take time, even with the generous salary you provide me, but—"

"There is no need, my dear. This was something I wished to do for you, and it gave me a great deal of pleasure."

"I cannot allow you to pay off my debts, Nicholas. You have already done too much for me."

"Not nearly as much as I should like." Aware of the probing stares of the chaperons, he restrained the urge to take her in his arms, but his voice grew husky. "Nor nearly as much as I intend. I want the right to take care of you, Verity. I want to give you everything you desire, and everything you deserve." He smiled ruefully. "I have fallen in love with you, my dear."

Her eyes misty, she gazed up at him. Nicholas wanted to make her his mistress, and wanton, immoral female that she was, she wished it, too. She ached to step into his arms and lift her lips to his again, to feel the searing heat of his mouth and the warm comfort of his arms. Only she could not do it. She thought fleetingly of her parents, of her mother with her foolish dreams, and of her father, who had wanted to give his little girl the world. She opened her lips to protest—but Nicholas covered them with his fingertips.

"Do not answer me yet. I know I've sprung this on you—and I meant to give you time to get used to the idea—but you look so enticing in the moonlight. . . . Verity, must we wait a year before we wed? I know you're still in mourning, but—"

He broke off at the sound of a high, near-hysterical laugh. Abruptly, Verity realized it had issued from her own throat. Nicholas wanted to *marry* her. Oh, heavens! She thought instantly of dozens of problems and reasons that they could not wed—but the knowledge that he wished to filled her with joy. A surge of elation rose within her and spilled over, lighting up her eyes and her smile. She wanted to fling herself into his arms.

"You are insane, Nicholas Lynton," she finally said, but her eyes were radiant.

"Then you are responsible, Verity Parnel. I was a staid, careful man until you dropped into my life. Now I find I cannot live without you."

It was her turn to gently touch his lips. "You must not say such things."

"I thought I was restraining myself admirably," he countered with a glance toward the chaperons. "Prepare yourself, my dear. When we are alone, truly alone, I intend to whisper words that will bring a delicate blush to—"

"Hush, Nicholas," she warned, already reddening as another couple strolled near. "I think we had best return inside, sir."

"Whatever you wish—but you will consider my offer?"

Her smile evaporated and a tiny frown marred the smooth lines of her brow. *Could* she marry him? Nicholas had effectively taken care of Lord Dinsmore and Ravenscar, but there were others to consider. What would Kate think of her brother wishing to wed a penniless girl? The ton would consider it a dreadful misalliance. And Bryce. He would not accept their marriage lightly. She shivered suddenly, drawing Nicholas's concern.

His hand on her elbow, he bent his head so only she could hear his words. "Whatever problems there may be, I am capable of shouldering them. Will you not trust me?"

They walked slowly toward the terrace door, both reluctant to return to the crowded ballroom. Just inside the door, Verity paused. She gazed at him, her heart in her eyes. "I do trust you, Nicholas, but I cannot marry you. At least not yet."

Chapter 15

Long after she should have been abed, Verity sat on the window seat of her darkened room, dreaming with her eyes wide open. She yearned for someone in whom to confide her wondrous news. Nicholas loved her. He wanted to marry her. Just the thought set her feet itching to dance, her heart singing. She wondered if Nicholas was also finding sleep impossible.

Dear, sweet, charming, utterly wonderful Nicholas! He'd been hurt when she did not immediately accept his proposal, hurt and confused. Knowing he would demand an explanation, Verity had carefully avoided him for the rest of the evening. Much as she longed to, she could not possibly accept his offer until she talked with Kate. If his sister disapproved of the match ... but she would not think of that now. Time enough in the morning to learn Kate's feelings.

A flicker of movement below caught Verity's eye. Then a pebble bounced off the window. Nicholas. She drew back, laughing softly. Did he think he was Romeo enticing his Juliet to the balcony? She was tempted to open the window and lean out. Pure foolishness, of course. Two more pebbles landed with slightly more force, striking sharply against the pane. If he were not careful, he'd break the glass.

Drawing her wrapper tight about her, Verity pushed aside the curtain and unlatched the window. She saw him clearly in the moonlight and her heart swelled with pride. He looked so handsome. The light breeze ruffled his dark curls and billowed the long sleeves of his white shirt.

"Come down and talk with me," he called, catching sight of her at the open window.

"Hush, Nicholas, or you will wake the neighborhood. Do you not realize the time?"

"I know only that it has been too long since I spoke with you alone. Come down, Verity."

"I cannot," she replied, laughing. "Go to bed, Nicholas."

"If I did, it would be only to dream of you."

"This is a most improper conversation, sir."

"Do you care, Verity? I don't mind if the whole world knows how I feel about you. Indeed, I'm much inclined to shout my joy from the rooftops." He grabbed hold of the ivy clinging to the wall. "Well, if you will not come down, I shall have to come up. Do you think this vine will hold my weight?"

She leaned out over the sill, her cloud of blond hair spilling down her shoulders. "Nicholas! You must not—good heavens, if you fell—oh, please don't try it."

He stepped back to peer up at her. "Then come to me. Good Lord, you are beautiful. I suspect you've captured moonbeams in your hair and stardust in your eyes, and would see for myself."

"And I, sir, suspect you've been imbibing brandy. Do go to bed, Nicholas."

"I could never sleep. Come dance with me in the moonlight."

She smiled, but shook her head. "You know I must not. Nicholas, have you been drinking? Are you intoxicated?"

"Only with your beauty. I drink to thee with my eyes."

"I believe you've been drinking with more than your eyes. Oh, do go away, Nicholas, before you are discovered."

A window slammed open on the second floor of the neighboring house. An elderly gentleman appeared, clad in his night rail and cap. He shook his fist out the window at Nick. "Stop that incessant caterwauling out there or I shall call the watch." An old shoe, thrown with considerable force, landed beside Nick.

Verity, hiding her amusement, leaned out her window. "I think he means it. Go to bed and we will speak in the morning."

He grinned up at her. "If you won't come down, then give me your promise that you'll marry me. Say yes, sweet Verity, that I may sleep and dream of my angel."

Her smile disappeared. "I . . . I cannot answer you—not yet. There is something I must do first. Please, allow me just a little time."

"What is troubling you, Verity? Can you not confide in me? Is it your mother? Are you concerned with what she will say?"

"No. My mother thinks you perfection. She adores you. You must know that she does."

"And her daughter? Does she adore me, too?"

Verity's hands gripped the edge of the sill. *With all my heart,* she whispered. Then, trying desperately to lighten the moment, she laughed. "There is not a woman in all England who does not adore you, sir, but you cannot wed them all."

"I want only one," he answered, his voice low, intent. "The question is, does she want me?"

The doubt in his voice twisted inside her like a knife probing a wound. "Nicholas . . . oh, please, just grant me a little time."

He stood silent for a moment, staring up at her, then sighed. "As you wish, my dear. Shall we say a week? That should give you sufficient time to weigh the advantages and disadvantages of marrying me."

"Nicholas! It's nothing like that."

But he was not listening. "A week it shall be. You

have my word I shall not press you for an answer until then." He bowed. "One week, sweet Verity."

She gazed after his disappearing shadow, wishing he had not looked so . . . so disillusioned. Slowly, she closed the window and drew the curtains. Perhaps she should have gone down and reasoned with him—explained her concern about Kate.

Besieged with doubts, she climbed into bed. All she wanted in the world was to marry Nicholas, but she could not if it meant alienating his sister. She'd given Kate her word that she had no intention of wedding him, and Kate had accepted her on those terms. Not only accepted her, but treated her with kindness and generosity. What would Kate say now? They had become friends, but that was a far cry from welcoming her as Nick's wife.

She remembered Kate's warning earlier in the evening not to take Nick too seriously. Had she spoken out of concern for Verity, or as a hint that such an alliance would be unacceptable?

And if she does disapprove? What then, my girl?

Verity shivered beneath the covers, feeling inexplicably alone and bereft. She lay still, listening as the house settled into silence. She heard a door slam below, and farther down the hall, the sound of a window shutting.

Bryce turned away from the window. Preoccupied, he crossed to the desk and lit a cigar. Blowing out a cloud of smoke, he considered the conversation he'd just overheard. Nick had proposed to the girl and expected an answer within a week. For a moment Bryce wondered why Verity had procrastinated. She'd be a fool not to wed Nick, but the delay gave him time. It remained to be seen if it would be sufficient for his plan to work.

He sat down, propping his feet on the edge of the desk. Judging by his cousin's behavior that evening, Nick truly loved the girl—which, Bryce thought, could work to his own advantage. He smiled in the dark. It would be a long time, perhaps years, before his cousin recovered from this entanglement.

Bryce inhaled deeply on his cigar. During those years he could borrow heavily on his expectations. And if his plan succeeded, his cousin would certainly return to Newbury, leaving the London house empty. Bryce could then offer to remain in Town, keeping an eye on the house and servants. After a reasonable period he would find some way to rid himself of Crimstock and the rest of his cousin's ancient retainers. With a few changes the old place would make an admirable establishment for a young bachelor.

He snubbed out the butt of his cigar. The future looked promising. Perhaps one day Nick would even thank him for his interference. After all, the girl *was* a thief, which Nick seemed to have forgotten. Well, Bryce would make certain he was soon reminded of her past.

Verity, having spent a sleepless night, rose late the following morning. She dressed carefully, choosing a blue and white striped walking dress, which Kate particularly liked and had insisted on buying. The maid used a matching blue ribbon to tie back Verity's curls, and as the clock chimed eleven, pronounced her ready. Still, reluctant to face Kate, Verity dawdled alone in her room. Her future, her happiness, depended on Kate's answer. She lingered yet another quarter hour before summoning sufficient courage to go down to the breakfast room. But Bryce was the only one at the table.

"Well, good morning, my little slugabed. Did you not sleep well? You look a trifle wan."

Smothering a yawn behind her hand, Verity replied, "I suppose I am still unaccustomed to the noise here, after the quiet of Brighton. Has Kate come down yet?"

"An hour past. She's in her room, dressing—but

you need not concern yourself. I rather doubt my cousin will wish for your company this morning. The American is taking her riding."

"Mr. Calvert?"

"The same, but sit down, Verity. You still look half asleep. Let me fix you a cup of tea." He rose, drew out a chair for her, then crossed to the sideboard. With his back to Verity, he took a small vial from his pocket. After carefully dropping a few drops of laudanum into an empty cup, he filled it with fresh-brewed tea. He added a small amount of sugar and a slice of lemon before carrying it back to her.

"Why, thank you, Bryce."

"It looks as though we are to be left to our own devices today, my dear. Nick left word he will not return until late. Some sort of business affairs, I understand. However, if you are in need of an escort, I am entirely at your service."

Verity glanced up at him. While Bryce was never directly rude to her, he generally treated her with careless disdain, often amusing himself at her expense. His concern that morning puzzled her.

"Nicholas suggested I make myself useful," he explained with a wry smile.

Thomas stepped into the breakfast room. "Excuse me, but Mr. Calvert has called for Miss Kate. She asked that you entertain the gentleman until she is ready. Shall I show him in here, or the drawing room, sir?"

"Oh, in here," Bryce replied, keeping a watchful eye on Verity as she sipped her tea.

A moment later the American strode into the room. Dressed for riding, he wore the traditional garb of an Englishman, but on Calvert the casual clothes only emphasized his masculinity.

Verity felt even more sluggish in the American's presence. She'd met him briefly at Lady Caroline's, but the crush of people had somewhat diminished his air of ruggedness. Here, in the muted ambiance of the breakfast room, he seemed overpowering.

But his manners were excellent. Flattered that he recalled her name, she suggested he join them for a cup of tea.

"Coffee, if you have it," Calvert said.

While Bryce prepared him a cup, Verity observed the man. She noticed the way the hard lines of his face softened when he smiled. It was no surprise Kate found him attractive.

"More tea, my dear?" Bryce asked. Without waiting, he whisked away her cup.

Verity hid her astonishment, but wondered exactly what Nick had said to make his cousin so solicitous. Whatever it was, it had worked wonders. Smiling, she turned her attention to their guest. "Kate told me you lived in America, Mr. Calvert. Have you returned to England to stay, or merely for a visit?"

"A visit only, Miss Parnel. I inherited some land here and came over only to arrange for its sale. As soon as my business is complete, I shall leave for Virginia."

"Calvert actually prefers that barbaric place to England," Bryce told her, taking his seat at the end of the table. "He could live here in civilized comfort, but instead he will go back and actually *work* on his land there."

"As my ancestors did here," Calvert replied, much amused. "You should come with me, Bryce. One finds a satisfaction in building something of worth that cannot be equaled by merely collecting rents or investing on the exchange."

His educated speech lay at odds with the rough, callused hand engulfing the delicate cup. . . . Verity yawned again, losing her train of thought. She blinked rapidly. Her eyes felt enormously heavy.

The door swept open, framing Kate. She looked a vision of loveliness in a close-fitting lilac riding habit trimmed with black braid. The colors were repeated on her wide-brimmed hat, and the ostrich plumes, curling around her dark hair, were dyed to match her skirt.

Giles Calvert rose at once.

"I hope I have not kept you waiting long," Kate said, smiling sweetly as she extended her hand.

He took the small, gloved hand in his own, and bowed. "I consider it a privilege to wait on you, ma'am."

Blushing, Kate turned to Verity. "Will you forgive me, darling, if I don't go with you to Mrs. Ellerbee's? Make any excuse you like, or send a note crying off for both of us."

"I shall send a note," Verity said, smothering a yawn. "Gracious, I can barely keep my eyes open this morning."

Kate studied her more closely. "Are you feeling ill, Verity? You do look dreadfully tired. Shall I send for the doctor?"

"No, it's nothing. I merely had trouble sleeping last night. You go ahead, Kate, and enjoy your ride."

"Well, do get some rest while I'm gone. We go to the theater tonight, and I hope to persuade Giles to join us." She slanted an arch look at the American as he stood talking with Bryce. Keeping her voice to a whisper, she added, "Is he not marvelous?"

Verity smiled, but it required an effort. As soon as Kate and the American left, she excused herself and returned to her room. She should write some letters . . . but the bed looked so tempting . . . perhaps if she lay down . . . just for a few moments, she would feel better.

She must talk to Kate, she reminded herself as she stretched out on the counterpane. When Kate returned, perhaps . . . Verity's eyes closed before she could complete the thought.

The maid woke her at five o'clock.

Verity dressed hurriedly. She couldn't believe she'd slept all afternoon and still she felt tired and out of sorts. She'd also missed the opportunity to talk with Kate—and there would be little chance to do so that night.

She was the last one down. Verity found the others waiting for her in the drawing room. The gentlemen rose as she entered, but her eyes sought only Nicholas, elegantly handsome in his evening attire as he stood near the fireplace with Bryce and Giles Calvert. He smiled at her. Even across the room she caught the warm intimacy in his eyes. Relieved that he was not angry, she turned her attention to Kate.

"Verity, my dear, you remember Christina Livingston? She is Lady Jersey's niece. Bryce thoughtfully invited her to join our party this evening."

The petite redhead, clad in a tightly fitting green silk gown, smiled at her. Verity murmured an appropriate greeting while wondering what had caused Kate's annoyance. There had been a tinge of sarcasm beneath her words. And Bryce—she glanced at him as he fussed with the drinks tray— why had he decided to join them? He loathed the theater.

Kate was speaking again. "Are you feeling better, Verity? Dulcie said you slept through the afternoon."

"I am ashamed to admit I did. I cannot imagine why I feel so tired."

"I'm not surprised," Bryce said as he handed Verity a glass of sherry. "You've both been keeping late hours."

Verity declined the drink, but Bryce insisted. "Drink it, my dear. A little sherry will fortify you for the long evening ahead. Believe me, I've seen *The Merchant of Venice* performed, and you will have need of it."

Miss Livingston, a puzzled look on her pretty face, remarked, "If you feel that way, I wonder you are so eager to attend."

Verity, taking a small sip of the sherry, wondered, too.

"My dear, one must attend the theater occasionally, if only to revile the performance."

Giles Calvert crossed the room to stand just behind Kate. "Well, I shall enjoy it. Plays in America are still something of a rarity. *The Merchant of Venice,* you say? I've always enjoyed Shakespeare."

Miss Livingston clapped her hands. "Oh, so do I. He has such a droll sense of humor."

Kate exchanged a quick look with Calvert, Nick hid a smile, and Verity covered her astonishment by sipping the sherry.

Only Bryce remained unmoved. "Come along, my little dilettante," he said, taking Christina's arm. "I'm certain you will enjoy the farce if not the play."

The Theatre Royal in Drury Lane was crowded, but Nick retained a private box, and he soon had his guests seated comfortably. The ladies occupied the three chairs facing the front of the box, with the gentlemen in a row behind them.

Verity, positioned between Kate and Miss Livingston, wished she had Nicholas beside her. Christina chattered endlessly, feeling it was somehow necessary to point out every notable person in the audience, while Kate remained unusually quiet. Verity tried to focus her attention on the stage, but the noise in the pit increased in volume until she thought her head would soon split, it ached so dreadfully.

At last the actors appeared for the opening scene of Shakespeare's drama, and the audience settled down. But still Verity could not concentrate. Her vision blurred slightly as she stared at the players. It seemed unusually warm in the theater. She plied her fan to cool her flushed cheeks, but the scant breeze helped only a little. She closed her eyes, feeling suddenly dizzy. She wished she could escape to some quiet corner for a few moments ... someplace cool. She sat perfectly straight, but kept her eyes shut. The noise receded . . . then she nodded and opened her eyes abruptly.

Scattered applause filled the theater, and actors scurried to change the props for the next scene.

"What a nasty fellow that was," Christina said. "I declare, this is not at all like the last play I saw."

Nick leaned over Verity's shoulder. "Would you care for something to drink? Lemonade, perhaps?"

Verity nodded and the other ladies readily agreed. Bryce stood up. "You must allow me to do the honors, Nick," he said, and disappeared out the back of the box.

"Your cousin is very obliging," Christina told Kate.

"Yes, isn't he?" Her eyes, however, were on Verity, who even in the flattering candlelight looked distinctly ill. "My dear, are you feeling faint?"

Verity stood shakily. "I think—if I could just get a breath of fresh air . . . it seems frightfully close in here."

Nick drew back her chair and offered the support of his arm. "We can stroll a bit in the hall if you would like."

Kate started to rise, too. "Shall I go with you?"

But Verity shook her head. "I shall be better directly. Please do not disturb yourself."

Giles held the door open for them. Clinging tightly to Nicholas for support, Verity stepped thankfully into the relatively peaceful quiet of the hall.

Nick led them away a few paces, then leaned against the wall, studying her critically. "If you wish to return home, I can have the carriage brought around."

"Thank you, but no. I should not like to ruin the evening for everyone."

Nick removed one of his gloves and felt her brow with gentle fingers. It was cool to his touch, but he misliked the feverish look in her eyes. "Are you quite certain, my dear? This play was never one of my favorites."

"But . . . Shakespeare is so droll," she murmured, making an effort to amuse him.

Nick smiled, but his eyes still reflected concern. "Miss Livingston and the others can remain if they wish."

"I shall be fine," Verity insisted. She gazed up at him and smiled weakly. "I fear I did not get sufficient sleep last night."

"I'm glad to know I was not the only one," he answered, and touched her cheek. He bent his head to kiss her, but Bryce swung around the corner.

"Come out for a bit of air?" he asked, juggling three glasses. "It's frightfully stuffy in here tonight. Here you go, my dear. This should see you right."

Verity took the lemonade and drank thirstily, the cool tartness seeming to soothe her parched throat. "Thank you, Bryce."

"My pleasure," he murmured, thinking of the vial of laudanum in his pocket as they stepped once more into the box. A round of applause marked the return of the players for the second act.

Verity took her seat. After only a few moments the room spun before her eyes. Dropping her glass, she slumped against Kate's shoulder.

Nick kicked over his chair. Beside her in an instant, he swept her up in his arms, tersely ordering Bryce to open the door.

Chapter 16

"What the devil is that bloody doctor doing up there?" Nick demanded for the third time within ten minutes.

Giles Calvert wisely ignored the question. Seated in a comfortable wing chair near the fireplace, he sipped his brandy, and wondered if Kate would think it cowardly of him to leave. Lynton's glass stood untouched on the sideboard while he paced the room like a caged tiger ready to bite off someone's head.

"Strange she should faint like that," Bryce remarked as he crossed to the sideboard and helped himself to the brandy. "I wonder if perhaps she had a bit too much to drink."

Nicholas rounded on him, his face dark with barely suppressed fury. "One more crack like that, and you shall meet me."

"Nick, old boy, do calm yourself. I meant no offense, but you must admit there are a number of ladies in Town who tipple a bit in secret. After all, how well do you really know Verity?"

"Well enough," he replied, his hands curling into fists.

"More than likely it was the heat, or something of that nature," Giles said. "Miss Parnel remarked—"

He broke off his words as the door opened again. Kate, looking unusually worried, entered and went directly to her brother. Laying a gentle hand on his arm, she assured him, "Verity will be fine. Dr.

Kearns is still with her, but he believes she needs only a day or two of rest."

"Well, that's a relief," Bryce muttered. "Did he say what caused her to faint?"

"Not . . . not precisely," Kate hedged.

"What, precisely, did he say?" Nick demanded.

"He thinks she may have taken some sort of opiate—perhaps to help her sleep."

"Seems logical enough," Giles suggested. "Perhaps she misjudged the amount and took more than she realized."

"Verity would not take anything of that nature," Nick said with such positive force, the others stared at him. "Her mother has been ill for some time and was forced to use all manner of drugs. Verity has a horror of them. She will not even take a powder for a headache."

Kate lifted her hands helplessly. "I know, Nick. She's told me much the same, but perhaps she took something by mistake. The doctor said that she—"

"The doctor! Some quack off the street. What do we know about him? Where did you find him, Kate?"

Thomas scratched at the door, then opened it. "Dr. Kearns is waiting to see you, ma'am."

"Show him in, Thomas," Kate directed. After a warning glance at her brother, she stepped toward the door to greet the slender, silver-haired physician. "Do come in, Doctor."

She made him known to the others, but he directed his remarks to Nick. "I was your uncle's physician for a number of years, Mr. Lynton. Please accept my condolences on his passing. He was a fine gentleman."

"Thank you, but I'm afraid I don't recall meeting you before. I believe Dr. Ingram was with my uncle at the end," Nick said, naming a well-known physician.

Dr. Kearns nodded, the barest hint of a smile turning up the corners of his mouth. His eyes, behind the thick spectacles, looked amused. "Your uncle disliked my diagnosis, Mr. Lynton. I strongly urged him to give up drinking and to curtail his diet. When he refused—well, he found a doctor more to his liking. It's often so when people hear disagreeable news."

Nick had the grace to flush.

"As for Miss Parnel, the indications are that she's taken heavily of an opiate, perhaps laudanum. She will sleep through the night. Although she should feel somewhat better tomorrow, I recommend that she remain quietly in bed."

"Yes, my sister told us as much. But what puzzles me is that Verity—Miss Parnel—does not hold with taking sleeping potions, or any sort of medication."

The doctor shrugged. "We cannot always know what even those closest to us do in private. However, there were no signs that she is a habitual user. Indeed, I suspect this may be the first time she's resorted to laudanum. And if that is the case, a sufficiently strong dose would have a debilitating effect such as we've seen with the young lady tonight. With your permission, I shall look in on her tomorrow. Now, if you will excuse me, I have other patients to see yet."

Giles Calvert declared it was time he took his leave as well, and Kate walked with both gentlemen to the door. Bryce, after one glance at his cousin's face, deemed it wise to retire, and retreated to his bedchamber.

Left alone in the drawing room, Nick paced restlessly. Why would Verity take an opiate? Was there something troubling her—something she felt she could not tell him? Did it have anything to do with her refusal to give him an answer? She needed time, she'd said. But time for what? Could Bryce possibly be right in saying Nick didn't know Verity as well as he thought?

He picked up his brandy glass and drank deeply,

the unanswered questions running relentlessly through his mind.

Late on Wednesday morning Verity opened her eyes, blinking against the bright sunlight flooding the room. Her head ached and her mouth felt as dry as cotton. She licked her lips while trying to recall what happened the night before. She remembered the heat of the theater, an overwhelming sense of dizziness, and then ... nothing. She turned her head slightly and saw Kate sitting near the window, a novel facedown in her lap.

Verity tried to speak, but her mouth was so dry, her voice came out as a raspy whisper. She struggled to sit up.

The rustle of sheets caught Kate's attention. Laying aside her book, she moved quickly to the bedside and placed a cool hand on Verity's brow. "So, you are awake at last. How do you feel?"

"Horrid," she croaked. "My mouth is so dry."

Kate poured a glass of water from the pitcher on the side table, then helped Verity to sit up.

The cool liquid felt wonderful sliding down her parched throat. When she'd finished, Verity handed the empty glass to Kate. "Thank you. What happened last night?"

Kate sat down on the edge of the bed. She took one of Verity's hands in her own and spoke gently. "You fainted at the theater and scared us half to death. Nick carried you out and brought you home."

Verity closed her eyes for a moment. "I'm sorry, Kate, to have caused you so much trouble. But I don't understand—I have never fainted in my life."

Kate hesitated, but met Verity's eyes directly. "We were concerned, of course, especially when we could not revive you. But the doctor who attended you advised us to just allow you to sleep. He was certain you would be fine this morning." She paused, then added, "He seems to think you had somehow taken an overdose of laudanum."

Kate watched her closely. Verity's eyes widened and there was no trace now of the enlarged pupils Dr. Kearns had pointed out the night before. Nothing showed except Verity's confusion.

"That cannot be . . . Mama used to take laudanum sometimes to help her sleep, but I never have."

"Well, dearest, try not to worry about it now. You're under orders to stay in bed and rest today. Dr. Kearns will look in on you later. In the meantime, do you feel up to a little breakfast? If you like, Dulcie can bring you a tray."

Verity, her stomach growling at the mention of food, realized how hungry she was. She nodded, still puzzling over Kate's explanation. "Perhaps I fainted because I ate so little yesterday."

"Possibly," Kate agreed, then smiled. "Now I had better go down and tell Nick you are awake before he wears a hole in the floor. He's been pacing all morning."

Kate found her brother in the library, several ledger books spread open on the desk before him. Working in his shirtsleeves, his hair rumpled, and a smudge of ink across his brow, he seemed absorbed in his accounts. But he looked up the moment she entered, his eyes full of concern. "How is she?"

"Awake and hungry. Both good signs, according to Dr. Kearns."

"Thank heavens," he said. "Does she remember what happened?"

"No, not at all," she answered, sitting in the chair in front of his desk. "Nick, do you think it possible Verity could have fainted because she'd not had sufficient to eat?"

"I doubt it. If that were the case, the smelling salts should have revived her. Did you ask about the laudanum?"

"She said she's never taken any, and I believe her. It's very puzzling, but at least she looks much better. I'm certain she'll be fine."

"We shall see what the doctor has to say, but I think I should stay home this evening in case she needs me."

"Nick! You cannot." Kate leaned forward, facing him across the desk. "Have you forgotten we are promised to the Duke of Sussex tonight—that he's giving a private dinner to honor the prince regent? Why, to cry off would be an insult he would not easily forgive."

"Bugger the prince."

"Nicholas Lynton," Kate cried, shocked to hear such words on her brother's lips. "Do you forget to whom you speak? And you dare talk of Bryce leading me astray."

"Forgive me, Kate. I am indeed sorry," he said, running a hand through his hair. "It's just that I'm so distracted, and after worrying over Verity, to have to deal with the prince and one of his interminable dinners—must we really go?"

"You know we cannot refuse," she said sympathetically while thinking her very proper brother must truly be distraught to have used such language in her presence. She'd heard the phrase from her husband—and worse—but never from Nick. Amusement lit her eyes, and then she giggled. "Bugger the prince? Really, Nick."

"It's not funny, Kate," he scolded, then his own lips twitched in amusement. "You will forget you heard me say such a thing, and I never want to hear that phrase on your lips again."

"Good heavens, no. Why, someone might ask from where I heard it."

Bryce, passing the open door, looked in. "Well, you two seem cheerful. Is our little bird recovered from her malaise?"

"Verity's much better," Kate said, looking over her shoulder at him. "She's having breakfast in her room. But do come in, Bryce. We were just discussing dinner this evening."

"Ah, this is the night of the duke's party for the regent, is it not?" He shot a commiserating look at Nick. "I don't envy you. I doubt you'll be allowed to leave before two in the morning—unless Prinny takes offense at some imagined insult. Well, I shall think of you while I'm dining at Whites."

"Really?" Nick could not quite hide his surprise. He knew his cousin didn't belong to that particular club—and even attending as a guest was an accomplishment. "You must be moving in the first circles."

Bryce carelessly brushed a speck of lint from his tailored jacket. "Lord Dinsmore asked me to join him. I rather suspect he wishes to talk about Uncle, but I have hopes for a game of whist later, so the evening will not be a complete waste."

"Be careful, Bryce," Kate warned. "Those gentlemen play for exceedingly high stakes."

"Thank you, my sweet, but you need not be concerned. There are few gentlemen who can match wits with me over the card table, and I feel my luck is in tonight. If you should return early, don't wait up for me."

Kate rose. "Well, I must look in on Verity. I shall see you both later."

Bryce held the door open for her, then followed her out at a more leisurely pace. His plans were developing splendidly. Nick and Kate would be occupied with the duke's dinner tonight, and Verity would be left home alone. Circumstances could not be more favorable.

He fingered the vial of laudanum he carried in his pocket. Perhaps just one more dose to ensure Verity would sleep through the night. He could not risk her appearing below stairs—nor could he risk entering her room. But if he managed to waylay one of the maids taking up a tray . . . a few more drops in a pitcher of water should do the trick.

He whistled as he climbed the stairs, pleased with his success thus far. Lord Dinsmore had been flattered when Bryce sought him out, and extracting a dinner invitation from the old man had been easy. They would be partners that evening at Whites, and if he played his cards right, Dinsmore might even put his name up for membership.

Bryce entered his room feeling optimistic. Luck was favoring him and the evening ahead looked promising. A pleasant dinner with Dinsmore, then Lord Ashford and Phillip Ravenscar would join them for a few games of whist. Bryce had heard those men drank heavily, and prayed it was true. He would encourage them, even buying the rounds if necessary. Then, when Ashford toddled home, Bryce would follow. Gaining entrance to the gentleman's house might be a problem, but with Verity's example before him, Bryce was certain he would find a way. And when he left Ashford's with a fat purse as a bonus, he would leave behind the little bird's note incriminating herself.

Knowing Lord Ashford, Bryce surmised the man would call the Bow Street Runners out as soon as he discovered he'd been robbed. It would only be a matter of time before Verity was exposed as a thief. Of course, she'd claim she was home sick in bed, but with no one to collaborate her story, who would believe her?

Bryce took the folded slip of paper from behind the satin lining in his jewel case and carefully placed it in the pocket of his vest. If Nick went so far as to call on Ashford and demand to see the note, it would be in Verity's own hand. Damning evidence.

A thunderstorm drenched most of London Friday morning, but at noon the sun broke through the clouds. Verity, who had spent two restless days in bed, insisted on getting up and dressing. She felt much better, though she still could not understand the illness that had affected her so badly.

Tuesday evening she had blacked out at the theater and could recall nothing. She'd felt better for a while on Wednesday, but in the evening she had again felt listless and sleepy. By nine o'clock she could not keep her eyes open and had retired early. She had awakened the day before with a dry mouth and aching head, then her symptoms had disappeared by late afternoon.

That morning, thank heaven, she'd felt her normal self, but she still felt puzzled by her illness. She'd vehemently denied taking laudanum, but she suspected Dr. Kearns did not believe her. Nor did Kate.

What did Nicholas think? Verity had not seen him for the past two days, and was eager to talk with him. She sat impatiently at the dressing table, allowing Dulcie to arrange her hair in becoming curls. Kate had told her Nicholas was concerned and had required frequent reports on her health. At least he worried about her, she thought, and touched the large bouquet of yellow roses he'd sent.

Kate had brought them up after breakfast, and teased her. "Perhaps if I spent a day or two in bed, Nick would send me flowers, although somehow I doubt he'd be quite so attentive."

"He is very thoughtful," Verity had replied, blushing.

"Indeed, but I believe his feelings run deeper than mere courtesy to a guest. Since your illness, Nick has behaved like a bear with a thorn in his paw. If he's not permitted to see you soon, heaven only knows what he will do."

Verity realized Kate had given her the perfect opening. Nervously, she pleated the quilt beneath her fingers. "Kate?"

"What is it, my dear?"

She swallowed hard, searching for the right

words. "I must talk with you. I . . . I have come to care very much for your brother."

"Well, I certainly hope so," Kate said with a laugh. She sat down on the bed and gently brushed Verity's hair back from her brow. "Has he proposed yet? I've been expecting an announcement any time this last week."

"You do not object?" Verity asked, relief flooding through her. "I would not answer him until I spoke with you. I was afraid you would, well, that you might not—"

"Nothing would please me more," Kate interrupted, and leaned over to hug her. Then, smiling warmly, she added, "I couldn't wish for a better sister. I know I said some terrible things to you in Brighton, but that was before I came to know you. I hope you don't intend to hold my poor judgment against me, for I thought we had agreed the past was behind us. Of course, if you insist, I will apologize properly."

Tears misted Verity's eyes as she returned Kate's hug. "Thank you. It means so much to me to have your approval."

"Foolish girl. I can tell you it wouldn't mean much to Nick. Did you really think he'd allow my opinion to weigh with him? He loves you too much to care what I think—and I do envy you that." A wistful note entered her voice, and she stood abruptly. Crossing to the dressing table, Kate busied herself with rearranging the flowers.

Verity watched her for a moment. "Kate? Have you met someone you care about?"

Kate finally turned. Her blue eyes glittered with a suspicious moistness, but she was smiling. "May I tell Nick you will be down soon? He's most eager to see you."

Verity had not pressed her, but now that she recalled the scene, she deduced the gentleman causing Kate's heartache must be Giles Calvert. And she knew he planned to leave for America in a few weeks. Poor Kate.

The maid stepped back to admire her handiwork. "You look lovely, Miss Verity—pretty as a picture."

"Thank you, Dulcie," she replied, critically studying her reflection in the looking-glass. Verity thought her face still seemed unnaturally pale, but certainly much improved since the previous day. She was suddenly thankful Nicholas had not been allowed in her bedchamber to see her—although he'd tried. Kate, considering such conduct highly improper, had refused him admission.

Verity rose. She would see Nicholas in a few moments. The thought brought a rush of color to her cheeks, and her feet fairly danced in anticipation. She straightened the satin sash on her primrose walking dress, took a deep, calming breath, and then walked slowly toward the door.

Deliberately, taking one slow step at a time, she descended the stairs, all the while rehearsing what she'd say to Nicholas. When she reached the hall, she heard raised voices coming from the morning room. All the words and phrases she had in mind disappeared as she recognized Bryce's voice. He would have to be at home that morning—and with Nicholas.

Verity stood just outside the door. She listened for a moment, hoping to hear Kate's voice. *She* would realize Verity wished to be alone with Nicholas, and make some excuse to leave them together. Then something Bryce said caught her attention. Verity held her breath.

"I tell you, Nick, Lord Ashford was fit to be tied. He stormed into Whites like an angry bull. He's bound and determined to find out who had the audacity to rob his house. He's already called in the Bow Street Runners."

She heard a low growl in response, but couldn't make out the words.

Bryce spoke again. "Then he told us the burglar

left a note. You could have knocked me over with a feather when Ashford said that. Of course, Ravenscar and Dinsmore were both at the table, and they naturally said the same thing had happened to them. I hate to be the bearer of bad news, old man, but the notes were all identical."

Nausea rising in her throat, Verity leaned weakly against the door. Was Bryce lying, or had someone deliberately framed her? *Why didn't Nicholas say something?*

Bryce, wondering the same thing, cleared his throat. "You do see what this means? While we were all out Wednesday night, your little bird took the opportunity to exact her revenge on Ashford. But she picked the wrong man this time. The Runners will find her. Stupid of her to have left that note."

Verity didn't wait to hear more. She hurried back to her room, nearly colliding with Dulcie in the upper hall.

The maid apologized, but peered closely at Verity. "Are you feeling poorly again, miss?"

Verity nodded, fighting the rising tide of bile in her throat. "I'm going back to bed. Please see that I'm not disturbed."

"Yes, miss," the maid said, then offered her assistance.

Verity waved her away. She closed the door of her bedchamber and stood leaning against it, a hand over her mouth. Ashford robbed, and a note left behind. Someone must hate her a great deal, she thought, but what hurt most was that Nicholas had not defended her. He had not said a word. He believed Bryce.

She supposed he couldn't be blamed. Not after hearing Bryce's story, but she wished—she very much wished Nicholas had said something in her defense. Expressed some small doubt. But he had her past to contend with, and he knew how much

215

she'd despised Lord Ashford. She couldn't blame Nicholas for not believing her. No one would.

One thing was certain. She could not stay in this house any longer. Verity moved away from the door. With leaden fingers she opened the strings of her reticule. She had sufficient funds left from the advance on her salary to take the stage to Brighton.

She dragged out her old valise and opened the wardrobe. She would not take any of her new dresses. She pushed aside the satins and silks and found the few old and mended gowns she'd brought to London. Her own dresses looked pitiful against the bright colors of the other gowns. They didn't belong here any more than she did.

After quickly changing into a drab gray walking dress, she carefully folded the rest of her clothes and packed them in the valise. Looking around the room, Verity realized she had only a few personal belongings. The silver brush and comb her mother had given her, a few pieces of jewelry with their paste stones, and a small bottle of cologne. She stowed the items carefully. Then she added a single rose from the bouquet Nicholas had sent, gently wrapping it in tissue. It was all she would have to remember him by.

She closed the valise, blinking back tears. She hesitated, wondering if she should leave Kate and Nicholas a note—but what could she say? Suddenly tired, unable to think clearly, she wanted only to escape. She tiptoed to the door and eased it open. The hall was deserted. Moving as quietly as possible, she crept to the servants' stairs at the rear of the house.

She stumbled once as tears misted her eyes.

Dulcie hesitated, but she was truly worried about Verity. She finally found her mistress in the library and told her Miss Verity was feeling poorly again. Concerned, Kate went up to see her at once. At first she thought Verity had merely stepped out, but then she discovered her things missing. Alarmed, she tried to think rationally. The first thing she must do, she decided, was tell Nick. She was halfway down the stairs when she heard loud voices coming from the rear of the house. Heavens, what now? Quickening her steps, Kate hurried toward the morning room. She heard Nick's angry voice as she swung open the door.

"You bastard," he swore with deadly menace, his eyes intent on Bryce. He drew his right fist back.

Their cousin stood just inside the door, facing Nick. Before Kate could speak, she saw Bryce's head suddenly rock backward, then he sprawled at her feet.

Kate stared from him to her brother. "Nick! What on earth are you doing?"

He ignored her, his eyes fixed on Bryce. "I want you out of this house within the hour."

Kate glanced from one to the other. She'd never seen Nick so furious. "Would someone please tell me what's happening?"

Bryce looked up as he removed his handkerchief and carefully dabbed at the cut on his lip. His effort to smile was more of a grimace. "I fear it's a case of being the bearer of bad news."

"Lies, nothing but lies, and if you dare repeat them, I swear you'll not live to see tomorrow."

"Nick, please," Kate begged, placing a restraining hand on her brother's arm. "Whatever you think Bryce may have done, there can be no reason for fisticuffs—not between cousins."

"Don't remind me that we are related!"

She turned to Bryce, still lying on the floor. "Oh, do get up before one of the servants comes in."

With an apprehensive glance at Nick, Bryce slowly stood. He still pressed the handkerchief to his mouth, and now Kate could see blood staining the white linen. She helped him to a chair, then glared at Nick. "Sit down. I demand to know what

217

has occurred, and I expect the pair of you to tell me without histrionics."

"Ask him," Nick growled. He strode to the sideboard and poured himself a cup of coffee.

Bryce picked up his own cup and sipped the tea. Then he looked at Kate. "I merely related an incident that occurred last night at Whites. Your brother found the news unpalatable, and took his anger out on me. I understand that, of course, and bear him no ill will. I myself felt quite distressed when I heard the story."

"Bryce, for heaven's sake, come to the point. What story?"

"Lord Ashford told us he'd been robbed Wednesday evening. The burglar broke into his house, but took only his purse."

"I do not see—" Kate began.

Nick interrupted her. "Our dear cousin claims the thief left behind a note—identical to the one Verity left me. *Ergo*, she must be the thief."

"I do not merely claim it—I saw the note," Bryce protested. He glanced uneasily at his cousin, misliking the confused look in Kate's eyes. "You can ask Ravenscar or Dinsmore. They saw it, too. The culprit must be Verity."

"But that's impossible," Kate said, looking at Nick.

"Exactly," he agreed, tight-lipped. "Would you like to enlighten him, or shall I?"

"Are you thinking she was too ill to go out?" Bryce asked. "I considered that, but I suspect her malaise was merely a charade. Once we left the house, she probably climbed out the window. After all, she's done it before."

Kate rubbed a tired hand across her brow. "She did not leave the house Wednesday night, Bryce. Nick was so worried about Verity, he asked Crimstock to keep an eye on her."

"That old man—he probably fell asleep. He wouldn't know if she was here or not."

Kate sighed. "Dulcie was with him. She told me they looked in on Verity every hour. It's why I gave them the day off yesterday."

Stunned, Bryce stared at his cup. After a moment he muttered, "Well, you must admit the evidence was damning."

"Yes, indeed," Nick agreed. The quiet tenor of his voice caused Bryce to look up. "But not in the way you mean. If Verity didn't rob Ashford, there's only one other person who could have, only one other who knew about that note. How did you manage it, Bryce? Did you keep Verity's note the night she broke in here? Were you planning, even then, to use it against her?"

Bryce stood up abruptly, tipping over his chair. He backed toward the door. "You're mad! Too besotted with that girl to see her for what she is—nothing but a common thief."

"I'm giving you fair warning—be very careful of what you say," Nick retorted, moving away from the sideboard. His hands curled into fists.

Bryce, too frustrated to care, sneered at him. "You should thank me, Lynton. I only tried to open your eyes, to save you from a disastrous marriage. That girl has you wrapped around her little finger—"

"That girl is going to be my wife," Nick interrupted, taking a step toward him.

Kate slipped between them. "Stop it, both of you. Bryce, I'm ashamed to think you would stoop to such despicable behavior, but I suspect I'm partly to blame."

She turned to face her brother, her face flushed. "I'm sorry, Nick, but when you first wrote me from Brighton, I feared Verity was somehow trying to entrap you into marriage. I asked Bryce to help me prevent her from succeeding. I was wrong about Verity, of course, but I never told Bryce so. If you are going to blame him, you must blame me, too."

For a moment there was silence. Then Nick

spoke. His anger had cooled, but contempt showed in his eyes as he glared at his cousin. "Whatever your reasons, you behaved like a cad. I want you out of this house. If I chance to see you anywhere, I'll cut you dead. You may consider yourself fortunate that I don't call you out."

Kate touched her brother's hand. "Nick, you are not thinking clearly. If Bryce remains in Town and it is seen we don't stand upon terms with him, people will gossip. For Verity's sake you must not do this."

"There will be gossip anyway unless I can figure a way to silence Ashford." He glared at Bryce again. "I should turn you over to him—tell him you're the real thief."

Bryce returned the handkerchief to his pocket and straightened his coat. With calculated assurance he faced his cousin. "Certainly, if you insist. Of course, then the whole sordid business of Verity's past would come out."

"He's right, Nick," Kate said. "But I have an idea." When both men looked at her, she explained. "Send Bryce to America."

"What? I won't go!"

"I will do nothing to help him—not after the way he tried to ruin Verity."

Kate smiled. "I don't think either of you has considered the advantages. Nick, with our cousin in America, you will not have to fear meeting him, or worry that he might gossip about Verity. Bryce, if you remain in England, and word of this gets about, you will not be received anywhere. Go to America. You said yourself there was tremendous opportunity in that land to amass a fortune."

"Granted, but I would need capital, and passage on a decent ship is not cheap."

"Nick?" Kate appealed to her brother, begging him with her eyes to settle this amicably.

He considered the idea briefly, then nodded toward Bryce. "I'll pay the passage, but I'll be damned if you get a penny more. You have what you stole from Ashford—that should be sufficient."

Relieved, Kate urged Bryce on his way. "You may still be able to arrange passage on the *Sea Witch* with Giles Calvert, but she sails tomorrow. I suggest you find him at once."

"It seems I have little choice," Bryce agreed. He faced Nick and offered his hand. "No hard feelings, old man?" He saw his cousin's eyes darken ominously, and hastily stepped back. "Will you at least permit me to leave my belongings here until I've made other arrangements?"

Nick, not trusting himself to speak, nodded. He watched as Bryce bid Kate good-bye and then left. They heard him whistling as he walked down the hall.

"He has audacity enough for six men—but at least now Verity will be safe."

"I hope so," Kate said, "but there is one problem. Nick, I didn't want to tell you while Bryce was here, but Verity has disappeared."

Chapter 17

Verity sat alone in the small garden at Brighton, one fat Siamese asleep in her lap, the other curled at her feet. All week she'd been fussed over, cosseted, and made much of, but all the attention did not make up for the fact that Nicholas had not come. She'd told herself she did not expect him. Even so, she had peered eagerly out the window at the sound of every passing carriage, and each knock on the door caused her heart to beat double-time.

That morning, however, she owned the truth. He was not coming. She'd been foolish to hope that Nicholas would somehow still believe in her. *She* knew she had not robbed Lord Ashford, but, even to her ears, Bryce's story had sounded convincing. How much more so it must have seemed to Nicholas.

After giving the matter considerable thought, Verity knew Bryce must be responsible for her predicament. No one else who knew about the incriminating note would have reason to wish her ill. Only Bryce, who stood to inherit if Nicholas did not marry. But she had no proof. If Lord Ashford set the Runners after her, and it seemed likely he would, she might be convicted of a crime she had not committed. What irony, she thought while her insides twisted with fear. And poor Mama. She'd seemed so much better of late, but her health was not strong enough to endure the scandal ahead. Verity feared the shock would be devastating.

Antony lifted his silky head at the sound of the door creaking open and footfalls on the path. Verity glanced around. "Good morning, sir. How are you?"

The Earl of Lewes came down the path to join her. "More to the point, how are you?" He bent and scratched Antony behind the ears, and immediately Cleo rubbed against his boots for her share of attention.

"I am well enough."

"Are you? I fear your mother is very worried about you."

Verity continued to stroke her cat's velvety fur, carefully avoiding the earl's eyes. She had refused to discuss her reasons for leaving London, except to say that she had no choice. She knew she owed her mother an explanation, but dreaded the moment when she must tell her the truth. She looked up at the earl now, sadness shadowing her eyes. "I know she must be disappointed—she so hoped Nicholas would propose."

"She still does, I think, but only because she wishes to see you happy."

Verity saw the caring and concern in his eyes. His lordship was a kind man, but she wondered if he truly understood the reason for her mother's melancholy. After a moment she said, "I think Mama would be content no matter whom I married. She simply dislikes the notion that I shall have to earn my living."

"Well, as to that, I do not believe it will be necessary," the earl replied. He fingered his perfectly tied cravat. "Your mother has ... that is, we agreed—Verity, my dear, I am shortly going to become your father."

A smile, the first in several days, curved her lips and warmed her eyes. Impulsively, she stood and kissed his leathery cheek. "I could not be more pleased, sir."

"Thank you. You are very sweet," he murmured, his face flushed with pleasure. "Lavinia said you would not object, but I confess I feared you might think it too soon."

She shook her head, touched by his worry. "I think even Papa would be pleased to know my mother will be looked after."

"You may be certain I shall take good care of her—and you, too, if you will allow me. I always wished for a daughter, but I never thought I would have one quite so lovely. I am a most fortunate man."

"I hope you will always think so, sir." She hesitated, hating to spoil his moment of happiness. If only she could think of some way to avoid involving her mother in the scandal ahead.

"Verity, if something is troubling you—I am not very good at this yet—but I would be glad to listen, that is, if you wished to confide in me. Of course, I don't want to pry into your affairs . . ." His words trailed off, and he tugged again at his cravat.

Verity squeezed his hand. "Thank you. Perhaps, in a few days, though I am not sure anyone can help. But let us not speak of that now. Instead, tell me your plans. Have you and Mama decided where you are to live?"

Before he could reply, Lavinia stepped into the garden, looking worriedly over her shoulder. She approached them, twisting her hands together.

Verity, recognizing the signs of agitation, rose quickly. "What is wrong? Are you ill, Mama?"

"I am fine, child, thank you. But someone . . . someone wishes to see you."

Verity's heart constricted. Could it be the Runners so soon? She wet her lips, suddenly finding it difficult to speak. "Who, Mama?"

"Nicholas Lynton."

For just a moment her heart lightened. Then she remembered the long week she'd spent waiting. If he believed in her, he would have come at once. She knew Nicholas. Some misguided notion of responsibility had brought him there to offer his assistance.

He might think her guilty, but he would not allow her to face the courts alone.

"Verity, dearest, he seems disturbed. Will you not speak to him? He's come such a long way to see you—"

"I have no wish to see him," she interrupted. *I cannot bear to see him,* her heart cried. "Please send him away."

"Now, darling, do be reasonable," Lavinia coaxed. She sent an appealing glance to the earl.

"I think we must not press Verity," he said, patting her hand in a fatherly manner. "I'm certain she has her reasons. Would you like me to speak to Nicholas?"

Verity nodded thankfully and watched Lord Lewes walk into the house. She longed to go after him, to see Nicholas just once more. But she did not trust herself. Even now she ached to fling herself into his arms and beg him to believe in her innocence.

Her mother was speaking, but Verity did not hear the words. She begged to be excused, then hurried up to her room. Crossing to the window, she sank down on the cushioned seat. At least she would have one last glimpse of Nicholas.

Her muscles ached with the strain as she held herself immobile, fearful of looking away in case she missed sight of him. Nearly an hour passed before he left. She saw him at once, tall, elegant as always, his long stride carrying him easily to the waiting carriage. She watched him with a hungry fascination, a desperate longing swelling in her heart. But he never glanced back or looked up.

Verity sat forlornly at the table between her mother and Lord Lewes the following afternoon. She'd made the effort to dress and come downstairs, though she had little appetite and her mind wandered. She glanced at her mother, but Lavinia's attention remained focused on the earl.

I should be thankful Mama is too engrossed with her wedding plans to worry over me, Verity thought. Certainly, she did not wish to be put through the sort of inquisition her mama had subjected her to in the past. Only . . . it would be nice if *someone* noticed how miserably unhappy she felt.

She toyed with the strawberries and cream set before her. Pining for Nicholas would accomplish nothing. She needed to make her own plans—go somewhere far away and change her name so the Bow Street Runners would not be able to find her. She glanced at Lord Lewes. He'd been extremely kind and offered his assistance. Perhaps he would be willing to lend her enough money to travel abroad. France would be best, she decided. She'd heard of many Englishmen fleeing there to avoid their creditors. Beau Brummell had done so, and dozens of others.

She would have to practice her French. Conversational phrases she'd learned at school ran through her head. *S'il vous plaît, je ne sais quoi, coup de foudre*—love at first sight. Nicholas had said he fell in love with her the first time he saw her . . . but she must not think of him. She took a bite of the strawberries, which tasted bitter in her mouth. Pushing the dish aside, she picked up her cup and sipped the tea.

Wythecombe stepped into the dining room, startling them all. That he had entered without knocking was strange enough, but he carefully closed the double doors behind him. He stood in front of them, his long face drained of color.

Lavinia stared. "Gracious, Wythecombe, whatever ails you?"

His mouth opened, but no words came out. He swallowed, fixed his gaze on Verity, and tried again. "Two men are here to see you, miss. They say they are from Bow Street and must ask you some questions."

She nodded, then carefully placed her china cup

on the table. So the Runners had come. Much sooner than she had expected.

Lord Lewes rose and offered her his arm. "Would you like me to come with you, Verity?"

"Thank you, sir," she said, welcoming the feeling of his warm hand on her cold one. She wanted to cling to him, but at the same time she hoped to shield her mother for as long as possible. Taking a deep breath, she said, "I think it would be best if I spoke to them alone. Mama, pray excuse me."

Aware that her mother, the earl, and even Wythecombe were watching, she drew her shoulders back and held her head high. She nodded to the butler and, after he opened the door, walked slowly into the hall. She saw the two men waiting near the door. Rough, burly men.

One of them removed his hat as she approached. He consulted a slip of paper, then looked at her. "Miss Verity Parnel, recently of Harley Street, London?"

She nodded.

"You will please come with us, miss. We have some questions to put to you regarding a burglary in Town."

"Where . . . where are you taking me?"

"Just to the Old Ship Inn, miss. If we have to take you back to Town, you'll be allowed to return here first. For now we just want to ask you a few questions." He opened the door, gesturing for her to precede him. A dark, closed carriage waited in the road.

She walked outside, blinking her eyes against the brightness of the afternoon. The Runners took their positions on either side of her. She felt dwarfed between them. Glancing back at the house, she saw the door remained firmly shut and the curtains drawn over the windows. Slowly, she climbed into the carriage.

They rode in silence for several moments. Then,

unable to bear the quiet any longer, she remarked, "I am surprised you found me so quickly."

"Well, we had a bit of help, miss. A Mr. Lynton gave us your direction."

Nicholas had turned her over to the Bow Street Runners! The ache inside her grew until she could scarcely breathe. So that was what he had come to tell her yesterday. She knew he had a high sense of duty, but she'd not thought he would willingly betray her. She sat in silence, hardly aware of the short drive to the inn. She walked through the lobby, unconscious of the curious stares of the guests, and followed the taller of the Runners up a flight of steps.

The men halted before a room on the second floor. The taller one, who seemed to be in charge, rapped sharply, then opened the door. He motioned her in. "The gentleman inside will ask the questions, miss. We'll be waiting out here."

Frightened, Verity hesitated. She wished now she'd allowed the earl to come with her. Praying for courage, she lifted her head and entered the room. It took a moment for her eyes to become adjusted to the dim light. She saw the tall gentleman waiting by the windows, his back to her. As he started to turn, she recognized him.

"Nicholas? I do not understand—" She glanced back at the closed door, puzzled. "They said I was to be questioned."

"So you are, my dear. I have any number of questions to ask. For starters, I want to know why you left Town without telling me. And also why you refused to see me yesterday."

She stared at him, struck speechless by his audacity. First he'd turned her over to the Runners, and now he calmly stood before her, demanding answers to his questions. He had misjudged her in thinking her a thief, but she'd obviously misjudged him as well.

She stepped back as though his very nearness offended her. "How dare you accost me in this manner? Did the Runners grant you a few moments alone with me as a reward for laying information?"

"It seemed the only way to have a word with you."

"Oh, you—you abominable, insufferable prig! I would not deign to speak to you if you were the last man on earth," she cried, and whirled toward the door.

He was there before her, and leaned lazily against it, blocking the way out. "You can answer my questions, or Bow Street's. The choice is yours, Verity."

"Why are you doing this," she demanded. "What do you want from me?"

"I thought I had made that much clear," he said. His blue eyes, blazing with desire, held hers for a moment.

Breathless, unable to think clearly, Verity turned her back on him.

Nick reached out and drew her into his arms, gently turning her to face him. "What must I do to convince you?"

"Let me go!" Her fingers curled into fists, and she beat against his chest.

Nick ignored the pummeling. "Never. You belong to me," he whispered just before his lips touched hers.

She felt the heat of his mouth, the persuasive movement of his lips on hers, and fought against it. Nicholas pulled her closer, enveloping her in the warmth of his embrace. She felt the hard muscles in his shoulders, the wide expanse of his chest, and struggled weakly. He lifted his head slightly, and then pressed his lips against her neck, trailing kisses from her ear down to the hollow in her throat.

She moaned, unaware that her fingers had relaxed and now clutched at his broad back, or that her body strained against his. She wanted only to taste his lips again.

Abruptly, Nick released her. He gently flicked her cheek with the tip of his finger. "I'm relieved to see that has not changed."

"What?" she asked unsteadily.

"The effect we seem to have on each other."

She reddened and stepped warily away, but this time he didn't try to stop her. Her glance fell on the four-poster. She realized for the first time that they were in a private chamber, and quickly averted her gaze. She moved toward the small alcove fronting the tall window.

"Verity, why did you leave without telling me," he asked, coming up behind her.

She shrugged, feeling his warm breath on her neck. "There seemed little point in staying. I overheard your conversation with Bryce. You could not wish to have a thief for a wife and ... and any other position would be unacceptable to me."

He smiled at that and touched a blond curl. "I seem to remember proposing marriage, nothing else."

"That was before," she stammered, moving away from the compelling touch of his fingers.

"But nothing has changed," he insisted, following her. She was trapped now in the alcove, and he waited patiently.

She stared stubbornly out the window. "How can you say so? I *heard* Bryce accuse me, and you never uttered a word in my defense. Nor did you come after me—not until nearly a week had passed. If you believed in me, if you thought me innocent, you would have come at once."

He heard the ache in her voice and yearned to comfort her in his arms. Lifting the curl on the back of her neck, he kissed her tenderly until he felt her quiver beneath his hands. "Obviously, you did not hear all of the conversation with my cousin."

"What ... what do you mean?" she asked, her breath coming in quick gasps.

Nick gently turned her to face him. "I—er—flattened him for daring to disparage your name."

"You mean you hit him?"

"Decisively. It seemed the thing to do. It appears you left too soon. Had you so little faith in me?"

She blushed, but met his gaze squarely. "Bryce sounded so convincing, and when you didn't say a word, I thought—"

"Hmmm. Better not to think so much. Try taking me at my word instead," he murmured, and kissed her again. When he had thoroughly silenced her, he picked her up and carried her to the sofa. "Now, little one, you have some questions to answer."

"The Runners," she gasped. "Oh, Lord, I had forgotten them. Nicholas, what am I to do? I cannot prove that I never robbed Lord Ashford—it will be my word against Bryce's."

"Bryce is somewhere on the Atlantic Ocean, sailing for America. He robbed Ashford and tried to blame you. When I confronted him, he decided a sea voyage might be beneficial to his health. With luck, we may never see him again. Now, once more, I am asking you, Miss Parnel, to do me the honor of becoming my wife."

"Oh, Nicholas, you must see I cannot. Lord Ashford will learn I wrote that note and then—"

"You may consign Ashford to the devil. I have taken care of him."

Verity gazed at him in awe. "You do not mean that you . . . you flattened him, too?"

Nick laughed. "No, little one. I'm sorry if that disappoints you, but I merely had a talk with him and recompensed him for his losses. Ashford knows it was Bryce who robbed him, but he will say nothing."

"Then—why the Runners?" she asked, glancing at the door.

"Merely to ensure that you answer my question. When you refused to see me, it seemed the only solution. And I promise you, Miss Parnel, if you do

231

not give me a proper answer, I shall turn you over to those men and see you hauled off to Newgate."

"I don't believe you!"

"You are learning, my dear. Actually, those stout fellows are the landlord's brothers."

"They are not really from Bow Street?"

"No, my darling. Just a couple of local men I hired, but I assure you they will obey me all the same."

"Oh, how despicable of you to frighten me. You deserve that I not speak to you at all."

"I'll wager you were no more frightened than I was when I discovered you had fled London—again. Verity, dearest, must I chase you forever?" He leaned forward to kiss her nose.

She turned her head slightly so that his lips met her own. For several enjoyable moments she willingly returned his ardor, reveling in the exquisite delight of his kisses. Then abruptly, she sat up. "Good heavens, I forgot about Mama. Nicholas, she must be nearly sick with worry. We must go at once—"

"We are not going anywhere until I have your answer. Your mother is safely below stairs with Lord Lewes and my sister. They are situated quite comfortably in a private parlor and will wait until we come down to toast our betrothal."

"Mama knew? And the earl? Oh, you are depraved, sir. Depraved, and despicable and devious—"

"I know. Even I am appalled at my behavior. But this is what you have brought me to. Will you marry me, Verity? I will not let you go until I have your promise."

She sat back in his arms, toying with the buttons on his coat. "I must consider this. How long do you suppose Mama and the others will wait?"

"As long as it takes for me to persuade you," he said, and lifted her chin. "What have you in mind?"

She lowered her lashes, then peeped up at him. "It may take quite some time . . . I may require con-

232

siderable convincing. Perhaps, if you kissed me again, it would help me decide."

"Witch," he said, but willingly obliged. "Well?" he asked some moments later.

Demurely, she kept her eyes downcast. "I still do not know. It's very difficult. When I think how you deceived me, and that you thought me a thief—"

"I still do," he interrupted, and kissed her again. When he lifted his head, it was to gaze at her adoringly. His voice husky, he whispered, "You stole my heart the night we met. You are a scoundrel, but I want you for my own. Say yes, sweet Verity."

An altercation at the door interrupted them.

They heard Kate's voice. "I demand you let me pass. My brother is inside."

"Sorry, miss, but we have our orders. No one goes in."

Verity giggled softly. "I think we had best go down."

"To announce our engagement?"

She looked up at him, loving the firm line of his jaw, the sweep of his lashes over his hopeful eyes. From the beginning her heart had known she belonged to him, but she had been afraid to trust him. Now she reached up and tenderly traced the curve of his lips. "Yes, Nicholas, oh, yes."